WRANGLING the COWBOY

USA TODAY BESTSELLING AUTHOR
KENNEDY FOX

Copyright © 2020 Kennedy Fox
www.kennedyfoxbooks.com

Wrangling the Cowboy
Circle B Ranch, #3

Cover designer: Outlined with Love Designs
Cover image: Wander Aguiar Photography
Copy editor: Editing 4 Indies

All rights reserved. No parts of the book may be used or reproduced in any matter without written permission from the author, except for inclusion of brief quotations in a review. This book is a work of fiction. Names, characters, establishments, organizations, and incidents are either products of the author's imagination or are used fictitiously to give a sense of authenticity. Any resemblance to actual persons, living or dead, events, or locales is entirely coincidental.

Each book in the Bishop Brothers World can read as standalones but if you wish to read the others, here's our suggested reading order.

BISHOP BROTHERS SERIES
Original Bishop Family
Taming Him
Needing Him
Chasing Him
Keeping Him

SPIN-OFF'S
Friends of the Bishops
Make Me Stay
Roping the Cowboy

CIRCLE B RANCH SERIES
Bishop Family Second Generation
Hitching the Cowboy
Catching the Cowboy
Wrangling the Cowboy
Bossing the Cowboy
Kissing the Cowboy
Winning the Cowboy
Claiming the Cowboy
Tempting the Cowboy
Seducing the Cowboy

Why you gotta be so heartless?
I know you think it's harmless

Girl, why you gotta be so in between
Loving me and leaving?

"Heartless"
-Diplo, Morgan Wallen, Julia Michaels

PROLOGUE
GAVIN

"Well, it's official. I'm joining a convent."

The bartender scoffs with an eye roll as she sets a shot in front of the brunette bombshell I've been eyeing. "You're too dramatic for your own good."

The soon-to-be nun downs the clear liquid and makes a face after. "I'm serious. I decided to take a chance and sign up for a dating app, and I swear to God..." She pulls her phone from her shorts pocket and unlocks the screen. "Alright, let's start with Dennis G. *Hey, beautiful,*" she mimics in a deeper tone. *"You like those braids pulled? I'll be your cowboy and let you ride me for a night."*

I nearly choke on my beer while I hold back my laughter.

"I mean, c'mon!" She groans. "That doesn't even make sense! You'd have to bend me over to pull my braids like reins, so he'd be riding me..."

My dick stirs at the image she created in my head, and fuck me, I like it.

"You're too literal, Maize," the bartender scolds.

Maize. Of course, she'd have a pretty name too.

I *should* stop eavesdropping and staring, but I can't. She's gorgeous, and her smart mouth has kept me hard for the past hour. After a job interview, I stopped by the Circle B Saloon to unwind before my long drive back to Houston tomorrow. I decided to sit at one of the tall tables to face the TV, and I haven't been able to take my eyes off the woman who's clearly had a rough day.

"Okay, how about this one from Gregory H." She clears her throat as she prepares to read another message.

The girl cracks up as Maize spews another horrific one-liner.

"I fuckin' quit. There are no decent, single men in Eldorado. They're either taken, swing for the other team, or talk like they dropped out of middle school. So, I'm joining a convent. At least then, my eyes would never have to be assaulted by an unsolicited dick pic ever again. And let me tell you, the last picture I got was crooked and scarred me for life anyway."

That has me doubling over with laughter, and there's no hiding it this time. Both girls snap their gaze to me as I try to control myself. I grab the neck of the beer bottle, take a swig, and act as if I wasn't listening to every word.

"Looks like one guy finds you amusing..." The bartender holds out her hand with a grin, but Maize frowns.

"I do," I say with a shrug, hoping to make her smile. "Mostly because you as a nun...I ain't seein' it."

"Really? Because I can totally picture her on her knees."

Maize's face turns beet red as she throws a straw toward the bartender. She giggles as Maize's head drops.

And now the image of *her on her knees* surfaces in my head.

"I meant, *praying!* On your knees praying," the bartender clarifies, but it's obvious she's full of shit. She's got a smart mouth too, and I quickly wonder if they're related. They do look alike.

"Excuse my sister," Maize says. "She gets a kick out of embarrassing me."

"I was right about you two," I drawl, grabbing my nearly empty beer and standing.

"Right about what?" Maize asks as I take the stool next to her at the end of the bar. She doesn't flinch when my arm brushes hers, and I take that as a good sign.

"I had a feeling you were related." I nod toward the other girl.

"My little sister," she confirms. "Kenzie."

"Her *favorite* sister." Kenzie smirks.

"My *only* sister," Maize counters, narrowing her eyes as she scowls at her again. "My pain in the ass sister."

With a palm to her chest, Kenzie gasps. "That's it. I'm cutting you off."

"Nooo!" Maize whines. "I'll read you another message," she bribes. "It'll be a really good one."

"Or I could just buy you a drink?" I interrupt.

Realization hits her as she sits taller and licks her lips. "Did you just offer to buy me a drink?"

Before I can respond, Kenzie speaks up. "Marry this man. Marry him *now*."

Maize glares at Kenzie, and I can only imagine what she wants to say to her right now, which I find comical.

"I mean, unless…do you want a dick pic first?" I flash her a smirk.

"Exactly how much did you hear?"

"I've been sitting over there for an hour, so…a lot," I admit, and her cheeks tint pink again. "It was very entertaining."

Kenzie sets a beer in front of me and a margarita in front of Maize, then looks at me. "I'll add them to your tab." She waggles her brows before leaving to help other customers at the opposite end of the bar.

"Oh my God," Maize groans. "I'm sorry about her. She assumes and—"

I reach over and put my hand over hers to stop her. "I offered, remember?"

"Yes, that's right." She nods, pulling her hand from under mine and grabbing her glass. "Thank you."

She's been burned by so many douchebags she doesn't even realize I'm hitting on her. I can't imagine any guy dumb enough to walk away from Maize, but lucky for me, she's single, and so am I.

"I'm Gavin, by the way," I say, holding out my hand and hoping to touch hers again.

"Maize." She takes the bait, and we shake. "Sorry I'm not more bubbly. You caught me on a rough night."

"No apologies needed, Maize. Maybe I can cheer you up, though."

"Oh yeah? With a non-crooked dick pic?" She arches a brow, grinning.

I chuckle, glad she's not giving me the cold shoulder. Though I've never had a problem getting a woman's attention, it's not out of the realm of reality. When I was a professional bull rider, women would flock to me, and I'd have to tear them off just to walk through a crowd. But I don't compete anymore. That life's behind me now.

"I'm too old to send explicit pictures to women."

Her eyes lower as she checks me out, then she tilts her head and studies me. "You can't be *that* old."

I suck in my lower lip as I soak in her delicate features. Light blue eyes, dark hair, and pale skin. She's undoubtedly my type, but something else about her has my blood pumping.

"I'm certain I'm quite older than you," I counter, taking a swig of my beer. "Why don't you tell me how old you are?"

"Because it's embarrassing. Most girls my age are married with a couple of kids already. And me? Well, I'm joining a convent."

"You're at least twenty-one, being that you're in a bar drinking. Definitely *not* over thirty." I tilt my head, looking at her eyes, skin, and lips. Fuck, she has the most beautiful face I've seen in a long time. "You're having a quarter-life crisis since, like you said, no husband and no babies. So, I'm gonna guess twenty-five." If I'm right, that means I'm ten years older than her.

Maize gulps down more of her drink as she watches me in amusement. "Sadly, you're correct. Well, in a few months."

I burst out laughing and shake my head. "You have plenty of time. Stop worryin'."

"That's so easy for guys to say! My grandma married my grandfather at nineteen, and they had five kids before she was thirty. Five! Granted, one pregnancy was twins, but still. I'm already behind."

"That was standard tradition thirty, forty, fifty years ago. But now, it's statistically proven that more couples wait to start their families and focus on their careers first. The average age of having their first baby is thirty. So, you still have *plenty* of time."

"Oh okay, so I only need to find a husband, convince him to marry me, get pregnant, and pop out a baby in the next five years. Noted."

"Or..." I counter, taking a long sip of my beer until it's empty. "You can just do whatever the fuck you want." Flashing a smirk, she tilts her lips up in amusement.

Before she can respond, Kenzie returns. "Another round?"

"Yes, ma'am. Keep 'em comin'. Maize and I have a game of pool to play. Loser buys shots."

"We do?" She furrows her brows as she sucks down the last of her alcohol.

"If you're gonna be a nun, you need to have as much fun as you can now. So, let's get started."

"I like him." Kenzie beams. "And if you don't marry him, I'm next in line."

"Oh, *puh-lease*. Everyone knows you and Grayson are gonna hate bang and finally admit your true feelings," Maize states.

"Don't you dare put that negative energy into the universe." Kenzie starts waving her arms around as if she's trying to push it away. "Grayson can go fuck himself for all I care."

If I knew who Grayson was, I'd be scared for him right now.

"Sounds like man-hating runs in the family." I grab the bottle Kenzie hands me.

Maize snorts and shakes her head. Once her glass is full again, I grab her hand and lead her to the pool table in the back. The pub is small and offers minimal seating, but I like it. It's a typical small-town country bar with Texas décor and pictures of cowboys on the walls. However, it's not loud and crowded, so Maize and I can actually hear each other talk and move around.

"Should I assume you know how to play, or do you need a personal hands-on tutorial?" I ask, setting my beer down. Grabbing two sticks, I hand her one, then pick up the triangle rack.

"You're quite cocky, you know that?" She bites her lip, and I notice the way her eyes rake down my body as if she wants to eat me like a snack.

"I prefer *confident*," I retort. "Though I'll say most women find that attractive in a man." I start gathering the balls from the pockets.

"Don't forget I'm becoming a nun, so my knowledge of men is lackluster at best." She sets her drink on the edge of the table and grabs the chalk. I have a feeling she knows her way around a pool table and just might give me a run for my money.

"I'd be willing to bet you know plenty. Though your execution on how to use it to your advantage might be the issue." I rack the balls and position the white ball to break. "Ladies first."

Maize narrows her gaze as she leans down and rubs the stick over her bridge hand. She pushes her ass out, which shows off her long, toned legs, and I tilt my head to get a better look.

"You keep staring like that, and you're gonna lose big time," she smarts off, then takes her shot. The balls bounce off the sides, and eventually, one goes into a pocket.

I smirk at her victorious expression.

"Looks like I'm stripes."

"Guess so. Let's see whatcha got." I fold my arms over my chest and watch in amazement as she sinks the next three balls before missing one.

We take turns calling pockets, and after fifteen minutes, we're each down to one. She talks shit the whole time, which I find cute as hell. This girl isn't trying to impress me with her body or by whispering all the dirty things she'd like to do to me. Not that I'd protest, but she's actually making conversation, and it's a breath of fresh air compared to what I'm used to.

Living on the road meant having my fair share of women available but being a bull rider—now retired—put a giant spotlight on me. Many saw the eight-pack and toned muscles and immediately stripped off their clothes. I won't deny I loved the lifestyle up until my last rodeo, but after a dozen injuries under my belt, I knew it was time to settle down.

"Corner pocket," she announces, taking her stance. I'll admit I'm a sore loser, and the thought of losing bruises my ego a bit. I find it hot as fuck that she knows how to play so well. But that doesn't mean I'm gonna give her the game.

Standing across from her, I rest my stick on the wall, then pull off my shirt. It's a bitch move since I know how she'll react, and it'll definitely distract her, but I like to play a little dirty.

"What are you doin'? We're in public," she warns.

Glancing around casually, I see three people at the bar and a couple at one of the far tables. I shrug and flex. "I don't think they mind."

Her throat moves when she swallows, and her hard gaze focuses on my abs as she tries to make the winning shot.

"You're tryin' to make me lose, aren't you?" She points at me and scowls. "It's not gonna work. I'm a nun-in-training and am completely *immune* to you."

"Is that so?" I puff out my chest to prove she's lying.

Maize blinks hard as if she's trying to look away but can't. "Yep. Doesn't faze me one bit. You're just wasting your time."

"Then why do you keep talkin' about it?" I challenge.

"Whatever. I'm not." She leans down again to focus on the ball. I shift my body until I'm in her line of sight, and when she goes to make her move, I grip the edge of the table as hard as I can. The veins in my hand pop out right before she strikes the cue ball, causing her to put too much force behind the shot, and the ball bounces onto the floor.

"Shit!" She slams the bottom of the stick against the floor and pouts. "You did that on purpose!"

Bending down, I grab it and walk over to her. Her breath hitches as I close the gap between us, and her eyes lower down my chest and stomach once again.

"I think you dropped this..." I hold the ball out for her, but she doesn't move.

Knowing I'm getting to her, I reach down and place the ball in her palm, then flash her a wink. "Wanna try it again?"

Finally, she blinks and steps back, putting at least a foot of space between us. "No, that'd be cheating. It's your turn."

"Alright." I grin as I take my position and call the pocket. Moments later, I sink my last ball.

She groans loudly, and I laugh.

"Problem?" I ask, looking over my shoulder.

She glares at me, shaking her head, and I bring my focus back to the eight-ball.

"Middle pocket," I say, then shoot it in perfectly.

"Looks like I'm buying shots," she says, defeated.

I put up our sticks, then tilt her chin up until our eyes meet. "Or we could skip them, and you could come home with me."

Maize looks like she's gonna pass out as she stares at me intently. I'm pretty sure I've shocked her into silence. The corner of my lips tilts up in amusement as I watch her mind spin out of control.

"It's a yes or no question, Maize. You look like you're trying to solve a trigonometric equation."

She wrinkles her nose and finally inhales a breath. "I-I'm a mess. You heard how awful I am with dating…" She holds out her hand, motioning to the bar. "And you witnessed firsthand how pathetic I am at flirting. I mean, seriously, it's sad. So, why would you—"

Before she can continue ranting, I cup her face, and our mouths collide. She's hesitant at first and barely brushes her lips against mine. When I slip my tongue inside, she finally relaxes into my touch. She tastes like lemon and salt, a combination of the alcohol she was drinking earlier.

My hand slides down her body as she wraps her arms around my neck, pulling me closer, and I know she wants this as much as I do. Maize releases a moan, and the sound goes straight to my dick. I want to hear that noise all night long—underneath me, on top of me, bent over in front of me. And there's no denying she does too.

"Maize, I need an answer before I embarrass myself here," I murmur against her mouth.

"Yes," she whispers. "Take me home with you."

"I need to pay my tab. I'll be right back," I say, somehow stepping back and releasing her. "Fuck." I adjust myself, then grab my shirt and slip it on. Maize giggles, and I notice the way she touches her swollen ruby red lips.

"Hey, Kenzie. I need to close out," I tell her, grabbing my wallet.

She gives me the total, and I hand her my card. Once I write the tip and sign the receipt, I slide it to her with a thank you.

"You're welcome. Don't forget to wear a condom!" she shouts as I make my way back to Maize, and I swear she's blushing more than before.

"You ready?" I hold out my hand.

"Dear God, yes." She grabs it, and I lead her through the back entrance to my truck. "I love my sister, but she's loud and obnoxious, which is sometimes cute, but typically embarrassing."

I chuckle as we climb inside, and I start the engine.

"She loves getting a rise outta you," I say, making my way down the street to Colt's apartment. Since I was only staying for one night, he let me use it while he visits his girlfriend in Dallas.

Five minutes later, I pull into the parking lot, and we jump out.

"You live here?" she asks as I scramble to find the key.

"No, it's a friend's place. He's not home, though."

As soon as I open the door, I flick on a couple of lights and lead her inside. "Do you want a nightcap?" I ask, gripping her hand in mine and leading her to the kitchen.

"No, thanks." She stops walking, and I quickly look at her. Maize grabs my waist and pulls herself close, then reaches for my face. I lean down and meet her lips as she pushes her tongue inside my mouth. She roams her hands over my body, lowering them to my belt buckle and zipper. Once she successfully undoes my jeans, I grab her shirt and pull it off. I wait a moment to take in how breathtaking her body is—perky tits, flat stomach, and slim waist. She's a fuckin' meal that I can't wait to devour.

"Goddamn, Maize..." I help her out of her tight jean shorts. "You're driving me insane."

"Take yours off *now*," she orders.

Once we're both down to only our underwear, I slide a hand between her thighs and feel how wet she is for me. I nearly combust when she coats my finger through the fabric of her panties.

Before I forget, I grab my wallet from my jeans. I pull out a condom, then drop the wallet on the floor. "Your sister's orders," I say, chuckling.

Maize shakes her head. "She acts like *she's* the older one."

Sliding my hands down her body, I grip her ass and lift her into my arms. Maize's legs wrap around me as my erection pushes against her. Our mouths crash together as I walk us through the living room and into the bedroom. Once she's flat on the mattress, I tower over her and sink my teeth into her neck.

"Fuck, I want you so bad," I growl into her ear. Flattening my tongue against her warm skin, I slide it over her jaw until I meet her lips again. "Say it, Maize. Tell me you want this as much as I do."

I hate that I need the reassurance, but after getting a glimpse of her doubts about men tonight, I need to be certain she does.

"I do, Gavin. I want it so bad. Fuck me...*hard*." She nearly begs as she arches her body up into mine.

"You got it, sweetheart." I move down her body and help her unsnap her bra. Covering her nipple with my mouth, I suck hard until she yelps. Then I move to the other.

"God, you're beautiful, Maize. I don't know if one night is gonna be enough to satisfy my craving for you. You're already like a sweet tooth I can't kick." I kiss down her stomach until I reach the edge of her panties.

Once I remove them, I slowly slide my tongue up her slit. Her breathing grows faster, and I know the moment I dive inside her, she'll combust.

I flick her clit before sucking it and tasting her. Gliding my hand up her thigh, I spread her wider and then push a finger into her pussy. She gasps, rocking her hips as I thrust.

As her sweet juices cover my mouth and face, I devour her like my last meal. It takes only a couple of minutes before her legs clench, and she screams out her release.

I'm well practiced with control and patience, but my willpower snaps the moment she comes on my tongue. Quickly, I remove my jeans, then slip on the condom. As soon as I line up with her entrance, I push inside.

The moment our bodies connect is fucking heaven.

She wraps her legs around my waist as I pound into her, over and over, giving her exactly what she asked of me. *Hard and fast.*

As she gasps for air and lets out little breathy noises, I know she's close again, so I don't slow down until she squeezes my cock. We rock together in perfect harmony as I rub her clit and massage her breast.

"Fuuuuck, Maize. You're so tight."

"Don't stop, oh my God, it's soooo good." She bucks her hips wildly as she fists the sheets. "I'm so close. Go deeper," she begs.

I lift one of her legs until it's on my shoulder and spread her wider so I can angle myself to get deeper inside her pussy. The moment I do, her entire body shakes, and she moans out her third release.

"Holy shit," she pants.

"I'm not done with you," I tell her, shifting back. "Roll over," I demand.

As soon as she does, I get between her legs and grip her hips. Maize arches her back and sticks out her plump ass for me.

"Spank me. *Hard.*"

Raising my arm slightly, I crack my hand against her cheek and smile when I see how red it gets. "Fuckin' perfect, baby."

I position myself between her thighs and return to paradise. With one hand, I fist her hair and yank her head back until my mouth touches her ear. "I've been fantasizing about doing this to you since the moment you mentioned it at the bar tonight. Bending you over and pulling your hair... fuck, I'd been hard for hours just thinkin' about it."

"Yes," she purrs. "Pull harder."

She looks up at me with big blue eyes, and I nearly lose myself right then.

"Don't push me, Maize," I growl. "I don't wanna hurt you."

"You won't," she assures me. "I want it hard and rough with you, Gavin. Don't stop."

I do exactly as she asks. I pull her hair as I fuck her from behind, slamming my cock so goddamn deep inside her pussy she'll be feeling me there for days. Then I smack her ass again to make sure my red imprint stays too.

The moment she clenches around my cock and gasps for more air, I wrap my hand around her throat and squeeze gently. She loses control, and seconds later, I do too.

My body aches from the best sex I've ever had.

I can say that with one-hundred-percent certainty, which, considering I haven't dated a woman in over a decade, is fucking insane. One-night stands, yes, but I never get attached. And I definitely don't think about round two the next day.

But I am. I want Maize for breakfast, lunch, and dinner. Then again for dessert. The taste of her pussy and sweet skin is still on my tongue, and I need more.

I half-open my eyes and see the sun blazing through the blinds. Why in the hell Colt doesn't have curtains is beyond me, but at least this way, I'll be able to fuck Maize and admire every perfect inch of her body.

When I roll over to find her, I'm greeted with an empty bed.

What the hell?

I feel around, but the sheets are cold.

No…she couldn't leave. I drove us here.

Deciding to check around the apartment, I pull on my boxers and walk to the kitchen. When it's empty, I check the bathroom. Then the living room.

Next, I notice her clothes aren't on the floor.

She *left*.

I check the time, and it's barely eight in the morning.

No note, no phone number for me to reach her, *nothing*.

Well, shit. There really is a first time for everything, and I can't say I'm a fucking fan of getting bailed on the morning after.

CHAPTER ONE

MAIZE

THREE WEEKS LATER

As I GET DRESSED for work, I can hear my parents chatting, and it makes me smile. I've been trying to soak in these little moments because eventually I'll move out and get my own place. My dad wants me to live here until I'm fifty, but that's not happening. It's one of the reasons I've been thinking about starting a catering business as a side hustle.

"Oh stop," Mom says with a giggle as I pull my hair into a tight ponytail. After all these years, they're still madly in love, and sometimes I wonder if that'll be in the cards for me. Not even my gourmet meals can snag me a man. I'm doomed to become a nun or be a single woman with twelve dogs and horses to keep me occupied. It's something I'm coming to terms with.

I'm picky, and I've got rules–well, a rule. I don't date men who work on my family's ranch. I got my heart broken and won't let it happen again. Most of the men in my small town are taken, too young, or related to me, so the pickings are really slim. Becoming a nun has been a running joke, but it *could* be my reality.

After I finish getting ready, I walk into the kitchen and pour a cup of coffee. I sit next to my dad, trying to wake up because I'll need to be on my

A game once I get to the bed and breakfast. As the head chef, I have four employees to manage and plan the meals for the week. My sole responsibility is to introduce all the guests to comfort food and Grandma's favorite recipes. They deserve an authentic Southern experience for breakfast, lunch, and dinner, and I take it very seriously.

"What's on the menu today?" Dad asks as he slips on his cowboy boots. He has managed the B&B since before I was born, and he takes pride in his work. Mom smiles, and I notice she's already dressed for work in black slacks and a pink blouse. When she moved to Texas permanently, she saw a need for childcare and opened the only daycare in Eldorado. It quickly transitioned into a private school and now boasts a long waiting list due to its popularity. Once my sister, Kenzie, graduates with a degree in education, she'll work there too.

We're early risers here—well, except for Kenzie when she's bartending at the Circle B Saloon until close. Right now, she's home from college, but she'll return in a few days. I'm not looking forward to it because I always miss her when she's gone.

"Breakfast consists of the normal spread of grits, biscuits, gravy, sausage, bacon, waffles, muffins, blueberry pancakes, omelets, and scrambled eggs. For lunch, I planned fried chicken, mashed potatoes, green beans, and rolls. Dinner is beef tips with gravy and rice, corn bread and veggies on the side, and finally, triple chocolate cake for dessert."

"I'm sure the ranch hands are gonna love that," Dad says with a laugh. "I mean, the guests."

"Oh, I'm sure they will." I cut my eyes to him, but all he does is shrug. The ranch workers eating at the B&B is a tradition my uncles started in their twenties. Uncle Jackson's to blame, but everyone knows he can't be controlled. After realizing he was gonna keep eating and inviting half the ranch to join him, Grandma made it a perk for the workers. By the time I got out of culinary school, I knew exactly what I was signing up for when I took the job.

I cook quadruple servings each day because the workers eat like horses, and I still need enough for the guests. There usually aren't any leftovers, so at least nothing's wasted. Knowing people appreciate my cooking does make me feel good, but I still give them shit for liking it so much. Then again, so does Dad.

Once my mug is empty and I'm more awake, I stand and grab my keys. Mom tells me to have a good day, and Dad says he's right behind me. I give them a wave and leave. Though the sun won't be up for another hour, it doesn't bother me. I enjoy getting up before the roosters and like the stillness of my surroundings.

When I arrive, the big farmhouse lights are dimmed, and I take my time turning them on. I walk into the kitchen to grind the coffee beans and then put them in the maker to brew. After I pull out the menu I've planned, I start pulling the ingredients from the cabinets. There's no canned food or anything pre-made served here. It's all mixed and made with love.

I've wanted to be a chef since I was a little girl, thanks to Grandma. As the fifth oldest grandkid but only the second girl, I spent a lot of time with her growing up. When I was five, she had me baking homemade blueberry muffins by memory. My childhood was different from my cousins because my biological mother passed away from cancer nine weeks after I was born. Dad had no idea I existed until I was left on the porch of the B&B. Raising a newborn wasn't something he knew how to do, so he hired Mila to be my nanny and help him adjust to being a single parent. They fell madly in love, and the rest is history. She raised me as her own and is the only mother I've ever known. Soon after, they were married, and Mila got pregnant with Kenzie. Once my sister was born, our family was complete. While I wish I knew more about my biological mother at times, I'm thankful for the family I do have.

Jane and Sandra arrive right on time and immediately take over for me, then finish with the omelets, scrambled eggs, and the muffins. I restack the plates, refill the silverware bin, and then bring out the vat of coffee to the dining area. The three of us work together like a well-oiled machine. While I'm in charge, I never have to micromanage because they know what I expect them to do each day.

We have a list of a hundred different recipes we rotate in and out, and we occasionally throw in new ones to see how people like them. The ranch hands are opinionated but no one has ever hated anything we've served. If they have, they've kept their damn mouths shut and rightfully so.

We run food out to the burners, and when I look up at the clock, I'm shocked we only have five minutes until breakfast begins. It never fails to amaze me how fast time passes when I'm here.

Dad enters and gives me a grin. "Smells good."

"Thanks, Mr. Bishop," Sandra says. I look over my shoulder and give him a big smile.

After everything is set and ready for the breakfast rush, we immediately start making the second and third rounds of food because it'll go fast. Soon, the dining room is full of chatter. Sandra checks every ten minutes and makes a list of what we need to replenish.

"More sausage and pancakes," she says at the door. "And coffee, but I'll get that going."

Each morning, the three of us do this dance. I usually cook on the flat top, and Jane is at the stove while Sandra makes her rounds to top off the food and drinks.

When I turn my head, my sister and cousin Rowan barge through the kitchen door, chatting about God knows what. Kenzie carries a plate holding an omelet, and she's stuffing her face.

"What are y'all doin' here?" I ask.

"Coming to visit you, of course!" Kenzie exclaims, then shrugs. "And eat."

"Thought we'd keep you company for a little while," Rowan says with a grin, propping herself up on the counter and swinging her legs back and forth. Though I'm working and don't need the distractions, I'm glad they're here so we can catch up anyway. Considering Kenzie is going back to college in a few days, I want to spend as much time with her as I can.

Rowan looks like she's floating on cloud nine, and I'm so tempted to say something about how annoyingly in love she is with Diesel, but I refrain.

As if she can read my mind, she speaks up. "Bite me."

"So, how's the sex?" Kenzie blurts. Rowan and Diesel have been inseparable, and while it's disgustingly cute, I'm happy for her.

"Kenzie!" I scold, knowing my employees can hear every word we're saying, but they keep our secrets like vaults. Oftentimes, they're so focused I forget they're still in the room. They both have kids a little older than us, so they're hardly fazed.

"What?" She takes a bite of her omelet. "You were thinking it too. I just care enough to ask," she states with pride.

I gag, and we all start laughing. Considering the breakfast rush is nearly over, I grab the ingredients to make the homemade rolls for lunch.

"Don't be a love hater. Someday, Maze…you're gonna find *the one*."

Just the thought of it has me rolling my eyes while I mix, then beat the dough.

"Speaking of which, Diesel and Riley are coming to the bar tonight with the new guy who just got hired. You should come. Kenzie and I are working," Rowan insists.

"Hells yes, you should!" Kenzie's face lights up, and she's way too excited about it. "Stay until after my shift so I can use my newfound drinking freedom to do it *legally*." She just turned twenty-one a month ago and takes every opportunity to remind us.

I glance at her. "I'm busy tonight."

"Doing what?" Rowan asks, doubtful. "Bingeing *Love is Blind* and shoving dark chocolate into your mouth doesn't qualify as busy."

I give her my best death glare, unamused by how right she is.

"But you gotta admit, it's a train wreck you can't look away from…" Kenzie says, referring to the show. "Cameron's my favorite. I'd marry him in a heartbeat."

"See?" I hold my hand out toward Kenzie. "I need to catch up."

Rowan doesn't buy my excuse, though. "You can do it tomorrow. Tonight, you're coming to the bar! No arguing!"

I plop the dough on the counter, then break it into pieces and roll it into balls. "Damn, I thought getting laid would make you nicer," I mutter with a smirk.

"Maybe you're the one who needs to get laid, meanie," she retorts.

"I *definitely* need to get laid," Kenzie adds, and the three of us burst into laughter. I know we're being loud as hell, but I can't help it. These two bring out the best in me.

"What's all this noise I'm hearing?" Dad enters, and I hope to all things holy he didn't overhear what we were talking about. I'd be absolutely mortified.

"None of your business," I quickly say. "Girl talk. No boys allowed."

"Pretty sassy for someone who still lives under my roof," Dad teases, not that I needed the reminder.

"Kenzie and I are gonna get an apartment in the city," I say casually, wanting to change the subject quickly.

"Not a chance in hell," he snaps. "Nice try, though." He reaches over and steals one of the apple turnovers that Kat delivered this morning. Kat's a family friend who provides the B&B with gluten-free pastries. While I could prepare everything, Grandma Bishop loves to support Kat's bakery, and it's something we've done for a long time.

"Dad…" I suck in a breath. "I'm almost twenty-five and live at home. Do you know how pathetic I sound? I need my own place."

He lifts his eyebrow. "You can move out when you get married."

This response causes me to snort, considering my very single relationship status. "And did you and Mom wait till marriage to move in with each other?"

I cross my arms and wait for his answer.

"Do as I say…"

"Not as I do," Kenzie pipes in and finishes his sentence.

"That's right." Dad kisses Kenzie on the head. "Your mom isn't ready to be an empty nester yet, and frankly, I think she'll go crazy without you two there, so until you're in a serious relationship, no talk of moving out."

Rowan looks at us with a tilted head. "My parents are halfway there. I wonder if they'll get all sappy on me when I move out?" she asks.

"Knowing your mom and dad, they're ready to relive their youth days and have their privacy back," Dad says with a chuckle. "They didn't exactly take the slow and steady route."

"Thanks for the visual…" Rowan groans. "Now I need to go throw up my breakfast."

Dad chuckles, then pats her on the shoulder. "Alright, well I'm gonna leave y'all to your girl talk."

Kenzie and Rowan continue chatting, and when the clock changes to ten, crumbs are all that remain. I add fruits and pastries to different baskets we keep out for the guests, as Sandra and Jane continue prepping for lunch.

"So, you never answered the question," Kenzie reminds Rowan. "How's the sex?"

"Mind-blowing," Rowan says, then snorts.

"I gotta clean up and get ready for lunch," I tell them, wanting no part of this conversation.

"Go for it," Kenzie shoos.

After the dining room is cleaned, Jane and I peel the boiled potatoes and then mash them. While I'm adding tons of butter to the pounds of russets, Rowan turns to me.

"So about tonight. I need you to commit."

I bite the inside of my cheek, then add salt and pepper. "You're not gonna let me get out of this, are you?"

Kenzie laughs at how demanding Rowan is being.

"Nope! You're joining us. The whole gang will be there, and you deserve to have a little fun."

"Fun?" I question with a smirk. She elbows me, and I grunt.

Soon the kitchen smells of fried chicken and cornbread. I realize how hungry I am, but I don't typically have time to eat until after serving lunch. When we place the hot food in the dining room, Kenzie and Rowan are the first to grab a plate.

"Ahh, now I see why you really came."

Rowan snickers. "Nah, this is just a bonus."

Kenzie takes a seat, then stuffs her mouth full and lets out a moan. "Mmm. So good."

Soon, guests trickle in and pile their plates, and chatter fills the room. Once Kenzie and Rowan finish eating, we exchange hugs, and I start on my cleanup list as I go over the dinner menu with Donna and Becky, the ladies who work the dinner shift.

I typically do the morning and lunch rush because it's so time-consuming, but I'll help in the evening too if I'm bored. We have a short meeting, then I post the menu for the rest of the week so we're all on the same page.

Jane and Sandra finish prepping as Donna and Becky start cooking. I go through the fridge and pantry and then write down what I'll need to order next week. Just as I'm wrapping up my list, Grandma Bishop walks in wearing her million-dollar smile. Immediately, she opens her arms and pulls me into a hug. I'm pretty sure I'm her favorite grandkid.

"Maize, sweetie, I've missed you," she tells me with a tight squeeze.

"I saw you Friday!" I remind her.

"Doesn't mean I can't miss you," she retorts, then pulls away and greets my employees. They're old friends who chat about the weather and their grandbabies as they work.

Dad walks in, sees Grandma, and laughs. "Mama. Whatcha doin' here?"

"I leave the house, and y'all act like it's a Christmas miracle. I'm not *that* old yet. But since you're so concerned, I was gettin' ready for my quilt club meeting and wanted to stop by and see you two on my way out," she explains, but her smile doesn't falter.

"Checkin' up on me, Grandma?" I ask.

She grabs my cheek like I'm five. "Always, dear."

This causes Dad to let out a howl. "Maize walks a straight line, just like her father. Now, Kenzie, she's a different story."

"Okay, well, if I'm being truthful, I heard you were making double chocolate cake for dinner. I told Scott that sugar wasn't allowed in the house anymore because it's not good for our waistline. So, I thought I'd just grab a slice and be on my way."

Dad snorts. "That's cheatin, Mama."

"No, no, it's not. I said no more sugar was allowed *in* the house. The B&B isn't home, is it? Technically, I'm still following the rules I set."

I cover my mouth to hold back my laughter, then point over to the fridge where the five cakes are waiting.

"That's why you're my favorite," Grandma says, and it causes me to beam.

Dad just shakes his head. "Wait till I tell Dad about your little scheme."

"You will do no such thing, John Joseph Bishop," she warns.

"Oooh, Grandma just pulled out the middle name," I quip.

Grandma lifts an eyebrow at me as she walks over and grabs a to-go box. After cutting the biggest slice of cake I've ever seen, she places a plastic fork in the container with it and then gives me a wink.

"You never saw me. I wasn't here." She waves her hand as though she's trying to pull a Jedi mind trick on us, and somehow, it works because neither of us will tattle.

I crack up, and Dad rolls his eyes. Grandma pats me on the shoulder, then waltzes out as quickly as she walked in.

"Grandpa showed up earlier. Trust me when I say he ate a stack of pancakes with extra, extra syrup," he tells me with a shit-eating grin.

"Oh God," I let out. "They're cheaters! Both of them."

"Not technically, just found loopholes. And they wonder where Jackson gets this shit from!" he exclaims. A bell dings at the front desk, so he hurries to fill his cup full of coffee, then leaves.

As I'm washing my hands, my phone vibrates. Once I dry them off, I pull my cell from my back pocket.

Rowan: See you tonight!

I laugh.

Maize: I said maybe!

Rowan: You will be there, or I'll kick your ass.

This makes me laugh.

Maize: Aww. How sweet. I'd like to see you try, though ;)

Rowan: I'm serious! Plus, who knows, you might meet a new man at the bar tonight. You just never know.

Maize: Oh pleaseeeee. We all know the only guys I'll see there are the regulars and ranch hands.

Rowan: Don't be a Debbie Downer. They're coming around nine. Be there or be scared. You deserve to let loose and have a little fun!

Maize: You know I'm an old lady and get up early.

Rowan: So it's time to change that. See ya there!

I send her a thumbs-up, something she hates, then I grab all the dirty rags and place them in the wash before telling everyone bye. Rowan doesn't like to take no for an answer, but I don't want to commit just yet. I'm so tired I might fall asleep before the sun sets.

Once I'm home, I kick off my shoes and relax on the couch. I close my eyes, knowing I need to shower because I smell like a mix of food and sweat.

"Are you sleepin'?" Kenzie asks.

I open my eyes and glance at her because I didn't even hear her come in. "Not yet, but if you would've left me a little longer, I might've been. Mondays are always so exhausting."

She gives me a half-smile. "Okay, just wanted to let you know I'm leaving. Get your ass rested so you can hang out with me until close."

I groan because she's just as relentless as Rowan.

She nods, then checks the time. "See you later, sis."

I give her a wave, then finally get up and head for the shower. Staying up late during the week isn't something I like to do because of how early I have to get up in the mornings, but I want to spend as much time with Kenzie before she returns to school. I really can't wait until she graduates in the spring and is home permanently. It's just not the same here without her.

After I clean up, I take an hour nap and reset my brain before I begrudgingly go to the bar. Though I may not stay until close like Kenzie wants, I hope it makes them happy to know their peer pressure still works after all these years.

CHAPTER TWO

GAVIN

Over the weekend, I moved all my shit into one of the spare ranch hand cabins. Though the new place is furnished, I still had a lot to pack and bring with me. I also couldn't leave Houston without my favorite saddle and rope. I thought I could pack up and move in with little effort, but it took an entire day just to load my truck. Then it rained during the whole damn drive to Eldorado.

This morning, I woke up extra early for my first official day on the job. I've already taken a shower and drunk a cup of coffee, and I still have forty-five minutes before I have to meet with Alex Bishop, the ranch manager. Instead of waiting around and watching the clock, I decide to head out.

The directions Jackson, my new boss, gave me are comical. The map he emailed me does not have any named roads—just barns, curbs, and cactus patches—and it looks like a five-year-old drew it. It's Southern directions at their finest. After I drive over nine cattle guards, I should see a metal building on the right.

Even though I live on the ranch, it's so massive it takes me nearly fifteen minutes to arrive where I need to be. The sun hasn't risen yet, but I'm grateful to see lights on in the shop and an old pickup outside. I park and enter, not sure what to expect.

Alex, who I met previously, is drinking a cup of coffee at a desk. He's Jackson's younger brother and about ten years older than me. Two guys in their mid-twenties give each other shit, and he watches them with a grin. After a moment, Alex notices me.

"Alright, if you ladies are done, Gavin's here," Alex interrupts them.

They both turn and size me up. By their expressions, I don't think they knew a new employee was starting today.

"Gavin, this is my son, Riley."

He didn't have to tell me because they look nearly identical other than their age. I take Riley's hand and shake it firmly.

"This is Diesel, he runs the cattle operation," Alex continues.

"Nice to meet you," Diesel says with a handshake and a grin.

"He's new to Eldorado and will be staying in one of the ranch hand cabins. He'll be working with Jackson on breaking in the wild horses. He has bull riding experience and trains riders too."

Diesel looks at me with a sly grin. "Bull riding?" His brows raise, a reaction I'm used to from people when they learn what I used to do. "Impressive."

"Thanks. It was dangerous work, won some competitions, got some trophies, but I'm retired now." People are always shocked by what I've accomplished. I've made enough money to do whatever I want, and I stopped riding bulls before I broke my back. However, I keep those details to myself.

"I bet you have some insane stories about traveling to rodeos and competing, huh?" Riley gives me a smirk.

"Or how much ass you got?" Diesel taunts.

The corner of my lips tilts up as I think about the past. It was a wild and crazy time. "You could say that. On both accounts."

"Maybe over a round of beers," Diesel suggests. "My girlfriend works at the Circle B Saloon in town and will hook us up. We could meet up after work."

Riley groans, and I'm not entirely sure why. Might be because Diesel mentioned his girlfriend, but I have a feeling there's more to this story than they're saying.

"Uh, sure. I've been there a couple of times." I pinch the back of my neck, thinking about the last time I was in town. Maize comes to the forefront, and I half-wonder if she'll be there. Wouldn't that be some crazy shit? I look at him. "How about nine?"

"Sounds good," he tells me.

One thing I love about this part of Texas is everyone's friendly, and I know Diesel's genuinely inviting me to make me feel welcome. It's just how people are around these parts, and the last thing I want to do is reject the offer and come off like a dick. First impressions are important.

"Alright, now that our team meeting is over…" Alex's lips tilt up. "I'm gonna give Gavin a tour of the property and get him settled in with Jackson and Kiera."

Moments later, Alex and I head out the door. Alex unlocks the truck that looks like it's seen better days, and we get inside. The bumper is bent with large scratches on the side. I buckle in, and as the sun rises, we begin the grand tour of the Circle B Ranch.

"Riley and Diesel like to rag on each other all the time. They've been best friends since they were kids," Alex explains. "And Diesel is now dating my daughter Rowan, something Riley has been against since he was five."

I laugh. "That actually explains a lot. Dating your brother's best friend…they better get married—or things might get really awkward between them."

"If he knows what's good for him, he won't break her heart," Alex clarifies. "He'll be roadkill otherwise. Rowan would murder him herself."

This makes me chuckle. I'm not a man of many words and usually listen and watch everyone else. Alex doesn't seem to mind and fills the silence with information about the ranch. I'm amazed they have thousands of acres of land. It's much different than the Houston area where I grew up.

Alex points out a large two-story home with a wraparound porch that sits off the road, telling me that's where his parents live. As we continue driving, we pass different barns, and he explains each one's purpose. Some hold extra feed for the animals while others house the equipment. An hour passes before we arrive at the training facility run by Jackson and Kiera.

When Alex parks, he turns and looks at me. "Jackson's a known prankster. Consider yourself warned."

I grin. "Thanks for the heads-up. It'll keep the days interesting at least."

"You say that now," Alex says as we head inside toward the office, where Kiera's sitting behind a big oak desk with a schedule book open. As soon as her eyes meet mine, she grins.

"God, I'm so happy you're finally here."

A minute passes, and Jackson walks in wearing a shit-eating grin followed by two young men. Twins. "Not gonna listen to any complainin' today," he warns them both. "Maybe your mom will."

Kiera groans with an eye roll. "It's too early for that. Don't start with me, or you'll be doing double," she warns.

Their jaws lock, but they don't talk back. I get the feeling they get themselves into a lot of trouble by their parents' reaction.

Kiera sweeps loose strands of blond hair out of her face. "Oh, Gavin, these are our two boys, Knox and Kane. You'll see them around doing the guided horse tours at the B&B. They also feed them in the morning and shovel shit in the afternoon, which will be the least of their worries if they keep driving me crazy."

Their faces contort, but they have manners and shake my hand.

"Nice to meet you," they say. There's no way I could tell them apart, even if I tried.

During my interview with Jackson and Kiera, they explained how busy they've been with training and how they desperately needed extra help with the wild horses. I went through all my experience, and a week later, they offered me a position. I had some other obligations at home first and couldn't start immediately, but they were willing to wait. When I got the call, there wasn't a doubt in my bones about accepting the job. The money was great, I'd have a place to stay, and the landscape was vast and beautiful. Though Houston will always be home, I was ready to escape to a small town away from the lifestyle I'd led. I fell in love with Eldorado the first time I visited. There's something magical about the ranch that I can't explain.

"I'll meet y'all outside," Alex tells the twins. One of them releases a grunt while the other rolls his eyes.

Kiera sighs once they're out of sight. "I wish they were more like their sister. Kaitlyn does things without being disrespectful."

Jackson chuckles and turns to me. "That's our youngest. She just left for her second year of college, but she'll be back during the holidays and breaks. I'm sure you'll see her around then."

The phone rings, and Keira answers and immediately begins scribbling on a notepad. "How about next week? Could probably fit you in on Monday. Yep. See ya then." She ends the call, then looks up at me. "I hope you're ready to start workin' this afternoon," she tells me.

"I sure am. Been looking forward to it," I admit, which seems to please them both. The exhaustion on their faces is evident. I'm glad I can relieve some of the pressure and stress they've had running this huge empire by themselves.

"Great," Jackson says, patting me on the back. "We've got a packed training schedule for the next five years."

My eyes widen in shock.

"That might be a slight exaggeration." Kiera snorts. "But the rest of the year and next will be really busy, though. Since our competitor closed shop, business has been booming."

"That's great." I smile.

"Have you eaten?" Jackson abruptly changes the subject, but Kiera doesn't seem to mind and goes back to her calendar.

"Actually, no," I respond.

Jackson immediately shakes his head. "Unacceptable." Swinging open the office door, he finds Alex standing by the truck talking to the twins and moves toward him. "Not feeding our new employee on his first day is ridiculous. The man has to eat!"

Alex rolls his eyes and flips him off. Jackson turns toward me. "Alex will take you to the B&B for breakfast. It's tradition. Then I'll show you 'round here."

Kiera comes outside and frowns. "Don't be a bad influence."

"Yeah, yeah. Haven't heard that all my life." He chuckles. "Really happy you took our offer. Now go eat. I'll see you back here in an hour."

"Is that a firm hour?" Alex asks. "Or do we have time?"

Jackson shrugs. "Take however long you need, considering it's his first day. Make sure he tries the blueberry pancakes," he tells Alex, then looks at me. "My niece makes the best stacks in Texas," Jackson says with a grin.

"Sounds like I need to." I smile. Alex and I climb into the truck while Knox and Kane ride in the back.

Alex drives us across the property on the road that leads to the shop.

"Sorry. I should've thought about bringin' ya to the B&B for breakfast since we were so close. Slipped my mind, though."

"No need to apologize. I should've eaten before I left the house. I typically do," I explain.

"Nah. Not anymore. Breakfast at the B&B is something you should add to your daily schedule. It's served from six to ten every day with enough to feed a small army—or rather all the ranch hands on-site." He chuckles.

Alex parks in the front by a ton of other work trucks. I check my phone and see it's just past seven. Knox and Kane climb out of the bed, and I follow Alex up the steps. Once we're inside, the smell of bacon and pancakes has my stomach growling. I didn't realize how hungry I was until now.

The tall ceilings and wooden floors of the B&B give me the same feeling as when I'd visit my grandma's house. We enter the buffet area, and I am surprised by the amount of food even though Alex warned me. We grab plates, and I notice the ample seating inside the dining room for the guests.

"There's seating outside too," Alex explains, piling sausage and scrambled eggs on his plate.

"Showing him how to do it right," a man says from behind, and my brows furrow.

He holds out his hand and takes mine. "I'm John, nice to meet you."

I glance at Alex. "Jackson didn't say he was a twin, did he?"

I shake my head.

"I'm the non-crazy one," John explains with a chuckle. "I run the B&B."

"Gotcha. I was slightly confused for a second," I admit.

John takes in a deep breath. "I'm sure you were. Most people are. Thankfully, Jackson's somewhat settled down in his old age, or I'm sure some sort of joke would've been played on ya. Trust me when I say it's not been easy having the same face as him."

His admission has me chuckling. "I can *only* imagine."

"Don't let me interrupt you. Enjoy your food. If you need anything, let me know," John says, then walks away to greet some of the guests who enter. It would be impossible to sleep in late with the delicious smells wafting through the house.

Alex and I sit at a table by the large windows that oversee the backyard, and Knox and Kane make their way to a bigger table. Though it's the last day of August, it's by no means cool, so hopefully, the temperatures will drop soon. The humidity here isn't like it is in Houston, but it's still hot as hell.

"So, how long has this place been here?" I ask, interested in the history of the B&B.

"Almost thirty years. It was John's idea to turn the old farmhouse into a nature getaway. Ever since we remodeled and fixed it up, we've been booked solid. Some regulars have booked the same weeks for the past few decades and have made visiting here a tradition in their family, which Mama loves."

I take a bite of the blueberry pancakes like Jackson suggested, and I swallow it down. My eyes go wide as I take bigger bites until my plate is clean.

"Good, huh?" Alex grins. "My niece, John's daughter, is the head chef. Took all Mama's recipes and added some of her culinary skills to them. She plans all the meals, and with her small team, she prepares hot food every day for every meal."

"You Bishops are the jacks-of-all-trades," I say, impressed with how much they've accomplished.

"Not to mention my older brother Evan is a doctor and so is his wife. So, if an apocalypse happens, you're in the right place." Alex says around a mouthful. It makes me smile.

Seconds later, Diesel and Riley enter, going back and forth with each other just like they were this morning, but now it all makes sense.

Alex shakes his head. "They act like that all the time."

Another guy I haven't met yet is following them. As soon as the guys see me, they walk up and give hellos and introductions.

"Grayson, this is Gavin. He's helping Uncle Jackson with the horses," Riley says, popping a piece of bacon in his mouth.

"Nice to meet ya." We say it at the same time, then laugh.

"I work with Diesel, but hope to one day be training horses too," Grayson tells me.

"I'm the best boss he's ever had!" Diesel nearly yells. Grayson rolls his eyes.

"Let's eat," Riley announces, getting antsy, and they follow him to sit with Knox and Kane.

I get up and put another stack of pancakes on my plate, then cover them with syrup. As I take a big bite of pancakes, I think about the night I had with a girl the last time I was here. I think I remember Maize mentioning someone named Grayson, and I wonder if it's the same guy. It's a small town, so it's possible.

I think about that night we spent together often and wish I would've asked her for her number. I've thought about her and the chemistry we shared. It's been impossible to get her out of my system, and it's not from a lack of trying.

We finish eating, and Knox and Kane decide to ride with Riley. Alex delivers me to Jackson, who's sweating his ass off with a shovel in his hand.

Alex rolls down the window. "Hey, old man. I brought Gavin back as demanded."

Jackson gruffs. "Thank you, captain obvious."

"Thanks for showing me around," I tell Alex as I get out of the truck.

"Anytime!" Alex says out the open window, then gives me a wave before leaving.

Jackson sets the shovel down and walks over to me, wiping the sweat from his brow. "How was breakfast?"

"Great. Reminds me of my ma's cookin'," I admit. "I think I ate ten pancakes."

"Told ya! Anyway, guess we should get you acquainted with the training area."

We walk over to the different sections and barns. Among the several corrals is enough room to train several horses at once. Before I got hired, Kiera and Jackson explained their experience and what they were looking for in an employee. For the past few years, they've been doing everything on their own with their kids' help. They want to expand, but without help, that's not possible.

"Right now, we're training eight horses. Two will be picked up by the end of the week, and one was delivered about an hour ago. The others are at different stages but only have a few more weeks to go. We're also getting some new mares on Monday."

I nod and make a mental note. We walk to the edge of the training area, and Jackson shows me an obstacle course set up for barrel racing. It's impressive, but it seems everything the Bishops do is.

"The kids usually feed the horses in the morning, and I make them clean out stalls in the afternoons. For the most part, they're doing different tasks around the ranch. They're good kids, but damn, they make me feel old."

I give him a side-grin. "My ma always said to be good growing up, or my payback would be having kids who were worse than me. Guess they're yours."

"Damn right they are," he admits, shaking his head. "Oh, that colt delivered this morning will be your first project. He's in the stable being fed but thought you could get started with him today. Spunky as hell and has a bad attitude."

"Just my type." I chuckle.

"Fireball should be a good start for you," he tells me, leading me to the barn.

The colt looks like he's around two and doesn't pay any attention to us.

"Apparently, he's a fucker, I mean bucker. Same thing, though." Jackson leans against the gate.

"Has he had any saddle practice?" I ask, wanting to know the history and what level we're starting on.

"The owners have done nothing but put a halter on him and led him on rides. He's an asshole, and they want him broken in enough for their grandkids to ride."

Fireball starts pawing his hoof on the ground, and I smile. It's been a while since I've been this excited about work. Jackson shows me the location of all the gear, then he leaves me to myself. Taking my time, I lead Fireball out to the arena, and we get started.

The afternoon passes by quickly, and I work with Fireball until we're both exhausted. I started slow with leading and saddle practice, and he hated every minute. Repetition is key when training and breaking animals. After we finish working, I rinse him down and put him in the pasture, where he immediately starts rolling.

"You are an asshole," I yell at him, then walk to the office, remembering I left my truck at the shop this morning. Jackson's got his feet up on the desk when I enter.

"Can you possibly give me a ride to the shop?" I ask, and he's more than willing.

We hop in the truck, and on the way over, he asks me how things went this afternoon.

I grin. "Great, but you're right, he does have an attitude. I think he'll realize who's in charge, though, hopefully."

Jackson chuckles. "He better."

He pulls up next to my truck, and I thank him before I get out and wave as he drives off. As I'm pulling my keys from my pocket, Riley and Diesel exit the shop. They look like they've both had a hell of a day.

"There you are," Riley says. "We both stupidly forgot to get your number earlier."

I pull my phone out, and we exchange info.

"Want me to pick you up on the way there?" Riley asks.

"Yeah, that'd be great. Just need to take a shower first."

Diesel looks down at all the dirt on his clothes. "Good idea."

"Awesome! I'll pick you up around eight-ish," Riley tells me, then turns to Diesel. "You need a ride too?"

"Nah, man, I'm gonna stay until close to hang out with your sister." He elbows him. Riley lets out a groan. A roar of laughter escapes Diesel, and I can tell he's getting a kick out of rubbing this in his best friend's face.

"I'm probably only going to stay for a drink, then go home, if that's cool with you," he tells me.

"That's fine. I gotta be up early for work in the morning anyway."

"See," Riley says with a finger to his chest. "Some of us *are* responsible adults."

Diesel laughs. "I'm responsible, ask my girlfriend."

Riley's ready to punch him in the face but doesn't. I tell them both goodbye and get in the truck and leave. I replay my day, and I realize I'm tired. By the time I walk up the steps and enter the cabin, I'm more than ready to wash off the sweat of the day.

I'm not used to being here yet, but I'm sure it will eventually feel like home. On the walls are photographs of horses and fences, rolling hills and old tractors. The décor is exactly what one would expect to see on a ranch. I go to my bedroom, grab some clothes, then take a shower.

By the time I'm finished, I still have a few hours before Riley arrives. I could have driven myself, but he's not staying that long anyway, so it's not a big deal. My eyes are tired, and I end up falling asleep on the couch until knocks tap on the door. I get up, and Riley's standing there with a smile. "Ready?"

"Yep," I tell him, grabbing my keys and walking out with him.

We drive over to the saloon, and Maize comes to mind. She was drinking her worries away, looking so goddamn gorgeous. I'm tempted to ask Riley if he knows her since this is a small town, but I don't. If we're meant to see each other again, we will.

"So how'd you end up here, considering you used to ride professionally?" he asks on the way.

"After I won a few championships, I was ready to get out of Houston. Eldorado seemed like the perfect place to settle down and not be in the hustle or bustle of a big city. It's the exact opposite of what I'm used to, and I love training horses."

"Oh, so you're from Houston. I didn't realize people were into riding and stuff there," he admits.

A lot of people think that, especially if they don't know the landscape.

"My parents live on the outskirts, not downtown or anything. But yeah, there's a lot of riding that goes on, and the Houston Rodeo is one of the biggest in Texas. It's a popular thing to do. When I watched the bull riders there as a kid, I immediately knew that's what I wanted to do when I grew up. Plus, I'm somewhat of an adrenaline junkie."

Riley laughs. "You'd have to be to get on the back of one of those animals."

We pull into the parking lot, and a small smile touches my lips when we walk inside.

"Looks like Diesel's already here," Riley mutters as we walk toward the bar. He's chatting with people, but Riley interrupts him. "Uh...anyway." He clears his throat. "This is Gavin. He'll be working with Jackson training horses."

Kenzie's eyes go wide, and recognition flashes behind them. I wonder if she remembers me from the bar that night, but she doesn't say a word. Neither do I. My heart races, and I wonder if Maize is here too.

I meet Rowan, and when I turn my head, I see Maize sitting there as pretty as ever. I have so many damn questions I can barely contain myself.

"This is my other cousin, Maize. She's the cook at the B&B."

I smirk, realizing I was eating her food this morning. "Ooh, the one who makes the amazing pancakes."

Maize slightly turns to shake my hand, and that's when she sees me. She blinks hard, as if she expects me to disappear. I wish she'd say something, and I open my mouth, but Rowan interrupts me, thankfully. There are too many people around to ask her what the hell happened that night.

"So, Gavin, where're you from?" Rowan asks, moving the conversation away from Maize, who's acting awkward as hell.

"Houston. But I've traveled a lot in the past twelve years or so. I've been all over the state."

"Gavin's a retired bull rider," Riley explains. "Trains riders now on the side."

"Oh my God," Kenzie gushes in the same tone she did the night I first met her. "That is so cool. I would love to see you ride."

I'm well aware of her personality and how she acts, and I smile at her. She has to remember me.

Taking a seat at the bar, I order a drink as Rowan walks up to Diesel. She's obviously Alex's daughter, and I don't doubt for a second he wouldn't kick Diesel's ass if he hurt her. Noticing the way they look at each other, though, I can tell it's the real deal. While I'm sipping my beer, Maize gets up and walks away, then Rowan follows her.

Diesel brings up my bull riding days, and I get lost in conversation. When I turn to order another drink, I realize Maize never returned. It makes me think that bailing on people might just be her thing.

CHAPTER THREE

MAIZE

"Hey, what's goin' on?" Rowan asks, coming into the bathroom where I'm hiding. "You look like you've seen a ghost."

"That guy..." I inhale sharply, hardly believing it.

"Gavin? What about him?"

"That's *Gavin*."

She blinks. "Right, I just said that."

"No, I mean, yes. That's the Gavin I slept with a few weeks ago," I reiterate.

"Wait..." She narrows her eyes. "The guy you bailed on the next morning?"

"Yes!"

Rowan quickly covers her mouth as if she's trying to hold back laughter. "Oh my God, Maze!"

"Shut up!" I smack her arm. "This is humiliating!"

"This is freaking awesome." She chuckles. "Did he recognize you?"

I sigh, rubbing my temples as a headache surfaces. "I don't know. I recognized him right away. That's why I quickly turned away."

"Well, go out there and say hi!" She pushes me toward the door, but I dig my heels into the floor.

"Hell. No!" I frantically shake my head.

"Weren't you just tellin' your daddy you were almost twenty-five years old and old enough to move out?" She cocks her hip and places a hand on it. "This isn't very mature." She snickers.

I roll my eyes and shrug because I don't care. I'm not going back out there. "I didn't realize how much older than me he was. He looks older, right?" I ask nervously.

She nods, agreeing. "He definitely does. Probably ten years older?"

"Oh my God." I drop my face into my hands. "I'm leaving through the back."

"I don't think so," she states firmly.

"Fine, then I'm staying in here."

"The bathroom?" She cocks a brow.

"Rowan, please! Help me," I plead.

"Alright, fine. I'll make sure the coast is clear." She pats my shoulder.

Slowly, she opens the door and peeks around.

"Okay, you're good," Rowan says. She faces me and waves me out. I immediately rush toward the employee exit.

"Thank you!" I whisper-shout, feeling relief as soon as I step outside.

I hope Gavin doesn't notice I ditched...*again*. I'm sure I'm a sight to see, scrambling out like I just robbed a bank. By the time I climb into my truck and head home, my palms are sweaty, and my heart is racing. Gavin working for Uncle Jackson means I'll eventually have to see him again. The dread nearly consumes me, and I'm pissed I got myself into this predicament in the first place. One-night stands aren't my thing, but I was convinced I'd never see him again because I thought he was only passing through town.

Cowboys are typically a hard no, and I should've stuck by that rule.

When I was eighteen, I dated a ranch hand named Timothy. It was love at first sight, or so I thought. My family was aware of our relationship and warned against getting involved because he wouldn't be staying long term. I foolishly thought I was enough for him to stay, but I was so damn wrong. When it ended between us, I realized how I'd been bamboozled by love. My heart was broken beyond repair, and I swore never to make that mistake again. I've avoided any men who've shown interest in me and worked on the ranch. Yet I find myself in this predicament. I just hope like hell he keeps our secret to himself and leaves me alone.

When I get home, Mom and Dad are watching TV on the couch. Before I'm bombarded with conversation, I wave, then rush to my room and dramatically fall onto my bed. The only thing that pulls me away from my humiliation is my phone vibrating. When I pick it up, I see a message from Rowan and hope she was able to come up with a good excuse.

Rowan: Totally random question for no reason, but when was your last period?

Maize: Uh...I don't know? Why?

Rowan: Well, any chance you could be pregnant?

What the fuck kinda question is that? Probably because all the blood drained from my face, and I rushed to the bathroom like I was gonna vomit the moment I realized Gavin was here.

Maize: WHAT? No!

Just the thought of being pregnant throws me into a panic. How the hell would I explain that to my family?

Rowan: Are you sure? Like 100%?

I think back to the incredible night we had together, but the small details remain a blur. We were greedy for one another, and he worshipped my body like I was a goddess. Gavin's the type of man you run away with for a summer, not the kind you settle down with. The bull riding culture creates fuck boys, and I bet he was one.
　Obviously, we were careful, but there's always a chance.

Maize: I'm on the pill, and we used a condom.

Rowan: Did you remember to take your pill?

These questions aren't helping the way I feel right now.

Maize: I think so...I mean, sometimes I forget, but typically I do!

Rowan: Oh my God...

Maize: Shut up. I swear. I'm not pregnant.

Rowan: Then take a test.

Maize: We hooked up like three weeks ago. It'd be too soon to know anyway.

Rowan: Maybe. I'm buying you a test, though, just to be sure.

I roll my eyes, though I know she will.

Maize: And when I prove to you I'm NOT, you owe me $100!

Rowan: Ha! You better cross your fingers and toes you aren't. Unless you want Mr. Brooding Cowboy as your baby daddy ;)

Maize: I hate you so much.

I roll over and bury my face in the pillow. I'll probably never be able to live this down. Thank God no one else knows about it other than Rowan and Kenzie. As the thought crosses my mind, I get a text from her.

Kenzie: Do you feel okay?

Maize: Yep, I just had to get out of there.

Kenzie: Okay good. Kinda worried me. Sidenote: I can't believe Gavin's working for Uncle Jackson. What are the odds?

With a groan, I reply. I was half hoping she'd forgotten that night, but Gavin isn't the forgettable type. Not with his dark hair, blue eyes, and pouty lips. She witnessed us flirting, saw us leave together, and knows I slept with him.

Maize: I don't know, but I'M NOT HAPPY ABOUT THIS.

Kenzie: Why? He's hot as hell and was totally into you that night at the bar. I'm ecstatic we have some real-life cowboy man candy to drool over. Might put in a good word to Aunt Kiera and see if she can hire someone more my age, though.

Maize: Ugh. Can we drop this?

Kenzie: I guess, but only because I gotta get back to work!

Then again, I can't deny how damn sexy he looked in those jeans and boots. I almost ask Kenzie if he's still there but decide against it. If I close my eyes, I almost remember the smell of his skin against mine. As soon as I think about rolling around naked in the sheets with him, I push it away. Even though my mind is all over the place, I somehow force myself to sleep.

The next morning, I'm in a weird mood. It's a reminder to keep my ass home regardless of how much Kenzie and Rowan pressure me to go out. Next time, I'm sticking to my guns and watching Netflix like I wanted.

I drink a cup of coffee and leave before Dad like always. While I grab the ingredients for breakfast, I'm distracted. My employees arrive on time, and I'm thankful because when they're around, I have no time to think about my complicated but nonexistent love life.

As soon as six rolls around, the dining room quickly fills up with people. At seven, I check the buffet status, and that's when I see Gavin. Our eyes lock, and I feel as if my feet are glued to the floor. I tuck my bottom lip into my mouth, wishing I would've just stayed hidden in the kitchen, then break the hold he has on me. When I glance over again, Gavin waves me over. While I contemplate turning around and pretending I didn't notice him, it's impossible with so many roaming eyes. My heart beats rapidly, but I push it down as I walk over to the table where he's eating alone. I try my hardest not to raise suspicion especially with my cousins watching.

Gavin smiles and speaks in a hushed tone. "We've met before, haven't we?"

Panic creeps in my throat, and I hope no one can hear him. Immediately, I shake my head. "No, I don't think so."

Gavin narrows his eyes. Damn those ocean-colored eyes seem to peer straight through me as he smirks. "I'm positive we ran into each other at the bar a few weeks ago," he insists.

I shrug and force a smile. "You must be confusing me with somebody else."

"You sure 'bout that?" He waits, giving me the chance to change my tune.

"I don't remember, sorry. But it's really nice to meet you. Oh, and I apologize for running out the other night. I wasn't feeling very well. But I hope you had a good time hanging out with everyone."

He clears his throat, then sips a cup of coffee. "Hanging out with your sister and cousins."

I keep a steady smile and don't react.

"Well, welcome to the ranch. Hope you enjoy your breakfast. I gotta get back to work."

By the time I return to the kitchen, my heart's galloping at full speed.

"Are you okay?" Sandra asks, glancing at the cold sweat that's formed on my brow.

"I'm fine. We need more ham and coffee," I say, wanting to forget Gavin completely, but knowing that'd be impossible. Pretending I didn't know him was dumb as hell, and I'm positive he didn't believe me. But if I keep up the act, maybe he'll drop it, and I can go on living in an alternate universe where I didn't have the best sex of my life with him. The chemistry we shared was undeniable, but I lost control with him, and it can never happen again.

I'm pissed he wanted to bring it up here. This isn't the time or the place, and it caught me off guard, which I don't appreciate. Once breakfast is over, I text Rowan, knowing she'll get a kick out of it.

Maize: So...I spoke to Gavin today.

Rowan: Did you? OMG! Details, now!

Maize: He asked if I remembered him, and I denied it.

I shake my head at how stupid it seems after I send the message.

Rowan: Wait, your plan is to pretend it didn't happen?

Maize: Exactly! Just avoid him like he has an STD, and then hopefully it'll be like it never happened.

Rowan: Uh. Good luck with that. Did you take that pregnancy test yet?

I growl and bite my bottom lip.

Maize: NO!

Rowan: I'm buying you one today!

The lunch rush flies by quickly, and I've never been more ready to go home and lock myself in my room than I am right now. Before I leave, I walk through the kitchen and confirm the night shift has everything they need. Donna and Becky assure me they have it under control, and I know they do.
"You headed out?" Dad pops his head up from behind the check-in desk when I walk by.
"Yes, sir."
"Before you go, can you check the garden? I think your mom mentioned something about the tomatoes and squash needing picked."
My eyes light up because it's one of my favorite things to do. "Sure, I'll be happy to."
I put on the pair of boots I keep at the B&B. After grabbing a tub, I walk out to the rows of vegetables and herbs we plant each season. Dad was right. I pull as much as I can, then drop it in the kitchen before going out and picking more. Getting my hands a little dirty relaxes my busy mind.

"Told ya!" Dad says when I return with my second load.

"In a few days, there will be even more," I explain and rinse them. After I finish, I say my goodbyes and head home. I think about Gavin and his cold stare when I denied knowing him. After I shower, I eat leftovers, then go to my room. Even if I used *Love is Blind* as an excuse to ditch, I wasn't kidding about catching up.

I flick on the TV and get comfortable. As I'm dozing off, Kenzie lets herself into my room.

"I knew it! I knew I heard Cameron's voice."

Grabbing a pillow, I throw it at her, but she quickly blocks it. She's entranced by the TV, but then snaps out of it and brings the attention back to me.

"You gonna tell me what really happened between you and Gavin, without the CliffsNotes?" She tilts her head and crosses her arms. "I wasn't born yesterday, Maze. I saw the way you two were flirting at the bar a few weeks ago, and considering you needed to be picked up after my shift, I think I know what happened. I'd never forget a face like that," she says.

I sigh. "You wouldn't believe me if I tried to make something up anyway."

"Because you're a shitty liar," she reminds me.

"That's what you think," I retort.

"Your face *always* gives you away." Kenzie smirks. "So quit stalling and tell me how big his dick was." She plops down on my bed, reaches for the remote, and pauses the show.

My cheeks heat, and her mouth falls open.

"Oh my God," she whispers. "He's humongous, isn't he?"

I nod, then cover my face before I glance at her. "The sex was amazing, but I can't get involved with him."

Kenzie places a hand on her chest. "I will trade you places in a heartbeat!"

I lean my head against the wall. "You're ridiculous."

"*You* are. If he'd let me inside, I'd go to his cabin right now and save a horse. So what's the hangup? You're allowed to have fun, Maze. Amazing sex never hurt anyone."

After sucking in a deep breath, I exhale slowly. "He's so much older. I knew he was when we hooked up, but it didn't matter at the time because it was a one time thing. Not to mention we're in two different places in our lives. I want to start my catering business eventually, and he could get bored of being in the middle of nowhere and leave. Not to mention my rule—I have it for a reason."

"Yeah, yeah. I know. Timothy ruined every opportunity for anyone who works on the ranch and wants to date you, even if they're the perfect man. So how old is he?"

I look at her. "Thirty-five, I think?"

"So what if he's closer to dad's age than yours. Big deal. There are some silver foxes out there that I'd let be *my* daddy."

Nearly throwing up in my mouth, I playfully smack her. "Oh my God, stop! That's not true." I burst out laughing at the face she makes. "You say that shit to get under my skin."

She smiles wide. "Of course."

I reach for the remote, but she pulls back before I can. "We're not done talking about this. I have to know what you're going to do about this now that he's here."

A small grin forms on my lips. "Pretend I didn't have the best sex of my life with him."

"And that's it?"

I nod.

Her eyes widen in shock. "Do you have brain damage?"

"No! It's just another heartbreak waiting to happen. Pretending lets me move on with my life. The right man will come when I least expect it."

Kenzie snorts and rolls her eyes. "But what if he is *the one*, and you're just being stubborn as hell?"

"Doubtful," I huff.

"People have sex with no attachments. You don't have to get married or anything. It's called having fun."

"Not for me, Kenzie. I'm good. Also please don't tell anyone. And I mean *anyone*. Rowan knows, but no one else."

She makes a zipper motion across her lips. "Secret's safe with me, but you gotta tell me why you called me to pick your ass up if the sex was so great."

I hesitate. "I was embarrassed that we slept together so soon after meeting. I'd never done that before. I knew I couldn't face him and didn't reach out because I wasn't sure what to say."

"You were living on the edge." Kenzie snickers.

I throw another pillow, but this time, it catches her off guard and smacks her. I snag the remote and flick on the show. Being preoccupied by Cameron, she kicks off her shoes and lies on the bed. We watch and laugh at the same things. Randomly, I'll think about Gavin and the way his lips felt on my skin. His strong hands on my body is something I wish I could feel again. Just the way his tongue twisted with mine makes heat rush through me. When the episode ends, I yawn.

"I'm leaving tomorrow to go back to school," she tells me.

I stick out my lower lip. "I know. I'm gonna be sad."

"Aw, I already promised Mom I would come back as much as I could." She hugs me.

"Good," I say. "Drive safe. Text me when you get to your dorm." I sound like Mom with the reminder.

"I will! Night. Love you," Kenzie says with a grin

"Love you too."

She shuts the door, and I let out a long sigh.

What Gavin and I had was special, but it can *never* happen again. Sex without some sort of attachment doesn't exist.

CHAPTER FOUR

GAVIN

ONE MONTH LATER

"C'mon, Racer. Don't gimme a hard time today," I plead with the colt who's giving me hell about wearing a bridle. He's a quarter horse, and they are usually the easiest breed to train, but it's hot as hell, so we're both agitated. He's not as wild as the others, which is why I start my days with him.

Maybe it's not just the heat that's annoying me.

It's been a month since I moved to the ranch, and though I've settled in comfortably, Maize's still trying to convince me she doesn't remember who I am. When we're in the same place, she actively dodges me as though I have a contagious disease.

And perhaps it pisses me off more than it should, but I've never had a woman who wasn't eager for my attention. She claims to have no memory of our night together, but I don't believe her, considering she screamed my name and begged me to fuck her *hard*. I haven't been able to get it out of my mind since it happened almost two months ago.

With working on the ranch and training Cooper advanced bull riding skills a few times a week, one would assume I'd be too damn exhausted to think about her, but every morning I see her at the B&B, and it's impossible not to. Maize barely glances my way as she walks in and out of the kitchen, refilling the buffet with her delicious pancakes and sausage patties. When I speak, she acts as if I'm wasting her time, and her responses are short. I'd be amused if she weren't lying to me. Regardless, I always smile at her, and though she tries to remain unfazed, the blush on her cheeks gives her away.

"That's a good boy," I tell Racer once I secure the bit in his mouth and put the bridle over his head. I slowly pet him and give positive reinforcements until he's used to the sensation. We've been working together for a couple of weeks, and he's already making good progress.

I train him for another hour—setting the saddle on his back and adding some weight so he can get used to it. Eventually, Racer will be used on guided tours.

After we're done, I put Racer in the main pasture to graze, and I get a text from Grayson.

Grayson: Meeting for brunch in ten.

On the early mornings when we're too busy to eat breakfast, we go after the rush. That usually means Maize isn't as busy, and I can attempt to get more than one-word responses from her.

Gavin: I'll be there.

I park at the B&B, a place that's become my second home, and get out of the truck. After I stroll inside, I immediately scan the area for Maize. Though I don't see her, I can hear her laughter. Once I'm in the dining area, I see Grayson sitting at a table with Riley and Diesel, and he's chatting with Maize and John.

"Mornin'," I bellow, tapping my hat toward Maize as she glares at me. "You look pretty today."

She sighs, then rolls her eyes before walking away without a word.

Yeah, I'm used to that reaction. Not sure why she's hell-bent on ignoring me or denying our night together, but I'm determined to figure it out no matter how long it takes.

"Tell me again how much game you've got." Diesel barks out a laugh.

"Trust me, it's not my *game* that's the issue. It's *her*," I counter, flashing an apologetic look at her dad before he murders me for talking about his daughter.

"I've raised that girl for twenty-five years, and I'm still trying to figure her out, so good luck." John chuckles before leaving us to ourselves.

"Great," I mutter.

Once I've filled a plate with food, I take a seat next to Grayson.

"Dude, I'm telling you. These Bishop women are as complicated as hell. Don't waste your time trying to figure them out because you'll go crazy tryin'. It's a goddamn miracle Diesel ended up with one," Grayson says, stabbing a hash brown with his fork.

"Hey, that's my sister," Riley warns. Before I arrived, it came out that Diesel and Rowan had been secretly dating. While they were taking it slow, Diesel learned he was a dad. When Chelsea, the woman he had a one-night stand with, brought their son to visit, she made a move. Diesel confessed he was in love with someone else. Shortly after, the whole Bishop family knew, and Riley blew a gasket, punching Diesel in the face. I would've loved to have seen it all go down.

"I'm just callin' it how I see it." Grayson shrugs, then looks at me. "Take it from someone who's under Kenzie's wrath for no damn reason, just walk away before she fucks you up for good." I can tell he's talking from experience by the pained expression on his face. "Thank God she's back at college now. I won't have to deal with her devil glares and bad attitude until Thanksgiving."

"Maize's too nice to hate you for no reason," Diesel says, then eyes me. "So, there's gotta be more to this story."

I haven't told anyone about our night together and don't plan to. Considering she won't acknowledge what happened, she probably wouldn't appreciate them finding out from me.

"She hasn't had the best dating experience," Riley explains. "And she won't give anyone who works on the ranch a chance."

"All I've tried to do is *talk* to her," I counter. "That's it."

"It'd be in your best interest if you didn't," Riley adds. "Trust me. I nearly knocked this one's teeth out when I found out he was sleepin' with my sister behind my back. I'm not sure I could actually hurt you, but I'd try if you broke Maize's heart."

I arch a brow at his cocky bluntness, and though he's right—he wouldn't leave a single mark on me if he tried—I'd rather not piss off the men I work with.

"Still bummed I didn't get to see it go down." I laugh as I dive into my scrambled eggs.

When our plates are nearly empty, Alex enters and gives us all a look. "There y'all are. We on a break I didn't know about?"

"Just re-fueling, Dad," Riley explains. "We're almost done."

"Good. We're running behind and have a shit ton to do today." He turns around and leaves before they can reply.

Diesel groans as he cleans up his mess, then puts on his hat. "Grayson, hurry up."

"I am!" he says around a mouthful, rushing.

Since their cousin Ethan left to finish his senior year of college, they've been shorthanded. Well, not really, but they were just used to slacking while Ethan was home for the summer.

"I really can't wait to train horses," Grayson mutters, popping the rest of his biscuit into his mouth.

"Why? Horse shit ain't much different than cattle shit." Riley snorts. "You'll be cleaning barns either way."

"I know, genius. But at least with horses, I'm bonding with them as I train and ride. Cows couldn't care less if you're around, and I'd argue that their shit is *very* different. Ever step in cow shit?"

Riley chuckles.

"Sorry to say, Grayson, but you aren't leaving me for a while," Diesel tells him with a crooked grin. "I need your assistance with all my bitch work."

Grayson rolls his eyes, and I wave before the three of them head toward the door. I'm fortunate enough to make my own schedule as long as I get my work done each week. Jackson and Kiera focus on their tasks, and I focus on mine.

Since the dining room is empty, I look for any opportunity to get into the kitchen with Maize. I notice the dirty dish tub is full and decide to take it back there. She can't yell at me if I'm helping.

I peek through the little window in the door to see if she's alone. When her employees are nowhere to be found, I kick it open and waltz in. Maize immediately spins around and pins me in place with a death glare.

"What do you think you're doin'?" She scowls, putting her hands on her hips. It's the cutest fucking thing ever.

"Helpin' you with these," I explain, glancing down at all the dirty dishes. "I'm a gentleman, ya know?" I set the tub by the dishwasher and spin around to face her.

"I didn't ask for your help, so you can leave," she tells me sternly.

"What's your problem, Maize Bishop?" I cross my arms over my chest and narrow my eyes. "You throw daggers at me like you hate me or something."

"I never said I *hated* you."

I take a step toward her. "So you like me then?"

Her nostrils flare. "Definitely didn't say that either."

"Then what is it? It's either one or the other."

"I don't know you well enough to have an opinion." She takes a step back as I inch closer.

Smirking, I continue, "Now that's not true. I think you know me quite well. You're just afraid to admit it."

"I honestly have no idea what you're talkin' about. As I've said before, you must have me confused with someone else."

I shake my head in amusement. "Trust me, Maize. I'd never forget you. *Or* our night together."

"Sure you weren't dreaming or something?" She barks out a laugh, but it's fake.

"Alright then, why don't you give me a chance? Let me take you out," I offer, watching her throat tighten as she swallows hard.

"I don't date men who work on the ranch," she informs me with a mediocre grin. "It's not personal."

Furrowing my brows, I move closer, studying her. "Is that so?"

"Yep." She quickly walks around me, and I turn to watch her unload the dishes. "I have a lot of work to do, so if you don't mind…"

"I *don't* mind. I already offered to help," I gloat, then stand beside her. "So let me."

This time, I don't give her a chance to deny me and quickly take over, rinsing off the crumbs before putting them in the dishwasher.

"Fine, whatever. I need to chop veggies for lunch anyway. Since Sandra and Jane are both sick with the stomach flu, my hands are full."

Realizing she's taking care of everything alone makes me want to do even more. I go back to the dining area and pick up the rest of the dinnerware, then load the dishwasher again. Thank goodness it's a large commercial one that only takes minutes to cycle through. After that, I wipe down each table and make sure they're set for lunchtime.

Once the dishes are finished, I have a hell of a time trying to figure out where they go. After a solid minute of looking, Maize finally takes pity on me.

"Over there." She points at a shelf. "On the right."

I look, and sure enough, there are the others. "Thank you."

"You really didn't have to stay."

"Seems like you needed some company today. It's quiet in here."

"I don't mind being alone," she says. "Silence doesn't happen much 'round here. My family usually stops in, or I turn on some music. I enjoy listening to it while I cook."

"You're really a great chef, you know," I tell her genuinely.

"You've chosen to eat the same things for the past month, so I can't really trust your judgment."

I cock my head with amusement. "So you notice what I put on my plate every day, huh? *Interesting*." I stroke my jawline, knowing I'm getting to her.

"No, and you're a lunatic. It's time to go now."

She's right. I've been here for over an hour and have a ton of shit to do, but I don't want to leave. "Okay, fine. Same time tomorrow?" I quirk a brow.

Maize huffs. "No! I already told you, I don't date men who work on the ranch, so you can stop doing"—she waves a frustrated hand in the air—"whatever it is you're doing."

"Only tryin' to be your friend." I cross my arms over my chest.

"I don't think that's a good idea."

"Why? You don't have any guy friends?"

"Not exactly," she breathes out. "And you're reminding me why I don't."

I slam a palm to my chest. "Ouch."

"Well, I warned you."

For a moment, I thought she would let her guard down, but she's smarter than that. As soon as she showed a sliver of her vulnerabilities, it's like she realized it and locked it away.

Maize Bishop isn't gonna make this easy, but I do love a challenge.

Once I'm back in the barn, Jackson strolls in with Knox and Kane behind him. They're laughing and smacking each other, but immediately stop when they see Kiera. I hold back laughter at how obnoxious they are, but even at twenty-one, they know to quit playing when their mother's around.

"What are you boys doin'?" she asks as Jackson kisses her.

"Making them clean stalls and organize the tack room. Then after that, they'll be washing all the work trucks and tractors."

Kiera's hands fly to her hips, and she scowls as if she knows this is a punishment. "What'd they do now?"

"Stole the Cotton's goats last night and hid them in our sheep barn," Jackson explains, shaking his head, but I can tell he's trying not to burst out laughing.

"Seriously?" she scolds, but then her expression softens. "That sounds like somethin' you'd do." Kiera teases Jackson. "Have them wax my car, too." She smirks before walking to the office.

"You're making this way too big of a deal, Dad," Knox complains. "The goats are back safe and sound. No one got hurt."

"Except when you pushed me and I tripped, nearly doing a face-plant in the gravel," Kane interrupts.

Although they're identical twins, they have different personalities.

Knox reminds me a lot of myself, confident and ready to take on the world, whereas Kane is more reserved and loyal. Though I have a feeling he gets roped into doing crazy shit with his brother, then has to deal with the consequences later.

"Too bad Kaitlyn isn't here. I'd pay her to do my half." Knox barks out a laugh.

"Who's Kaitlyn again?" I ask.

"Our little sister. She left for college right before you arrived," Kane explains, but I remember Jackson telling me about her.

"How old is she?"

"Nineteen. Just started her second year of college," he answers.

"Don't get any ideas," Jackson snaps.

My eyes widen at his demanding tone. "No, sir. Absolutely not."

Aside from the fact that Jackson's my boss and I wouldn't want to lose his trust, nineteen is too young. Plus, the only woman on my mind right now is Maize Bishop. Her being twenty-five is pushing my minimum dating age limit, but she's mature, and our chemistry is undeniable. I find so many things about her sexy as hell. Though I've had flings with younger women, I'm done with all that foolishness. I want to put down some roots and start a family—sooner rather than later.

Perhaps Maize's not at that stage of her life yet, but she was the one who pointed out she was behind because she's not married with kids. She laughed as if it were impossible for her to find a partner in five years, yet here I am. I'd be willing to let her call the shots if she'd actually give me a damn chance to prove that what we had that night was real.

CHAPTER FIVE

GAVIN

TWO MONTHS LATER

I'VE BEEN WORKING at the ranch for three months, and I thought Maize would've admitted she remembered us being together by now, but she hasn't budged. I've helped her in the kitchen a few times, but she went back to pretending I didn't exist afterward. Though I don't have time to play her childish games, I've come to accept Maize Bishop's stubborn as hell.

Way more stubborn than most of the wild horses I've trained.

I try not to let it bother me, but every time I see her, memories of her soft skin pressed against mine flash through my head. It's damn near impossible not to think about when she's around. I could understand if she was embarrassed or even regretted being with me, but why lie? I'm determined to find out, even if it takes me years.

Now it's the day before Thanksgiving, and all the Bishops are working double-time to finish their chores so they can eat and be with their families tomorrow. Luckily, I don't have as much to do—the stalls are shoveled, food and water stocked, and the tack rooms organized. Though I've been working with Cooper, he went to visit family in Alabama this week, so I just have to worry about the horses.

"Gavin! Wait up," Grayson shouts as I walk toward the B&B.

"What's up, man?" I'm already on the porch, reaching for the door.

"You got holiday plans?" he asks.

"Not really. I'll call my parents and work out after I feed the horses, but that's it. Why?"

"John and Mila invited me to eat at their house. You should come," he says as we walk inside.

"Not sure that's a good idea. Maize hates me enough as it is."

He shrugs. "So? Kenzie wants to murder me, and I've been invited for the past three years. We shoot daggers at each other, then eat pie."

I snort, heading toward the buffet. I'm starving, and the turkey potpie Maize made for lunch smells delicious.

"You don't think John and Mila would mind an extra person?"

"Nah, they told me to invite you too. Everyone eats with their families, then we show up here for dessert."

I like the idea of seeing Maize outside of the B&B, where she can't disappear or make excuses for why she can't stick around. She'll have to play nice in front of her parents.

"Alright, I'll go."

I load a plate, and Grayson fills his too. "Cool, I'll let Mila know to add a chair for ya. But get ready to nap for three hours after."

Chuckling, I find a table and take a seat. I look around, wondering where Maize is today because she's usually in the dining area during the rush.

"She's in the kitchen," Grayson tells me without asking. I blink and furrow my brows. "Maize. She's prepping all the desserts for tomorrow. Kenzie's helping with dishes while Sandra and Jane refill the buffet and prep for dinner."

I skipped breakfast and opted for a protein shake, so I didn't get to see her this morning. "So I assume you ran into Kenzie then?"

She's been away at college and came home a couple of days ago.

"Like an asteroid."

Laughing, I shake my head and dig into the best potpie I've ever had.

"So, tell me the truth about you and Maize. There's way too much..." He waves around his fork. "Sexual tension. Did you two meet before or something?"

I keep my head down and focus on my food.

"Dude, that's a yes." He points at me.

"That's a 'mind your own damn business.'"

He scoffs and acts offended. The kid is ten years younger than me, and I don't have the energy to gossip like a teenager.

"I knew it." He beams, and I roll my eyes.

"Kenzie's hated me since the first day we met, and I honestly have no idea what her problem is."

"You ever thought about askin' her?"

"I have a million times, but she's determined to bust my balls." He shakes his head, swallowing down his food. "She tells me to 'fuck off,' 'eat shit,' and—my personal favorite—'go to hell, jackass.' I'm convinced she's confused me with someone else because I didn't do a damn thing to her."

That seems suspicious, and I halfway wonder if they slept together, and *he* doesn't remember her. It's not out of the realm of possibilities, considering Maize claims she doesn't. Except I think Grayson's being genuine, which makes it worse.

So I ask him. "Any chance you two hooked up, but when you officially met at the ranch, you didn't recognize her?"

"Not possible. I'd remember Kenzie."

"You sure about that?" I challenge, finishing the last of my food.

Grayson wrinkles his face. "About eighty percent."

I chuckle. "Or maybe you did something else to her? Ran over her dog, called her fat, fucked her best friend?"

"Jesus," he mutters, laughing. "I mean, I don't think so. But I wish she'd tell me already."

"Well…" I stand, grabbing my empty plate. "Good luck with that."

"Ha, thanks." He follows as we put up our dirty dishes. "I'll see you tomorrow then. Lunch is at one."

"I'll be there."

We walk toward the front door and wave to a few guests on the way.

"Oh, and dress nice," he warns me. "Everyone's expected to be in their Sunday best."

"Seriously? Alright."

"Yep. Slacks, button-up, nice shoes."

"I'll see what I can do. See ya later, man," I say, then we go our separate ways.

After digging through my closet, I finally find something "nice" to wear. I can't remember the last time I dressed up, but I have a couple of pairs of black slacks and a few button-up shirts.

Once I've showered and dressed, I grab the flowers I bought from the grocery store yesterday and head to my truck. I arrive at John and Mila's at the same time as Grayson, and we walk to the front door together.

"Lookin' pretty sharp," he taunts as he knocks on the wood.

"I know how to clean up when I have to."

Grayson looks at the flowers. "Those for Maize?"

I grin. "Nope."

Mila answers with a smile and moves to the side to let us in. "Hey, boys. Glad y'all came."

"Thank you for the invite," I tell her, handing over the bouquet. "These are for you, Mrs. Bishop."

"Oh, Gavin. You didn't have to do that." She sniffs them and smiles wide. "They smell lovely, thank you."

"Of course."

Grayson and I follow her to the kitchen, and I immediately smirk when I see Maize's expression go from happy to annoyed. By her reaction, she didn't know I was coming.

"Maize, can you find me a vase, please? Gavin was so sweet to bring these for me," Mila asks, setting them down on the counter.

Maize studies me, and replies, "Sure, Mom."

"John's just finishing up some paperwork at the B&B and will be home any minute. Then we can dive right in," Mila explains.

"Where's Kenzie?" Grayson asks.

"Actively avoiding you." Maize snorts, carrying a crystal vase. "Wish I could say I was doing the same." She glares at me.

Grayson puts a hand on his chest over his heart. "You mean she hasn't missed me? I'm hurt."

I chuckle at his sarcastic tone, knowing damn well he wishes she *would* miss him. I'd almost feel bad for him if I wasn't dealing with my own Bishop woman issues.

John enters just as Kenzie comes down the stairs.

"Ugh, come on. I was hoping this would be the year I had something to be thankful for." Kenzie slams her shoulder against Grayson as she walks to the dining table.

"I'm here, so you do." He winks at her, but all she does is roll her eyes, then takes a seat.

"Where would you like me?" I ask, not sure if it's assigned seating or not.

"Preferably outside." I hear Maize mutter as she carries a hot dish.

"Across from you?" I ask loudly. "I'd love to."

She groans as she sets the food on the table.

"Mrs. Bishop, do you need some help?" I follow Maize into the kitchen.

"Take this," Maize says, handing me a scalding ass bowl without warning.

"Oh shit." I quickly set it down and grab a potholder off the counter.

"Warning, it's hot," she muses.

"Gee, thanks."

This girl really is trying to kill me. Though I don't know why, because she's the one who denies everything. If anything, I should be the one pissed at *her*, considering she bailed on me the morning after.

Once the food is on the table and we all sit, Mila says grace and thanks Grayson and me again for joining them.

"Dig in," she announces.

John passes the turkey, then we pile on corn bread stuffing and roasted veggies. Once I take a bite, it's confirmed it tastes as delicious as it smells.

"This is amazing," I say, smiling at Mila.

"Maize makes the best turkey," she confirms.

I look at her from across the table, then smile. "Should've known."

"Uh, *excuse me*. I helped," Kenzie blurts out, causing us all to laugh.

"Adding the marshmallows to the sweet potato casserole doesn't count…" Grayson teases. Kenzie gives him a death glare and looks like she's going to knock him out.

"You weren't even here, so zip it." Kenzie snarls, and I swear, the tension between them could be cut with a knife.

Everyone chats while we finish eating, then Mila offers seconds.

"I'm always ready for more turkey." Grayson pats his hard stomach.

"Don't forget about dessert later," Mila reminds him.

"No, ma'am. Maize's sweet pumpkin pie with homemade whipped cream is unforgettable."

Kenzie rolls her eyes and stands, then takes her empty plate to the kitchen.

"I made extra this year…" Maize says, pointing her fork at Grayson. "Just for you."

"You're my favorite Bishop, Maze. Don't tell the others…" he whispers, and she laughs. I hate that it makes me jealous, knowing she's sweet and kind to him but treats me like a walking STD.

I watch the way she lets her guard down, and as soon as her gaze meets mine, she looks away, but not before I see the faint blush on her cheeks.

When we're all stuffed to the max, I help clear the table. Kenzie and Maize rinse the dishes while Grayson helps Mila put the leftovers in containers. John and I break down the table to its normal size.

"Your house is beautiful, Mrs. Bishop. I love the modern décor. Much different than the B&B," I tell her once everything's clean.

"Thank you. We had fun decorating." She smiles at me. "You want a tour of the house?"

I glance around and notice Maize's reaction, and she tenses when Kenzie speaks up. "I'll give you one, Gavin! Let's start with my sister's room."

Maize elbows her in the ribs, and Kenzie dramatically coughs. "Shut up. I better do it, or you'll be telling him all kinds of embarrassing childhood stories about me."

With an unapologetic shrug, Kenzie smirks. "Well, duh." She looks at her incredulously, which makes me wonder what they're hiding.

With a sigh, Maize walks around me and tells me to follow her. I hear Kenzie chuckle, then she tells Grayson off, which makes me smile. These Bishop sisters don't make anything easy.

"You already saw the dining room and entryway..." She waves a hand to the left as we walk down the hallway. "The living room is here, though we don't get a lot of time to hang out or watch TV. Most of us are usually working or sleeping."

"Looks cozy, though," I say, shoving my hands in my front pockets so I don't do something stupid like reach out and touch her.

She takes me through the rest of the lower level, then we go upstairs, and she points out her parents' and Kenzie's room.

"Mine's at the end of the hallway."

I silently follow her, not taking a second alone with her for granted. This is the most she's talked to me since I moved to the ranch.

"It's very you," I admit after she opens her door and allows me to peek inside. Three walls are a neutral tan color, and one is a bright teal. Pictures of her and Kenzie on the ranch are framed and hung on the walls along with dreamcatchers. A white comforter is neatly spread across her bed, and fuzzy teal pillows are stacked high.

"You don't even know me," she states.

I study her. "I know enough."

She swallows hard with her eyes locked on mine, but too quickly, she lowers her gaze and breaks our contact.

"It's embarrassing to live with my parents at my age," she blurts out. "I just turned twenty-five and still sleep in my childhood bed." Maize groans, then shrugs. "But until they can marry me off, I'll stay here."

Bringing a hand to my chin, I scrub my fingers over my beard as I remember a similar conversation we had at the bar. "Marry you off, huh? To who? What happened to becoming a nun?"

Maize blinks hard, then shakes her head as if she has to remind herself not to react. "What? No, not like an arranged marriage or anything. But when you work on the ranch, it doesn't make sense to move away. Especially when I work as much as I do," she explains, leading me back toward the staircase. It's amusing she ignored the nun part and is still playing her little game.

"Doesn't hurt that it's cheap rent."

"That's definitely a perk," she says as we enter the kitchen, and when she checks the time on the wall, she adds, "Crap, I gotta go to the B&B and set up the desserts."

"Let me help. It'll go faster," I offer, not giving her room to argue.

She sighs. "Alright, fine."

After Maize announces we're leaving, they tell us they'll meet us there in twenty minutes. It will give me more alone time with her.

Since the B&B is only half a mile from her house, she leads me to a side by side, and we climb in. The silence slices through the air on the way over, and once we enter the kitchen, she gives me orders, and I quickly step into action.

"Pies over there, cakes and cookie bars on the other table, then fruit on the third one." She pulls items from the fridge, and my eyes widen at the assortment of desserts laid out.

"Shit. You feedin' an army?" I grab two pecan pies and inhale the sweet aroma.

"Just wait till you see *all* the Bishops together. There are a lot of us..." she says. "Then add in the ranch hands too."

As I help her move tables around the dining area, I wonder how everyone will fit in here, then remember the rocking chairs and tables on the back porch.

Once we've set the desserts out, Maize puts the serving utensils in each dish and directs me to find the dessert plates. Then I grab the whipped cream and start the coffee maker as ordered. Once I've done what she's asked, I head out of the kitchen and hear her talking to someone.

"Elle! It feels like it's been forever." Maize hugs her, and I immediately see the Bishop resemblance. Elle has long, dark hair and features similar to Maize.

"Came to see if you needed help, but I see now that I'm interrupting..." Elle looks me up and down, and Maize quickly turns around.

"No, no. Gavin's training horses with Jackson and Kiera. Mom invited him to dinner."

"Mm-hmm."

"Nice to meet you, Elle. I'm Gavin." I hold out my hand, and she quickly takes it.

"A pleasure. I'm Elizabeth, but only our grandmother calls me that." She smiles.

I chuckle. "Noted."

"Elle works with Dr. Wallen," Maize explains. "Which is why I hardly ever see her anymore."

"I met him shortly after I started here. Seems like a nice guy. I bet you're learning a lot from him," I say to Elle.

"Yeah, well..." She inhales sharply. "We don't call him Dr. Dickhead for nothing."

My eyebrows raise in curiosity.

"Speak for yourself," Maize chimes in. "The rest of us call him Dr. VetDreamy." Maize chuckles, giving Elle a hard time, but the thought of her thinking he's good-looking annoys the fuck outta me.

"Do *not* call him that," Elle warns. "Just because he's good-looking doesn't take away the fact that he makes my work life miserable."

"It can't be *that* bad." Maize waves her off.

"Not for you, maybe. You have a great view." Elle smirks at me, and Maize gives her a dirty look.

Deciding to play along, I step next to Elle and wrap my arm around her. "Glad to see someone appreciates me 'round here."

"Is Maize being rude to you?" she asks.

"If by that you mean she ignores and tells me off, or straight up groans any time I speak, then yeah, I guess so." I shrug, giving Elle my best puppy dog face.

"Maize Bishop!" Elle scolds, folding her arms over her chest. "I know your mama taught you better than that. Be nice to the new trainer. He seems sweet."

Maize perks a brow, and her nostrils flare with rage. "I'm *plenty* nice."

"That's you being nice?" My eyes widen with a grin. "Shit, I'd hate to get on your bad side then."

"Keep talkin', and you will be," she snaps.

"Okay, I'm sensing some kind of...tension here, so I'm gonna go find me some pie," Elle says, then quickly walks away.

"Unbelievable," Maize mutters before storming off.

I don't let her get too far before following her into the kitchen. "You ever gonna tell me what your problem with me is?" I ask as she grabs something from the fridge.

"My problem is you're always around. I'm not interested, and you aren't getting the memo." She slams the door and turns to face me.

"Whoa, whoa, whoa…" I hold up my palms to stop her before she runs off. "You're not interested? I didn't ask you out or anything." The last time I offered to take her on a date was a couple of months ago.

"I can read between the lines, and I'm good with body language."

"Is that so? Enlighten me then. What am I insinuating?"

She sets down the container and puts her hands on her hips. "You're intrigued by me and want to ask me out again even though I've given you a million signs I'd say no. Yet, here you are."

"The only thing that intrigues me is you refusing to admit we've met before. Why is that?" I cross my arms.

"Because we haven't." Her upper lip twitches, and it gives her away. It's obvious she's full of shit. It's only a matter of time before she confesses the truth. The sooner, the better.

"Okay, have it your way then." I shrug and walk away. Before going through the door, I look over my shoulder and smile. "I have a feelin' you'll be remembering very soon." Then I flash her a wink and leave.

The B&B fills up with Bishops, and for the next hour, I eat Maize's delicious desserts and chat with everyone. I hear her talking to someone behind me, but fight the urge to look since I can feel her eyes on me. She may not like that I called her out, but too damn bad.

"Gavin," Grandma Bishop sing-songs my name as she opens her arms and wraps me in a tight hug. Though she's not *my* grandma, it's what everyone calls her.

"Happy Thanksgiving," I say, squeezing her back.

"How was your dinner at John and Mila's?"

"Delicious. Maize didn't disappoint one bit," I emphasize her name, knowing she's listening close by. "Her desserts are even better."

"She's a precious gem, ain't she? We're lucky to have her." Grandma Bishop smiles proudly. After another minute, she excuses herself to make her rounds.

"You keep talkin' about me, then wonder why I think you're obsessed with me," Maize quietly says so no one can eavesdrop.

"Obsessed? You keep avoidin' me and say there's no reason for it," I retort. "Our night together is nothing to be embarrassed about, Maize."

"You're absolutely delusional."

I take my time and check out her body before meeting her intense gaze. "Then why do you always have goose bumps when I'm around? Coincidence?" I pop a confident brow.

She narrows her eyes while simultaneously rubbing her bare arms. "Shut up. I don't."

I chuckle, bringing a hand to her shoulder and sliding it down to her wrist, feeling the bumps against the pads of my fingers. "Right. I believe you."

Maize groans, creating space.

"Stop denying it, sweetheart."

"You're so full of yourself. Even if we had met before, I doubt it would've been anything memorable. So perhaps my mind did me a favor and blocked it out." She flashes an *eat shit* grin, then stalks off.

Moments later, Grayson comes over and pats my shoulder. "Wanted to officially welcome you to the Bishop wrath."

CHAPTER SIX

MAIZE

FIVE WEEKS LATER

AFTER AN INSANE AND BUSY CHRISTMAS, I'm excited I get to spend New Year's Eve with my cousins because I'm not working for once. I did an enormous dessert bar on Christmas Eve and then served a special brunch on Christmas Day. Since I gave my employees the holidays off, my mother and Kenzie helped. Having them around is always fun since we love baking cookies together, but it took four twelve-hour shifts to prepare everything.

Having Gavin at our house for Thanksgiving was awkward and tense. Thank God that pregnancy test Rowan made me take months ago came back negative, or shit would be hitting the fan right now. Giving him a tour and then him later confronting me was irritating as hell. I don't understand why he won't drop it and put the past behind us. It's been four months, and if I have to see him every day, I'd rather him not have the satisfaction of knowing I *do* remember.

How could I forget?

Still doesn't mean I want to admit it.

Denial, denial, denial.

That's my motto.

It wouldn't be that hard if he'd just stay out of my way, but he shows up at the B&B every damn day looking like a Southern temptation. If I don't push him away with my attitude, I'll end up right back in his bed.

And that *cannot* happen.

The last time I let a smooth-talking cowboy sweep me off my feet, I paid the price. Seeing him every day afterward was hell, and I won't allow it to happen again.

But tonight, I'm going to let loose and drink away my thoughts of Gavin Fox. It's no wonder they called him "The Fox" when he was bull riding. Not only was he talented, but he had the looks to back it up too.

The worst combination.

My phone dings with a text, and I see it's my sister.

Kenzie: You coming soon? It's starting to fill up!

Kenzie and Ethan are bartending tonight, so Elle and Rowan are supposed to meet me there to drink and hang out.

Maize: Be there in 30.

I finish getting ready, leaving my hair down in beachy waves, then put on some red lipstick. It's a contrast from my everyday look, which consists of a ponytail and mascara. It'll be nice to dress up and hang out with the gang.

Before I leave, I find my mom in the kitchen and wrap my arms around her. "Happy New Year, Ma."

She pats my hands before spinning around with a smile. "You headin' out?"

"Yep. Gonna keep Kenzie company."

She snickers. "I doubt she'll need it at the bar."

"True." I laugh. "Dad at the B&B?"

"He should be home at any moment. I told him the house would be empty tonight, so he better hurry. And hopefully, he'll bring wine."

I exaggerate a gag. "Gross, Mom."

"What? You think just because we're older, we don't need *alone* time?" She quirks a brow. "We had to get creative when you girls were younger."

"Aaaaaand that's my cue to leave." I kiss her cheek, then grab my bag and hop in my truck.

By the time I arrive at the bar, the parking lot is packed, and I have to park on the street. I enter and squeeze my way through a ton of people drinking and dancing.

"Finally!" Kenzie scolds when I manage to find a seat. "Thought you were gonna bail on me."

"Are Rowan and Elle here yet?"

"No, but they're on their way. Hopefully, this crowd weeds out soon, though."

Ethan comes up and hands me a coaster. "They will. Most of them stop in and have a few drinks before they go to house parties."

"Start me off with a Jack and Diet," I tell her.

Moments later, Elle walks in, and I hug her. "I'm so happy you could make it."

"Only because Dr. Dickhead gave me off tomorrow." She rolls her eyes like she's surprised.

"Which means you need to take full advantage and drink!"

She orders a cocktail, then turns to me to catch up. "So, you gonna tell me more about this Gavin?"

"There's nothing to tell."

Kenzie snorts, then strolls to the other side to help a customer. After Kenzie embarrassed me at Thanksgiving, I told her to butt the hell out. She's the only one who knows the whole story, and though Elle is aware of the one-night stand, I've kept the details to myself. I was with her and Rowan the morning after it happened. Elle begged us to help birth a calf, so I arrived hungover as hell and asked them if they knew anyone named Gavin. Since they didn't, I had hoped he was just passing through, and I'd never have to see him again.

My luck would have it otherwise.

"When we were officially introduced at the ranch, I acted like I didn't know him, and he's been torturing me ever since," I say quickly before sucking down half my drink.

"But you *do* know him."

"Yes, but I don't want him to know that! I want to pretend our night never happened, but he's hell-bent on not letting me."

Elle laughs, sipping her own drink. "Well, it sounds to me like Gavin wants round two."

I groan, shaking my head. "Not happening. I'm already embarrassed enough."

"Perhaps you're just so memorable, he can't get you out of his head." She shrugs with a cocky grin. "I mean, you are a total babe."

"Well, he can find another *babe* because it's not gonna be me," I say matter-of-factly.

Elle smiles and chews on her straw, looking behind me. "Speakin' of the devil."

I quickly glance over my shoulder and see Gavin with Grayson, Diesel, and Rowan behind him.

Fuck me.

Of course they'd invite him. Dammit.

"Hey!" Rowan rushes toward us and wraps her arms around us.

Kenzie squeals and takes their drink orders.

"Hey, Maize." Gavin's hoarse voice makes me shiver.

"I see you've turned your obsession into stalking."

"Is it really stalking if this is the only pub in town?"

I turn and see his flirty grin, which causes me to look away and motion for Kenzie to refill my glass.

"Let me buy you a drink," he says, taking the seat next to me.

"That's not necessary." I inch away from him.

"Maize, shut up and order the expensive shit." Kenzie waggles her brows.

"Round of shots?" Gavin asks, and I relax my shoulders. "For everyone," he confirms.

"Vodka," I say. Gonna need it if he's determined to bother me all night.

Kenzie pours the liquor, and soon we're three shots in. Diesel and Rowan are in their own little world as Grayson taunts Kenzie at the other end of the bar. Elle is playing pool with some guy, leaving me alone with Gavin.

"Looks like you're stuck with me."

"I've noticed." I groan, taking a sip of my drink. At this point, I can't taste the Jack or the Diet Coke.

"C'mon, I'm not that bad. You should give me a chance like you did four months ago."

I nearly choke and hope he doesn't notice, but by the sly grin on his face, I know he does.

"You're delusional."

"You keep sayin' that, but I'm not buying it, Maize Bishop."

I roll my eyes, not giving in to this little game. Maybe if I keep drinking, I'll be able to tune him out.

"Hey, we're all going to Wyatt's for the ball drop," Rowan tells me. "Wanna come?"

"Y'all leavin' now?"

"Yeah, we're gonna drink and eat snacks there," she confirms.

I look at Kenzie, then back at Rowan. "No, I'm gonna stay with my sister." Though she's a grown-ass woman and can take care of herself, I don't want to leave her here without company on New Year's Eve.

"Okay, babe. Text me if you change your mind." She kisses my cheek, and I watch as all the guys and my cousins walk out the door.

"You aren't going with your friends?" I ask Gavin, shocked he didn't even consider it.

"You're all the company I need." He smirks before taking a drink and looking at me over the neck of his beer. It shouldn't be sexy, but as I watch the way his throat tightens, I realize I must be drunker than I thought.

"I'm not here to entertain you, so go to the party." I wave my fingers toward the door. I can't be trusted alone with him.

"Who said I expected you to? You're quite presumptuous." He turns his body toward mine so our knees touch.

"I'm presumptuous?" I balk. "I beg to differ considering I keep telling you to go away and you never do."

"I'm just sittin' here," he says calmly, motioning for Kenzie with his empty beer bottle. "You're the one who keeps lookin' at me like I'm your next meal."

I shake my head. "You've lost your mind."

"That's not what you said the first night we met."

"Okay, now I *know* you've lost your damn mind."

"What can I get you lovebirds?" Kenzie asks casually, and if looks could kill, she'd be dead.

"Maize and I are gonna shoot some Fireball."

"No, we are not," I interject.

"It's no fun playing drinking games by myself," Gavin says, giving me a sly grin. I want to slap it off his sexy face. "You only have to drink if you lose anyway, so what do ya say?"

Kenzie waggles her brows when I glance at her. I sigh with a shrug, giving in. "Fine."

She lines up four glasses, then fills them full. "Have fun, you two." Flashing a wink, she moves to the other side to help more customers.

"Alright, Cowboy. What's this game?"

"Ever heard of two truths and a lie?" he asks.

"Unfortunately, yes. You really wanna play this game with me, though? I'm pretty good at reading people," I say matter-of-factly, but it's the booze talking.

"So you keep sayin'. And now I'm even more certain I do." He chuckles, scooting my shot closer. "If you don't guess the lie, you drink."

"And if I do, you drink."

"Let's play. Ladies first." He gestures toward me, and it takes me a minute to think.

"Okay. When I was six years old, I fell off a four-wheeler and sprained my ankle. I'm left-handed. And…" I tap my lips, thinking of the final one. "I've never had a one-night stand."

The corner of his lips tilts up, and I wonder if he's going to guess right or not.

"Jesus, you're playin' dirty. Alright, well, then I'd have to say your lie is the last one." The corner of his lip tilts up.

"Wrong. I was eight, and it was a horse." I glance down at his shot then back at him.

Gavin shakes his head "Oh, I see you're *really* doin' me dirty. Two can play that game, darlin'." Without arguing, he downs the shot.

The alcohol is definitely buzzing through my body because I can't take my eyes off him. His buff biceps, the way his veins pop in his arms, and how his eyes focus on me as if I'm the only one in the bar are hypnotizing.

"Your turn."

"Okay, get ready to lose." He flashes an arrogant smirk. "I rode my first bull when I was nine. I won my first championship when I was nineteen.

I've never had a one-night stand, then left the morning after without as much as a goodbye."

I glare at him, knowing he purposely said that last one to see how I'd react. Well, too bad for him it won't work.

"Nine years old? Bullshit. More Fireball for you," I tell him confidently.

Gavin grins, placing it to his lips, but then sets it down in front of me. "Wrong, sweetheart."

"No way! Nine years old?"

"Yep. Believe it."

Groaning, I swallow down the shot. If I'm not careful, I'll drink too much and let my guard down, which cannot happen.

"Well, we're one and one. What's the tiebreaker?" I ask, noticing two shots left.

"How about I ask you a question, and if you tell me the truth, I take both of these."

"And if I lie?"

"You kiss me at midnight."

I sit up straighter, keeping my eyes focused on his. Is he for real?

"How will you know if I'm telling the truth?" I ask.

"Because I already know the answer."

"I might be drunk, but I'm not stupid," I tell him.

"Never said you were, but you wanted a tiebreaker, and I gave you one."

"How about we each take one and call it even?" I grab one of the glasses and hold it up.

"Why? Afraid you'll actually have to be honest for once?" he challenges, and I can hear the hurt in his tone.

Instead of answering, I down the whiskey, then slam the empty glass on the bar. "You don't know me, Gavin."

He leans in close, causing heat to ripple through me. Then his mouth lowers to my ear. "I know enough to know you like your ass slapped." Gavin licks his lips, then continues, *"Hard."*

I squeeze my eyes shut, and flashes of our night resurface. Every time he's near, memories flicker through my mind, and as much as I've tried to ignore it, with him so close, it's impossible.

For a second, I want to give in to the desire and have a round two, but nothing good would come of it. He's older, more experienced, and more likely to break my heart. It won't end well.

"Excuse me," I say, pushing off my stool.

I rush to the bathroom and look at myself in the mirror. I'm completely red and flushed, and I'm pissed at how my body reacts to him. Our night together was the hottest sex I've ever had, but I'll be damned if I give in to his good looks again.

After I wash my hands and steady my breathing, I step into the hallway and gasp when I see Gavin leaning against the wall with his arms crossed.

"What are you doin'?" I stutter.

"Making sure you weren't running off on me again."

"Again?"

Gavin moves toward me, closing the gap between us. "Yes, *again*. The morning after we had sex, you bailed on me. No note, no explanation, just up and left. And I want to know why."

"I have no idea what you're talkin' about." I hold my ground, not giving in. "Perhaps you have me confused with another girl you slept with." I shrug, acting as if his accusations don't faze me.

"Trust me, I'd never forget you, Maize. We drank, I kicked your ass in a game of pool, and by the end of the night, I had you screaming my name in bed."

His words have a shiver running down my spine. Damn him.

"So you wanna tell me why you keep denyin' it?"

"Because it didn't happen." I snort.

"It's almost midnight."

I nearly get whiplash with his topic change. Kenzie shouts that there are thirty seconds left.

"Yeah?"

"Since you're so hell-bent on refusing we were together, then perhaps I should remind you what it was like." Gavin flattens his palm on the wall next to me, and when his mouth moves closer to mine, my breath hitches. "Let me kiss you," he whispers.

"That's not a good idea."

"Everyone should get kissed on New Year's Eve. Even a frustrating, gorgeous woman like you."

"Maybe I want someone else to kiss me." I shrug, mocking a smile. "You're not really my type. No offense."

"You sure about that? I was your type the first time."

"Again, that never happened."

People chant the countdown, and we're only seconds away.

"Ten, night, eight..." he says. "The opportunity might not come around again, Maize."

Five, four, three, two...

Without thinking, I fist my hands in his shirt and pull his face to mine. Our lips collide, and Gavin quickly catches on, reaching down and gripping my waist. As our bodies mold together, he slides his tongue inside my mouth. I taste cinnamon and inhale his musky scent as fireworks erupt between us. His hand cups my cheek, and he tilts my head back to deepen the kiss. Every nerve sparks with electricity as our mouths battle for more. We release moans as we devour one another, similar to the first time but more heated and desperate. Memories of how he touched me and satisfied my every need rush through me, and it's then I know I'm losing my resolve.

Slowly, I pull away and lick my lips. I blink, unable to look at him as we stand in the dimly lit hallway and try to catch our breaths.

"This doesn't mean anything's changed between us," I blurt out, finally glancing up at him.

He slides his tongue along his bottom lip. "I beg to differ."

"After a bad experience, I don't get involved with men who work on the ranch, so get whatever thought you have in that head of yours out because it's not happening," I say sternly, though by the smug look on his face, he's not buying it. "We had one night. Let's just end it at that."

"So that's why you've been lying?"

Inhaling a sharp breath, I finally nod. "Fine, yes. I froze the day you showed up at the bar and decided to bail instead. I never expected to see you again, especially not on my family's ranch."

"Just to confirm, you do remember?"

Nodding again, I admit it. "Yes, but like I said—"

He dips his head and brings our mouths together again. Softly, our tongues tangle, and then all too soon, he backs away.

"Nothing's happening," he finishes my sentence. "Got it." He flashes me a mischievous wink.

Hearing Gavin say those words is like a punch to the gut. Even though I'm the one who said them to *him*, knowing my secret is out in the open makes me feel more vulnerable than before.

"It's not you, Gavin. I mean, it is but not because I wasn't attracted to you. You're older than me, you work for my uncle, we both work long hours, and if shit hits the fan between us, we'd be stuck seeing each other all the time. Trust me when I say that isn't a good time."

"Maybe if you'd give me a chance, it won't end like your past relationship did."

"I can't risk that. I'm sorry." My heart couldn't take it again.

"Well, if you change your mind, you know where to find me." He bites his bottom lip. Damn those lips are gonna get me into trouble—*more* trouble. Considering we've already hooked up and now have kissed again, I'd say it's already messing me up.

"I'm sure you have no problem getting women. You had fun chasing me until I admitted I remembered you, but now that it's all out in the open, you can stop this little cat and mouse game and go back to hooking up with belt buckle bunnies."

Amusement is written all over his too-perfect face. "You're gonna be fun, aren't ya?"

"Excuse me?"

"You're more stubborn than the bulls that tried to buck me off. I've had dozens of injuries, been stomped on, and had one charge and flip me on my back. And still, I think you're gonna be the hardest to break in. But I like a good challenge." His smirk only fuels my annoyance even more.

"I'm not some animal you can train," I snap with a scowl.

"No, sweetheart, you aren't. You're going to be more work. But Imma prove that I'm worthy of a real chance. Don't worry, I'm up for it. But don't you dare think I'm going away anytime soon, sweetheart."

Gavin grabs my hand, presses a kiss to my knuckles, then winks before walking away.

I blink hard as I stare at his ass in jeans that fit him like a glove.

Wait, what in the hell just happened?

CHAPTER SEVEN

MAIZE

THE LAST MONTH and a half have been a mix of emotions, but mostly excitement and dread.

Lately, I've been trying to keep myself busy to ensure my mind focuses on anything other than Gavin and the way his lips felt against mine New Year's Eve. Trying to forget him is proving to be a lot harder than I ever imagined. Nine times out of ten, I want to punch him for being so handsome and smelling so damn good.

As I'm cleaning up after the lunch rush, the night crew comes in and begins prepping dinner. They're busy chopping onions and having a conversation about their teenage daughters, which has me snickering as I wash dishes. Over the past month, I've been doing a lot of soul-searching. I'm not getting any younger, and if I ever want to move out, I have to hustle harder. Though I've been dreaming about starting a catering business, I've done nothing to pursue it. I typically don't make resolutions, but I promised myself I'd make it happen this year. It's scary but exciting, and I'm not sure where to start, but I think I'm ready.

Once I finish cleaning, I tell everyone goodbye. Just as I'm heading through the dining room, Grandma Bishop enters as if an angel called her. "Hey, sweetie."

I tilt my head, wondering what she's doing here. Grandma's always up to something and is in the know with all the town gossip. "So, I've got some news. A little birdie shared something with me today."

My blood pressure rises, and I hope to all things holy she didn't catch wind of what happened between Gavin and me because I'd literally die. "Oh really?"

I try to play it cool, but I'm actually crumpling as my heart rate rushes.

"So, I was at my quilting club meeting and was chattin' with Rebecca Blanchard. She mentioned the rodeo was coming to town in a few months, which we all know is typically a big deal and brings lots of business to the B&B. But she *also* mentioned something else."

My palms are sweaty, and my mouth goes dry. Any time someone mentions the word rodeo around here, Gavin's name comes soon after. I nearly stop breathing as I wait, and the anticipation might kill me. Grandma eats it up as I wait. Sometimes she's so dramatic.

"Come on, just go ahead and spit it out," I finally say, the dramatic pause being too much.

"Maize Grace! Watch your manners. This is my story, and I tell it how I want." She gives me the evil eye, then goes back to being nice granny. "Anyway. Rebecca told me about the barbecue contest, and she mentioned you should enter your famous smoked brisket. The one you did for the food drive fundraiser last year. It was incredible, Maze, and we all took a vote and believe you could win first place." Grandma beams as if I already had the trophy.

"You really think I have a chance or are you just saying that?" I ask, nearly laughing that my food was the topic of their conversation at their meeting.

"I can admit I give a bunch of frivolous compliments, but honey, I'd never set you up to humiliate yourself. If your brisket wasn't worth a lick, I wouldn't mention it, because I can't have you embarrassing yourself or the Bishop name," she confirms with a nod. "You went to that fancy culinary school for a reason. So, you need to enter and kick some ass."

I burst out laughing. "Grandma, you just said ass."

"I'm old enough to have earned that right."

"This is very true."

She grins at me and places her hand on my shoulder. "The last day to submit the application is Friday, then the judges choose who qualifies to compete. I think the grand prize is five grand, and I know you've been wanting to start that little catering business, which I fully support. So I think this could help with startup costs. Even though I've offered to fund it, I know how proud and independent you are, just like your dad."

My whole face lights up thinking about what that money could buy for my business. While Grandma has been super supportive, she's right. I want to do this on my own. It's the Bishop way.

"So whatcha think?" she asks, beaming.

"It would be an amazing opportunity. And if you think I have a chance, then heck yes, I'll do it," I say, and she wraps me in one of her infamous hugs.

When we break apart, she looks me in the eyes. "Honey, I think you're a shoo-in to win. Plus, once you start your business, there are tons of ladies at church who want to hire you. They've got daughters who are getting married, birthday parties, and holiday events that none of them wanna cook for. Don't blame 'em, though. It's easier to have someone else do it these days."

I snort. "You all deserve to be pampered."

"I'm no spring chicken anymore. It's why I love my grandbabies so much. Always willing to help." Grandma pulls a packet of papers from her giant purse and hands it to me. "Here's everything you need. Turn this into the Chamber before the deadline."

"Yes, ma'am," I say, flipping through the big packet. "I'll make sure I fill it out tonight."

Grandma waves goodbye, and when she's out of sight, I let out a loud squeal. I'm smiling so wide my face hurts.

Dad rushes into the dining room and looks spooked. "Are you okay? I heard screaming."

"Fine, just fine! Grandma thinks I should enter the rodeo's barbecue contest." I hand the packet to him, and he flips through it.

"So who's gonna be on your team?" he asks.

My eyes go wide. "Team?"

"Yeah, it says here you have to put a team together and list their names. It has a place for five to ten people." He gives the papers back to me, and I scan over them.

"Well damn," I mutter, and he doesn't correct me. "Um, you wanna help?"

He chuckles. "Of course, as a last resort, though. You should ask your sister, Rowan, Elle, Riley, Zoey, Knox, Kane, and force Diesel to help too. And if they say no–"

"Then I'll threaten them," I say.

"If you want, but I was going to say, I'll get your uncles involved. And either they'll cook because I'll tell Mama you need to put together a team, or they'll force their kids to help."

"Good idea! Guess I've got some work to do once I get home," I say, wondering if I should group text them or do it individually. I'm not in the mood for excuses, but I think they'll be on board to help without kicking their asses. One thing's for certain, us Bishop's usually stick together.

"Let me know if you're able to round them up or not." Dad grins, and I leave with a pep to my step.

It's been a few days since my cousins said they'd help me at the rodeo, and it only took a few friendly threats. Elle was even able to commit after she told her sexy as sin boss she needed off. I've got Riley, Elle, Kenzie, Kane, Knox, and even Diesel. Rowan's planning to close the bar during that week because it'll be really busy. I should find out any day now if I've been accepted, and if not, Grandma will have a few choice words with the Chamber of Commerce. No one crosses that woman when it comes to her grandkids, and I mean absolutely no one.

Today is Valentine's Day, and I'm already dreading it more than usual. I've decided not to go onto social media so I can avoid the ridiculous photos of couples so happily in love with candy and flowers. I'm already gagging thinking about it. Even though I'm a known love hater, as Rowan says, I still like making the day fun for the B&B guests.

The weather is brisk, and I crank the heat on full blast on the way to work. When I step out of my truck, frost crunches under my feet as I walk, and I honestly can't wait for the spring flowers. Once I'm inside, I immediately get started. After I mix the strawberry pancake batter, I pull out the giant heart molds and the smaller ones for the sausage patties. Each year, we get tons of compliments by keeping the theme.

My employees arrive, and it's a madhouse when breakfast starts, but then again, when is it not? We're running back and forth between the buffet and the kitchen, and I swear we make hundreds of heart-shaped pancakes. The next time I go into the dining area, I see Riley and Diesel ragging on each other as Knox and Kane instigate the situation.

"He totally called you a pussy," Kane taunts.

"I did not." Diesel shakes his head.

"Shhh," I say, rushing over to them and grabbing Kane by his ear like he's a kid. "We have guests in here, so you need to shut the fuck up," I whisper. "I will tell your mama in a heartbeat that you're using that language in the B&B."

He rolls his eyes but straightens up as soon as Dad comes into sight. "Y'all behaving?"

"Yes, sir," they all say in unison. I give them an evil look, then smile sweetly at my dad. He nods and walks away as I return to the kitchen.

Just after eight, my cell phone buzzes like crazy on the counter. It's from an unknown number, but I answer it anyway.

"Is this Ms. Maize Bishop?" a man asks.

"Yes, it is."

"Great, I just wanted to call and congratulate you on being accepted to compete in the barbecue contest at the rodeo. We would've gotten back to you sooner, but we had a ton of applications to sort through this year. You're still interested, correct?"

My heart flutters with happiness. "Oh my God, yes, absolutely!" I throw my hand up in the air, giving a fist pump as Jane and Sandra glance over at me.

"Fantastic. We'll have a pre-meeting in a few weeks that you'll need to attend. Please make sure you read over the rules for your team so you're not disqualified. We're happy to have you on board and can't wait to try your brisket."

"Thank you. Thank you so much."

The call ends, and I let out a hoot. I know I'm being loud as hell, but this is the best news I could've received today. I thought I wouldn't get picked for a few days because I hadn't received a call yet, but now that I have, that means I need to start preparing.

Knowing I have to tell Dad the good news, I go and search for him. He's in the dining area pouring coffee into a mug.

"What's going on?" He grins.

"They chose me for the contest!" I'm so excited my voice is an entire octave higher than usual.

He gives me a side hug. "See, told you! You're gonna win this, sweetie! I just know it!"

"That would be incredible," I admit, imagining it, then notice we need more bacon and biscuits. "Gotta get back to it."

I'm floating on cloud nine as I slap bacon strips on the griddle. Since Grandma mentioned it, I've been trying to perfect my honey barbecue sauce, but honestly, the meat is so juicy and tender that it's not even needed. When I deliver the food to the buffet, I see Gavin enter. His eyes meet mine as I carefully stack a pile of hot buttermilk biscuits under the lamps.

He winks at me, but I can't let his presence distract me, so I immediately turn around. I know what he's doing, so I'll keep avoiding and ignoring him the best that I can.

Twenty minutes pass, and Dad announces that we need more coffee. After I grind some beans and fill the giant container, I carry it out there, and that's when I overhear Gavin and Grayson's conversation.

"Yeah, I'll be at the rodeo for sure," Gavin says, then continues. "I'm still training Cooper. He's trying to qualify so he can compete at the next level."

"Oh yeah, hasn't he been riding for a while?" Grayson takes a huge bite of pancakes.

"He's determined and listens. He has what it takes," Gavin tells him.

"Well, he's got a world champion giving him instruction. I might come watch." Grayson smiles.

Gavin pauses for a second, and I don't even dare to look at him, though I don't mind eavesdropping. "Determination can be deadly, though. Most don't realize how dangerous it really is out there, and the moment you get sloppy, is when you could lose everything, including your life. Rodeo life, though, I really loved it."

I swallow, fill the sugar packets and stirrers, then go back to the kitchen, not wanting to hear any more. If he loved it so much, why would he want to stay on the ranch? Eldorado is small and simple. Moving from big town Houston to here is probably nothing more than a temporary getaway for him. I give him a year before he gets bored and finds some other place. I wasn't good enough for Timothy. Considering Gavin's history, I don't think I'm enough to make him stay. Or at least that's what I keep telling myself while keeping my distance. At this point in my life, I'm not looking for a fling.

The rest of the morning goes by in a blur. As I'm preparing for lunch, I call Grandma to tell her the good news, and she's ecstatic for me.

"If you ever need a taste tester, call me," she says with a laugh before we say our goodbyes.

Sandra washes the dishes, and considering how many people were in and out today for breakfast and lunch, I decide to do a deep clean. It's something I typically do once a week. Since Jane has already swept, I grab the mop and bucket and then drag it out to the main room.

I freeze in place when I see a dozen white roses in a vase on the buffet table. I look at them like they're a poisoned apple, then glance around, confused. Slowly, I walk up to them and notice a card is attached with my name written in chicken scratch. My eyes go wide, and I just hope Dad isn't around to witness this because it would cause too many questions.

I open the envelope.

Happy Valentine's Day, Maize. If you'd let me, I'd make it worth your while, since you no longer have amnesia.

I hurry and tuck it in my back pocket, and then grab the roses and take them into the kitchen.

"Whoa!" Sandra says with wide eyes.

"I know, I know." I set them down because while they're beautiful, they're also heavy. The sweet smell fills the kitchen, and I try to steady my breathing. My heart pounds hard because there's only one florist in town, which means Gavin *had* to speak to them about sending flowers. This is exactly how rumors start around here.

"Who are they from?" Donna questions, pulling me from my thoughts.

"Didn't say." I'm being truthful because his name wasn't actually written, just insinuated.

"Someone's got a secret admirer." Dad speaks up from behind me, and I nearly jump out of my shoes.

I roll my eyes, wishing I could disappear. "I guess."

"Hmmm." Dad rubs his chin. "I wonder who it could be."

"I dunno!" I look around, trying to find my escape. "I gotta get back to mopping."

I rush to the dining room and have never moved so fast in my life. I'm thankful I took the card because I know Dad would've peeked, and that's the last thing I need right now. After I'm done with my tasks, I grab the roses and tell everyone goodbye.

I'm tempted to text him on the way home and demand he stop, but I realize I don't have his number. Truthfully, it's probably a good thing because it means I can't drunk text him. Knowing we'll be at the rodeo together excites me but also makes me anxious. He's well-known in the area, and the last thing I want to witness is women flocking to him. Hopefully, I'll be too busy to even notice.

When I park, I look over at the roses. It was a sweet thought, and while I want to be angry, I'm not sure I can. If we were two different people, maybe we could work. Part of me wishes it was possible, but the other knows it's not.

CHAPTER EIGHT

GAVIN

"He's bein' a bastard, ain't he?" Jackson asks, hanging on the railing.

"Oh yeah," I respond, nearly breathless.

A new colt was delivered last Monday, and he's my special project. They named him Demon for a fuckin' reason too 'cause he's a little shit and doesn't want to cooperate. If he keeps it up, we'll be doing laps around the corral for the next two weeks. One thing I've learned while training horses is to have patience and be gentle. These animals don't trust humans on instinct. It's something that's earned.

"Rodeo's next week, right?"

I glance at him over my shoulder. "Yes, sir."

"Good deal. I'm gonna try to watch your trainee ride. Hopefully, he places. Anyway, I'll let you get back to it."

"Alrighty, thanks," I say, then slowly walk up to Demon as he backs away. Eventually, his curiosity gets the best of him, and he takes a few steps forward. Holding out my hand, I let him sniff me and keep my movements slow. The last thing I want is to spook him.

I touch the softness of his nose, then create some space so he can get reacquainted with learning. Right now, he's ready to bolt, and if the gate was open, he would.

After a minute of staring each other down, I grab the rope and start lead practice. He trots around in circles, and I swing the extra ends of the rope in the other direction, and he turns around. We do this for thirty minutes, and then I give him a break. Demon eyes me.

I click my tongue, encouraging him to come toward me. I clip the rope to his halter and lead him around the pen, then we go back to our training.

As he makes his way around the pen, I notice Maize from my peripheral. She's watching me train, and a smile forms on my face. She's no different than the horses—resentful, hesitant, but also interested—and I'm determined to break her too. The chase keeps me going, but I also like the thought of being with her too. I may be a retired bull rider, but I'll always be a champ, and I'm ready to win her over.

When I turn my head, our eyes meet, and she freezes in place. She's carrying bags, and I'm sure she's bringing Kiera and Jackson breakfast. Sometimes she does that when they're not as busy at the B&B. Wiping the sweat off my brow, I keep my eyes on Demon. As he does laps, she moves closer and hangs on the gate.

"Hey," she coos, her voice soft and sweet.

"Hi." I don't stop my training session even though I want to do nothing but pay attention to her right now. Not sure what it is about Maize Bishop, but the chemistry we share and the way she makes me feel are different from all the other women I've ever been with. She's not the type you have a one-night stand with and forget, but rather the kind of lady you bring home to meet your mama.

"What're ya doin' for lunch?" she asks.

"No plans," I say with a half-grin.

"Why don't you come down to the B&B and eat? I know this sounds silly, but you lived rodeo life for a long while, and I'd like your opinion on something."

I lower my arms, and instantly, Demon stops trotting and stands twenty yards away and stares at me. Bringing my gaze to her, I walk closer. "About what?"

"I cooked the brisket I'm entering into the contest and want you to try it since you've been all over the state. Barbecue is a whole food group in Texas, and I know you've probably eaten truckloads of it." She hesitates. "I just don't want to go embarrassing myself. The only thing is, you'll have to promise to be truthful no matter what."

I study her lips, then meet her soft eyes. Something about Maize drives me absolutely fucking crazy, and right now, all I want to do is swipe my lips against hers until we're both breathless.

"So, what do you say?" she finally asks.

"Sure. I'll be there, but you owe me one," I tell her with a wink.

She chuckles, a sound I don't get to hear too often. "Add it to my tab. See you at eleven."

Once Maize is out of sight, I go back to Demon, and we try saddle training next. When I look down at my phone, I realize it's nearly time to meet Maize. Quickly, I finish up, then I pop my head into the office and let Jackson know I'm going to the B&B for lunch in case he comes lookin' for me.

On the way over, I can't stop smiling because this is a step in the right direction. Though Maize and I have played tug-of-war for months, her reaching out for my help feels like progress. She's smart to ask me because I *have* eaten a lot of barbecue over the years. It's a staple at every damn rodeo I've ever been to.

I pull up to the B&B and park. Though it's only the end of April, it's already hot as hell. Can't even imagine how summer's gonna be, but I'm not looking forward to it because I'll be working outside. When I enter, I immediately smell the smoky meat wafting through the whole place. My mouth begins to water, and my stomach growls.

As soon as I sit at a table in the corner, Maize steps into view and looks around the room. When she spots me, she smiles, then holds up her index finger and walks away. I get up and pour myself some sweet tea, and when I return to my seat, I notice she's carrying a tray full of food toward me.

"Whoa," I say with a grin when she sets it down.

The laughter that releases from her sounds so sweet. Maize hands me a set of silverware and sits in front of me. Before I take a bite, I notice she's fidgeting with the hem of her shirt. She's so nervous about me eating, not something I've witnessed since being here. I push the fork into the meat and watch the juices run from it. It's tender as can be as I eat it. The taste isn't like anything I've had before, and I swear it's the best damn barbecue I've ever had.

I grab the dinner roll and dip it in the barbecue sauce, take a few bites of smoked sausage, and finish off the brisket like I haven't eaten in a decade. Maize's cheeks turn pink as she bites her bottom lip. "Okay, so what do you think?"

With the rest of the bread, I wipe it across the plate until it's perfectly clean. "Do you have more?"

"You're just saying that," she chides, crossing her arms.

I place my hand over hers and lean forward, lowering my voice so no prying ears can hear. "You're gonna win this, sweetheart. It's the best I've ever had. Cross my heart."

Her smile grows wider. "Really?"

"I wouldn't lie. The texture. The flavor. It's not dry at all like some briskets are. And the sauce, holy shit, woman. I'm tempted to get down on one knee and ask you to marry me right here, right now."

She pulls her hand away, and I realize I crossed the line, but I don't care. It's the damn truth.

"So, about those seconds…?" I linger, not just referring to her food.

Standing and scooting in her chair, she grabs the tray, leaving my tea, then walks away. I almost thought she was pranking me until she returns with a heaping pile full of her soon-to-be award-winning barbecue. "I gotta go help my employees, so I'll be right back. Okay?"

I give her a nod and dig in. It's so delicious I eat every morsel, not wasting a crumb. About an hour passes before she comes back.

"There's no way you ate all that," she says, her eyes wide.

I lean back and suck in a deep breath. I might've gone overboard, but it was too good to pass up. "I did, and now I'm full as hell and have no idea how I'm going to work for the rest of the day. I can already feel the food coma coming. It was so good, and if I had any room, I'd eat more." I throw her a wink.

"You're not shitting me, right?" she asks again.

"Never. You'll win, hands down. I'd even bet on it." I hold out my hand, hoping she shakes, but she doesn't do anything but smile wide.

"Thank you," she whispers. "Means a lot to me. I'm just nervous about all this."

"Shouldn't be. You're a pro, Maze. That prize is yours," I stress, wishing she'd believe me. I look around and notice the B&B is empty. It's just her and me. The place is a mess, so I stand and help her pick up the remaining dishes left on the tables. We grab as much as we can so we don't have to make another trip, and I follow her to the kitchen area.

Maize sets the dishes in the sink and then steps slightly out of the way to give me more room to add what I'm carrying. Our arms touch, and electricity shoots through me. She must've felt it too because I notice goose bumps form on her arms. Though she denies anything between us, moments like this remind me there is something. Nothing she could say would make me think otherwise because her body gives her away every single time.

"Maze," I whisper, watching her breasts rise and fall. I place my palm on her warm cheek and brush my thumb against her skin. She swallows, and I'm tempted to kiss her, but I don't want to press my luck when I'm gaining ground.

My phone rings, and I glance down to see it's Jackson. I'm sure he's wondering where the hell I ran off to because I've been gone for a while. "I don't want to go, but I have to," I admit.

"I know," she whispers.

I look down and reject the call, not ready to go just yet, but knowing I have to.

"Do you want a hand?" I ask.

She tilts her head. "Not unless you want Uncle Jackson bursting through those doors and dragging your ass back to the training facility. You've helped me more than enough already."

Leaning over, I place a soft kiss on her head, then turn away just as her employees are walking through the door with baskets of veggies from the garden.

"See you later," I say, then leave. I sent her flowers on Valentine's Day, and the note I left wasn't a joke. I would make it worth her while if she'd let me.

When I get in the truck, I call and let Jackson know I'm on the way. Apparently, a mare's being delivered this afternoon. It slipped my mind that I needed to check her in, but I got to the barn in record time.

Jackson pulls hay down from the loft, and I grab a few bales and help distribute it to each stall. It's a revolving door with training now that three of us are doing it. Kiera and Jackson have been happy with how much we've grown the facility, and the word has traveled fast. We're booked nearly two years in advance, and the waitlist is a mile long too. Wouldn't be surprised if they hire a few more people to keep up with the demand.

Before long, a truck with a gooseneck horse trailer comes traveling down the rock drive. A man parks and pops out of the cab and walks over to me. "You Gavin?"

"Yes, sir," I tell him.

He nods. "I'm Billy Gibson. Own the ranch a ways down. Ready to unload her?"

"Sure am. And very nice to meet you."

Billy goes to the back and lifts the bar to the trailer gate. The mare instantly starts throwing her hoof out, ready to kick one of us. She's pissed.

"We call her Angel," he tells me with a thick Southern accent.

I chuckle. "Sarcasm, I assume?"

"Absolutely, son."

"Perfect, I've got one named Demon right now. They'll probably get along just fine."

Just as I'm assisting Billy, I see Grayson and Diesel pull up in the old beat-up Ford. They go inside the office, and I do a walk around of the horse. We like to make a note of any injuries before accepting them. I lift her hooves, and she's not having it, but thankfully, she's not too big or hard to handle yet.

"Whatever you do, don't walk behind her," he warns and pulls me back.

"Thanks," I tell him.

"She might've kicked your balls right off. It's one of her bad habits," he explains. "Her only goal is to take out anyone or anything that gets behind her flank. My dog learned his lesson real quick."

I nod and check the other side. "Noted. Well, she looks good."

"Y'all gonna earn your money with this one," he says, patting her.

It makes me chuckle. I've yet to meet a horse that was easy to break. "You'll just need to sign some paperwork inside, and then you'll be all set," I explain and point toward the office. He gives me a head nod and goes that way.

As Angel is tied to a post, I take a step back, crossing my arms and looking at her. She's a beautiful gray leopard appaloosa with a black mane and white socks. Holding my hand out, I allow her to make the first move and sniff me. Once Angel seems calmer, I lead her to her stall. By the time she's settled in the barn, I walk to the front, and the owner is long gone.

Diesel and Grayson step out of the office, ragging on each other.

"If it weren't for me, you wouldn't even be at work this morning," he tells Diesel.

"And that's why you're my right-hand man," Diesel explains. "You keep me in check."

Grayson rolls his eyes and grins. "There's Casanova."

"What?" I chuckle.

"I heard Maize got roses on Valentine's, and I've been meaning to ask you if you sent them," Diesel says.

I tilt my head at them because there's no damn way either would know 'cause Maize's sealed like a vault. "I'm not the type of man who kisses and tells, boys. So, you need to go on with all that rumor mill shit."

"You're no fun," Diesel whines.

"I'm plenty of fun, or at least that's what the ladies say." I shrug and laugh.

"The rodeo's next week, right?" Grayson lifts his cowboy hat and smooths his sweat-covered hair down before setting it back on his head.

I nod, answering him with Maize on my mind. I wonder if we'll ever be anything more, and chasing women isn't in my forte. Feeling the constant hot and cold from her is a new experience for me, and I'm not sure I like it. Though I do enjoy the chase of it all.

"How's Cooper doing? Nervous yet?" Diesel asks.

"Actually, he's doing really well. Wouldn't be surprised if he placed. I know the competition won't be easy, though. As long as he stays on his A game and gets out of his damn head, he'll make it happen," I explain. "We're actually meeting tonight to continue our lessons. Most of it's mental, but a large portion is physical too. You ever thought about riding?"

Diesel's a big guy with lots of muscle, and with the right training, he could probably go far.

He snorts. "Hell no!"

"Big D here's too much of a pussy," Grayson snaps with a chuckle. "He nearly cried when he saw a spider in the truck last week."

I burst out laughing.

"I did not!" Diesel scowls and takes off running after Grayson, who's way too fast for him. I remember being pretty much the same at their age.

Diesel bends over and picks up a rock and throws it at Grayson. It nails him right in the back of his head. Wanting to retaliate, Grayson starts throwing them back.

"What in the fuck are you two doin'?" Jackson yells.

I cross my arms and watch them chase each other like kids.

"Nothing!" Diesel says, finally dropping his ammunition.

Jackson looks at me and shakes his head. In that split second, Grayson nails Diesel in the forehead.

"What the hell!" Diesel screams and starts the chase again.

Jackson claps his hands to get their attention, but they're lost. Seconds later, he puts two fingers in his mouth and lets out the loudest ear-piercing whistle I've ever heard. They both stop moving.

"Get your asses in the truck and get the hell outta here. Actin' like rowdy children," he demands, but he's smiling.

"Learned it from you!" Diesel pops off, and Jackson rears up like he's going to charge them.

It's enough to scare the shit out of them, and they climb into the truck without hesitation. When I see the look on their faces as they back out of the drive, I chuckle. They're giggling like schoolkids, and so is Jackson.

I shake my head, and Jackson pats me on the back. "Guess it's time to get back to work."

"Yes, sir," I confirm, then head to the barn. One thing about working on the Bishop ranch is that there's never, ever a dull day around here.

CHAPTER NINE

MAIZE

I can't believe today's the competition. I've been counting down to this ever since I got that phone call, and now it's finally here. My nerves have gotten the best of me all week, and I've been a wreck, trying not to overwhelm myself. I know what winning could do—give me the opportunity to jumpstart my business.

When I was in culinary school, it was very competitive. I received job offers from many of the chefs who taught me after I graduated. I could've gone anywhere—San Francisco, New York, Dallas, or Chicago—and worked for upscale restaurants and fine dining experiences only, but the stress would've been too intense for me to handle. Instead, I explained I'd be working for the family business. Though it wasn't what they wanted to hear, it was respectable, and I don't regret my decision. Being under pressure like that isn't for me, which is why I don't enter cooking competitions.

When we arrived with the pit early yesterday morning and saw the competition lined up, I was ready to drink tequila straight from the bottle. Diesel and Riley got the wood loaded and the pit to temperature as I prepared the meat. Some contestants have been smoking meat longer than I've been alive. They take it seriously and want to win just as much as I do. Learning there were close to thirty teams nearly gave me a heart attack.

Mom, Dad, Grandma, and I arrived before the sun rose this morning. After we parked, I added more hickory to the pit as my parents put up the canopy with chairs, so we didn't bake in the sun. I brought a checklist with timelines for my team, and as soon as Kenzie saw it, she rolled her eyes. My cousins have been the best support system and have helped me so much, but not without complaint.

Dad gets up and stretches as Knox and Kane check the temperature of the food. Kenzie micromanages them, using her soon-to-be teacher skills, and it makes me chuckle.

"You okay?" Dad asks as I unlock my phone and check the time. I swear only ten minutes have passed since I last looked.

I shrug. "Yeah. I guess. As good as I'm gonna be until this is all over."

"Honey, you're gonna do fine. And even if you don't win, I'm proud of you for trying. It's hard to put yourself out there and allow people to judge and be critical of something you're so passionate about," he says, patting me on the back. "It smells delicious."

"You wanna try the first cut when I pull it?" I lift my eyebrows, already knowing the answer to that question.

"Damn right," he tells me.

I look around him, and Kenzie gives me a thumbs-up. We're on track to having the juiciest brisket to date. If I don't win, I will swear until my dying day the judging was rigged.

Dad walks back to his seat, and Elle comes up to me. "Almost ready?" She checks the time on her smartwatch. "We have about two hours before we have to pull the meat and deliver the plates to the judge's area."

"I know. Actually, only one hour so it can rest beforehand." I bite my bottom lip, knowing that the juices will run out without adequate time to sit, making the meat dry. The last thing I want to do after smoking it for twenty-four hours is to ruin it at the end, and damn, it's so easy to do.

The twins are responsible for making sure it doesn't get dry and checking the internal temperatures. Right now, it's just a waiting game. I've done this process at least a hundred times since I knew I'd be competing, but it still makes me anxious. If something can go wrong for me, it usually does.

"Girl, you got this," Elle encourages, noticing my mood. Kenzie walks up and bumps her hips against mine.

"Can we eat yet?" she beams.

"Not yet. I made an extra brisket just for y'all, though," I tell her, knowing they'd want some after smelling it all day.

"Seriously, if I could cook like you, I'd probably already be married," Elle says with a smile.

Her joke makes me laugh, and it's exactly what I needed. "But then you wouldn't be available for that hot boss of yours."

She rolls her eyes. "Don't even. He's still being a total and utter dickhead. Because I took today off, I have to work the next three weekends. How in the fuck is that fair?" I can tell she's upset.

"Oh no. I'm sorry," I offer.

She shakes her head. "Not your fault. That's just how rude he is."

"Sometimes that attitude makes them even hotter," Kenzie quips, giving her a nudge. When I hear Uncle Jackson and Kiera, I turn around with wide eyes.

"Oh my gosh, what are y'all doin' here?" I ask.

"I had to come and see my honorary daughter kick some ass," Jackson howls. He sometimes calls me his honorary daughter because I couldn't tell Dad and Uncle Jackson apart when I was a baby. Honestly, though, some adults can't tell them apart now, especially when Uncle Jackson reels it in and tries to trick people.

"I might not win, though. I'm trying not to get my hopes up," I admit.

"You're doing the best you can, sweetie. That's enough," Kiera says and grins. As we chat about the weather, I overhear Riley and Diesel talking to Grandma. "So when you gonna give me more babies?" She glares at Riley.

Immediately, his face turns red, and Diesel nudges him. "Oh, come on. Don't pretend you're not banging every day."

Riley's eyes go wide. "My grandma is literally right there." He points at her, though she doesn't look offended. She raised Jackson, who was a total hellion, so she's pretty much immune to everything.

"And that's why I didn't say the f-word. I got respect for Grandma Bishop." Diesel lifts his cowboy hat and gives her a curtsey. I snort and shake my head.

"Thank you, Adam. But we're not done with this conversation, Riley," Grandma continues.

Somehow, Riley finds his escape, and Diesel follows in his shadow. The two of them are hilarious together and will be best friends until they're old and wrinkly. Now that Diesel and Rowan are more serious, so much more has been added to their friend dynamic.

I let out a calm breath, double-checking my phone, the meat, and starting all over. It's the chef version of pacing. "Maize, why don't you go check out the rodeo and walk away for a little while?" Dad suggests, noticing my unease. "We've got this under control. The boys are doing what they're supposed to, and as long as Mama is over there watching them, they won't mess this up. She's literally your own Southern mob boss right now." He chuckles.

I look at him with big blue eyes. "Daddy, you sure?"

"You need a break before you drive yourself crazy."

Sucking in a deep breath, I nod. "You're probably right."

"Of course, I am, sweetheart. Fathers always know best."

"Okay, okay, don't go getting a big head or anything," I say, then take off my apron and hand it to him. "The brisket needs to be pulled soon. Elle knows when."

He salutes me, and I give a small wave, then walk past the rows of pits toward the main area. I make my way past horse trailers and temporary corrals.

In the arena, hooves pound against the ground, and when I'm closer, I see it's barrel racing. The young teens' age group is competing right now. It brings me back to riding when I was younger, and I realize how much I miss it. I can't remember the last time I saddled up and took one of the trails. In high school, it was my escape and gave me a chance to think. Now, I spend most of my time in the kitchen.

Leaning against the gate, I watch this girl, who's probably no older than twelve, race her horse. Her brows are furrowed, and she wears a serious expression as her ponytail sweeps in the breeze. When the young girl finishes, a small group of people stand and cheer, and that's when I see Sarah Cooke.

Groaning, I roll my eyes. Even though it's been years since I graduated high school, I will never forget how she treated me. Sarah was the real-life Regina George, all the way down to the blond hair and the clique of girls who followed her around.

I notice Gavin and Cooper sitting with them, and I shake my head. It slipped my mind that Cooper's family was friends with hers. Though I shouldn't be staring, I can't help but watch the way she flutters her long eyelashes at Gavin when he speaks. He has her full attention as he sits next to her. She says something, and he gives her a smirk, and it's more than obvious how intrigued she is by his presence.

My skin feels as though it's burning when I see Sarah flirting with Gavin. Not being able to handle it, I walk across the stadium and keep my eyes forward. Outside of the arena, a carnival has small rides for kids and a petting zoo with ponies, chickens, a kangaroo, llama, and ostrich. I watch a few toddlers with their parents inside the pen, and it's absolutely adorable. As I'm leaning against the cool metal, I feel someone stand close to me, way too damn close. I turn my head, ready to tell whoever it is to give me some space, when I see Gavin.

"Thought that was you," he says with the same smile he gave Sarah.

"I was about to tell you to back the fuck up," I say, putting my attention back on the kids. From my peripheral, I see Sarah and Cooper waiting for him. My jaw locks, but I'm not sure if he notices or not.

"How are things going so far?" He keeps his eyes on me. "Wait, aren't you supposed to be cooking right now?"

I laugh and meet his gaze. "The brisket is almost done, just waiting for Elle to pull it, then we'll plate it. My nerves were so bad that Dad forced me to take a break to get my mind right. Though I'm not so sure how much it really helped."

"Gavin," Cooper speaks up, then points toward the food area.

"Your friends are waiting," I mumble, glancing over at them. Sarah looks like she wants to claw my eyes out, and it makes me smile.

"We were going to get corn dogs and sweet tea. Have you eaten yet?"

I shake my head.

"You should come with us," he offers. His arm brushes against mine, and I hurry and tuck my hands in my pockets, hoping he didn't notice the goose bumps.

"I don't want to interrupt anything."

A hearty laugh releases from him. "What're you talkin' about?" He turns and looks at an impatient Sarah and Cooper. While I don't want to be petty, I will never forget what she did to me. Sarah stole the only guy I liked in high school just to prove she could. Because of her, I was forced to go to the Jingle Bell Ball alone. *Bitch.*

"Nothing," I say, refusing to allow Sarah to get the best of me. He holds out his arm, and I hesitate but grab it.

"Ready?" he asks.

"Absolutely," Cooper tells him. "I'm starving."

Sarah's eyes burn into me, but she doesn't say anything. Gavin moves past them and leads us to the food truck area. Immediately, the sweet smells of homemade cotton candy and fried everything float through the air. We stop in front of one of the trucks that's well-known in town.

"What would you like?" he asks.

I shrug. "Whatever you're having."

Cooper follows him as he waits in line, but Sarah stays behind. Though I haven't spoken to her in over a decade, she moves closer to me.

"Hey, Maize. How've ya been?" she asks.

I don't even look at her. "Great."

She crosses her arms, and I notice she's staring at Gavin. "The things I'd do to that man." There's a slight pause. "I mean, unless you two are a thing."

"We're not official," I admit, just in case she asks him.

"So, are you two exclusive?"

This causes me to turn to her. "I'd rather not talk about this."

Thankfully, before she can respond, Gavin walks up with two giant corn dogs in one hand and two bottles of water in the other.

"I thought you wanted tea?" I say as he hands me my food and drink. "Thank you!"

"They were out, and it would take twenty minutes. Didn't want to wait." He gives a quick eye roll, then grins.

"That's a bummer."

Cooper hands Sarah an order of cheese fries. With his mouth full, Cooper chats about competing later tonight and how he's feeling nervous. I quickly check the time and realize I need to get back as soon as possible.

"I'm sure you're gonna place," Sarah says.

Cooper beams as he takes another big bite of a cheeseburger with a donut bun. My eyes go wide because I've never seen anything like that before.

"How's that taste?" I ask. I'd never thought about combining those two things, and instantly my mind reels with how to incorporate that for breakfast at the B&B.

"Delicious," he tells me with mayo in the corner of his mouth.

A breakfast sandwich served on a donut might be added to the menu next week.

Gavin chuckles and hands Cooper a napkin as he goes on about riding. Sarah glances at me, then she focuses on Gavin. She laughs in all the right places and looks up at him with her big brown eyes. It's pathetic. After we finish eating, I listen to Gavin talk about rodeo life and how he nearly broke his hip.

My phone buzzes, and I pull it from my pocket then answer.

"Where are you?" Kenzie asks. "Brisket has been resting for thirty minutes, and we're waiting for you to cut it open, or at least that's what Grandma says."

"I know, I know. I'm heading that way now," I say, grinning as a rush of excitement streams through me, but I stay calm.

"Okay, hurry your ass up. It's your time to shine, sis," she tells me before ending the call.

Gavin's eyes meet mine. "Everything okay?"

"Yeah, just fine. I need to get back," I admit.

"I'll walk with you." He turns to Cooper and Sarah. "I'll meet up with y'all at the arena in about thirty minutes." Without waiting for a reply, Gavin walks away with me.

"You were quiet back there." He glances at me.

I give him a smile, realizing we're alone. "I am now."

We're almost to the competitive cooking are, and I stop walking and turn to him.

"Thanks for lunch," I say before continuing.

"Anytime. Least I can do, considering you feed me nearly every day."

This makes me laugh because in a roundabout way, it's true. Time seems to sit still as the warm breeze brushes against my cheeks.

"What are you doing later? After you submit your entry?"

My heart races at the prospect of him wanting to hang out with me at his stomping grounds. "Cleaning up, then probably going home. Won't find out anything until tomorrow when they make the official announcement."

"After you're done, I'd love it if you came with me and watched the guys ride the bulls tonight. Starts at five."

I brush fallen strands of hair from my eyes and grin. "Yeah, I'd like that."

He seems pleased with my answer, considering I've been pushing him away for months. "Oh, I don't think I have your number."

My smile widens. "Of course, you don't."

With raised brows, he pulls his phone from his pocket, and I take it, plug in my number, then hand it back.

"Text me when you wanna meet up," I say, tucking my lips in my mouth, then turning away.

"You better believe it," he says, but I don't look back at him.

CHAPTER TEN

GAVIN

As soon as Maize's out of sight, I send her a text.

Gavin: This is my number. Lemme know when you're free.

I imagine the little smirk she likes to throw at me.

Maize: Will do.

Gavin: Good luck! See you soon!

When she makes it back, I know it'll be hectic for her. Maize's a perfectionist when it comes to her cooking, so I can only imagine how anal she's being right now. I'm sure Riley and Diesel will tell me all about it, considering they were wrangled into helping.

I text Cooper and meet him at the barrel racing area where his cousin's competing. My mind wanders, and my body buzzes from being with Maize, but I try to push it away. When I come into sight, Sarah and Cooper wave, and I climb the stadium stairs two at a time and sit. For the next couple of hours, we watch the teens compete like fearless savages. They take corners so tightly that they look like they'll slide right out of the saddle.

Every so often, I pull my phone from my pocket to see if I've gotten a text from her yet. Tonight, she'll either be in a great mood or a shitty mood, depending on how things go. Either way, I'm determined to show her a good time.

When there's a break between age groups, Cooper stands and yawns. "I'm gonna go to the RV and take a nap." He rubs his eyes. "Need to reset my mindset before I ride."

"That's a good idea," I say. "Want me to come get you an hour before?"

"Yeah, that would be good." He gives me a nod, then leaves.

Sarah grins when Cooper walks away, leaving us alone.

She scoots closer, and I can feel the warmth from her body. "So."

I smile, and before I can say a word, my phone vibrates. Immediately, I pull it from my pocket and see a text from Maize.

Maize: Food is delivered, and we cleaned up. Judges are eating, and now I'm pacing. UGH.

Gavin: Awesome! So, you're ready to hang out?

Maize: Yes! Please! I need to keep my mind busy.

A smile touches my lips, and I think of a few ways to do just that.

Gavin: Wanna meet me at the mutton busting area?

Wanting to be alone with Maize, I stand and politely excuse myself. Sarah's face contorts, but she quickly smiles and tells me goodbye.

Maize: I'll be there in 10 minutes.

Once I'm out of the arena, I hear a crowd yell, followed by an eruption of applause. Parents and spectators are way more excited watching the toddlers ride sheep than the stadium is watching teenagers race barrels. It's adorable, and it's where I first realized I wanted to ride bulls when I was older.

I lean against the metal railing and see a sheep loaded in the shoot. A boy, barely five, sits on top of the fuzzy animal with a helmet and full gear. He holds on for dear life with his arms and legs. They open the gate, and the sheep zooms into a full sprint, trying to get the kid off his back. Five seconds later, the little boy is on the ground throwing a fit with elephant-sized tears. I chuckle, and so does everyone else.

As I turn, I see Maize walking toward me wearing a sexy smile.

"There's my champ," I say when she's closer and wrap my arm around her. For a second, I think she's going to pull away, but she doesn't. Instead, she leans in, giving me an awkward side hug, then creating space. Just like the curious horses.

"I haven't won *yet*," she reminds me, just as the next sheep bursts out with a little girl on its back. She holds on tight and ends up staying on until the announcer tells her to let go. There's a time limit to stay on just like in bull riding. She gracefully slides off, gets up, and dusts the dirt from her jeans, then gives a thumbs-up to the audience.

"Yes!" Maize hoots and hollers, then throws a fist pump in the air.

I chuckle.

"I love seeing girls break barriers like that."

"Around the states, mutton bustin' is gender-neutral. But she totally kicked ass."

When she walks past us, Maize claps loud and compliments her. I love her enthusiasm. A few more kids ride, and we decide to sit in the stands. We're so close the softness of her skin brushes against mine.

"If you're this excited about mutton bustin', you're gonna have a hell of a time in an hour."

She licks her lips. "I'm sure I will. Honestly, I've never watched the bull riders."

I tilt my head. "Why not?"

"Wasn't interested in the big egos." She shoots me a wink.

I clap my hands together and laugh. "Some of the assholes who ride love being in the spotlight, but most of the people who hung out with my circle kept to themselves. It was more about winning than being a celebrity. Super competitive."

She lightly elbows me. "I was just kidding. With my schedule, it just never interested me to take a day off and come out here. Plus, most of the girls my age flocked to the men who were in town just passing through. It's not my vibe, if you know what I mean."

I tuck hair that's blowing in her face behind her ear. "I understand."

"You were an exception," she says. "The *only* exception."

Placing my hand on my chest over my heart, I grin. "Means a lot. I'm honored. Shouldn't I get a trophy or something, though?"

She snorts. "Sometimes you're an ass."

"I'm not trying to be. Scout's honor."

My phone buzzes, and I realize it's the alarm I set to wake Cooper. He has an hour to get ready before he has to check in.

"Wanna walk with me to get Cooper?" I ask.

She nods, and we walk down the bleachers. I place my hand on the small of her back as we move through the crowd. There are more people here now than there were earlier, and that old excitement I'd feel before competing comes back. This time, it's a little different. While I'm not riding, I still have skin in the game because of Cooper. If he places, he'll get the qualification he needs to go to the regional championship, which is a big deal. Though it won't be easy, if he continues to rank, he could follow in my footsteps and make it to the world championship.

We walk past rows of trucks and horse trailers, and I can hear the generators buzzing from the campers. Most of them are luxury fifth wheels or buses, all bought by rodeo winnings and sponsors, I'm sure. These guys travel across the state to try to rank, and each time they win a title, they get paid too.

Maize looks at the different rigs, and she's amazed by how luxurious they are.

"Cooper is staying on-site even though he lives here?" Maize asks as we continue forward.

"Yeah. Considering you ride a few times during the rodeo, it's typically easier to be here than to commute."

When we make it to the giant fifth wheel, I get ready to knock.

Maize glances over at me. "Do you miss it?"

I look at her and contemplate my answer. "At times, but it's dangerous as fuck and a rough sport. It's well-known that each time you go out there, it's not a matter of if you'll get hurt, but when. After I went pro at eighteen, I pressed my luck a lot and knew I had to call it quits before I ultimately regretted it."

"Do you? Regret it, I mean?"

I don't have to think about it. "No. Retiring when I was at my prime was a good decision. I'll always be known as a two-time world champion who stopped riding after my final win. I still get calls for interviews and reunion rides, all which I've declined. I've broken too many ribs and tore too many muscles and ligaments over the years to have the desire to do it again. And concussions? I've lost count. Trust me when I say I don't regret stopping."

Maize's expression softens, and she shoos me forward. I tap on the door, and seconds later, Cooper opens it wearing just his jeans.

"Oh, sorry. I didn't realize a lady was present. I'll be right out." The door clicks shut.

I turn to Maize. "So, do you know the rules?"

"Of what?"

"Bull riding."

She shakes her head. "I know some, but you'll have to give me the CliffsNotes version, so I know what's going on."

A few moments later, Cooper comes out fully dressed in a nice button-down shirt and jeans. Of course, he has on his black Stetson and flashes his million-dollar smile.

"Ready?" he asks us.

I chuckle. "Ready as you are, cowboy."

Cooper leads the way, and we follow him.

"You gettin' nervous?" I ask Cooper, and he slows down his pace, stepping in line with us.

"Truthfully?"

I answer with a nod.

"I'm kinda losing my shit inside because what if I get hurt?"

I point at my temple. "You gotta get your mind right before you go out there. We talked about this before. Each time you get on a bull, it could be your last. It's why you have to respect the sport. When you're out there, what do you need to focus on?"

Cooper swallows hard. "Safety, my form, and the animal."

I pat him on the shoulder. "That's right because you already know the risk."

The lights from the arena splash across the ground, and I hear the noise of the crowd. Just seeing all the people causes a spike of adrenaline to rush through me. It's probably only a tenth of what Cooper is feeling. When Maize notices my shift, she grabs my hand and squeezes, but I stiffen.

"Great. Now I'm getting nervous," she tells me with a chuckle.

"We're gonna stay on the ground floor and watch. I'll be with Cooper when he climbs on the bull until they let him loose. Now, about those rules," I say, my voice dropping an octave.

I think I see her shiver. "I'm waitin'."

Cooper goes to check in, and Maize and I stand in the dirt by the bleachers. When I look down, I notice she's wearing cowboy boots, and it makes me smile.

"There's a rope around the bull's neck with a bell on it. The bell is supposed to help the rope drop when the cowboy falls off. We use this stuff called resin to make the rope stickier, so it's easier to grip."

"Learn something new every day." She gives me a genuine smile. "So why eight seconds? I always hear that being talked about."

I nod. "Ahh. Yes. Well, eight seconds is the amount of time it takes for a bull to wear out and for the adrenaline to decrease. So, it's a quick spurt of them being powerful motherfuckers, and then they kinda calm down after it. Trust me when I say seconds feel like minutes." Though I don't tell her that time seems to stand still in the same way when I'm with her.

Her mouth falls open slightly, and I can tell she's impressed. "That's insanity."

An announcer comes on the loudspeaker, and Cooper returns. "I'm rider number eight. I'm gonna go sit on the bench and meditate or some shit," he says with a grunt.

"You're gonna do just fine. We've practiced this over and over."

He gives me a nervous grin and leaves Maize and me to our conversation.

"So judging. The rider is judged up to twenty-five points, and so is the animal." I point over to where the judges are sitting. "Perfect score is a hundred, but it's as rare as getting struck by lightning or winning the lottery."

"Well shit," she mumbles.

Her response makes me laugh. "You know how you always see riders with their arms up in the air?" I lift my hand and show her.

She snorts and mocks me. "Mm-hmm, the typical cowboy riding a buckin' bronco pose."

"That's the one, and it's for a good reason. Once the gate opens, you can't touch yourself or the animal. You can only hold on with that one hand, and the other has to stay free, or you don't get scored."

"You get disqualified? That's messed up."

"Basically. Takes a lot of practice to keep that other hand away because you want to hold on with both because it's a long-ass fall to the ground."

Maize glances over at me. "I think I have a newfound respect for these cowboys. I had no idea it was so intense."

I take my hat off and tip it at her.

"Wait, how'd ya know what bull you're gonna get?"

"Ahh. Good one. You're matched up. At some competitions, you can choose, but usually, it's random."

"So it's not like Tinder where you can swipe right or left?" She snickers, and I join in on her sentiment.

Soon, the first rider is being loaded in the chute. Though the announcer says something, and the clock starts, I'm brought back to the last time I rode as soon as the gate opens. The bull was known for cycloning, which I fucking hated more than anything because I understood its dangers. When I fell off, he charged after me, and thankfully, one of the rodeo clowns deterred him. The moment I looked that big angry fucker in the face and stood on my feet, I decided right then it was my last ride regardless of how I placed. Little did I know, my score was ninety-seven, and I ended up winning the whole damn competition on one of the most notorious bulls at the championship.

The only thing that brings me back to reality is Maize's gasp. The guy falls and gets up and runs as fast as he can to the edge, where two people help him climb up. The clowns make a show out of getting the animal's attention, and the crowd goes wild. If it weren't so risky, I'd find it entertaining. Maybe one day, I will.

More men go, their scores not that high, and I know it's getting close for Cooper. I take Maize's hand and lead her to where the rest of the riders are impatiently waiting for their turn. Cooper comes and stands next to me, and I let go of her hand so I can give him a pep talk.

"The scores on the board right now, you can beat them. You've got the upper hand. Stay out of your head. Keep focused, and you can win this and qualify. Guaranteed. Don't be passive in that chute, Cooper. You gotta be aggressive and take control of that animal. If you need anything while you're in there, you tell those guys who are helping you load."

He nods and lets out a howl. "I think I'm ready."

The man before Cooper gets ready to go, and the chute boss lets him know he's next. Cooper waits to be situated on Troublemaker, a fire engine red bull who's already pissed as hell. I never understood why and how they got names like this. Doesn't make anyone feel good about getting on their backs.

Maize stands off to the side, and I shoot her a wink as I climb the metal railing and keep giving Cooper positive reinforcements. Safety is what I'm focused on right now because the last thing I want is for my rider to get hurt. We've practiced for months, and he's got it as long as he doesn't psych himself out when he climbs on.

"You've got this," I tell him one last time, then go stand next to Maize, watching his every move.

Cooper puts on his helmet and mouthpiece, then gets in the bucket shoot. The guy who's gonna be pulling on the rope to tighten it for him hands it over. He grabs the opposite side of the railing and puts his foot on the bulls back to let him know he's there and is about to get situated. After a few seconds, he sits, putting his feet forward so he doesn't break an ankle. Cooper starts loosening the rope and warms it up, then he asks for it to be tightened. The bull is already losing his mind, moving around and kicking the gate. A spotter holds on to Cooper, making sure he doesn't fall or break something before they let him go.

I've done this process a hundred times, but my nerves are fucking wrecked because it's all so unpredictable. Maize stands next to me, and I don't think she's taken a single breath.

He gets the rosin hot by roughly running his hand up and down it, and I can tell it's getting real sticky. After he taps his fists against the rope, the helper releases it, giving him enough slack to grab it when he's ready. The music is loud as hell, and the crowd is already excited. Funny how when you're in the pen, you can barely hear anything other than your heart and erratic breathing.

Once he's finished warming his rope, Cooper puts his palm in position and wraps it the way I taught him. At any second now, he'll give the nod, letting them know he's ready for the chute to be opened. Those ten seconds pass so slow, but when he does, it all goes by so fast.

His positioning is perfect with a straight back and his chin tucked. With his toes forward, Cooper rides with total control. I watch him and glance up at the clock. Five seconds. Six seconds. And right as it switches to eight, the buzzer goes off, and he purposely falls. He quickly bounces up with a big ass grin on his face and rushes out, waving to the crowd. I cup my hands around my mouth and yell his name. He sees me and points right in my direction, happy as can be.

Maize's beaming when I glance over at her. "He's going to win, isn't he?"

"Yeah! He just won this whole damn thing! There's no way the competitors can catch up to his score now."

She squeals and wraps her arms around me, and I love seeing her so excited about a sport I'm so passionate about.

Cooper eventually finds me, and he's on cloud nine. "I did it. I kept it simple just like you said. I felt like I was fucking flying!"

I pat him hard on his back. "Fuck yeah. You placed, man. That means if you keep it up, you could go pro, join PBR, and become a world champ."

Cooper gives me a tight hug. "Thanks, Gavin."

"You're welcome. Now get ready to go out there and smile real big for the cameras when you get your fuckin' buckle. Congrats. You made me proud."

Cooper's family meets him by the stands, and he goes over to them. They're head over heels excited for him, just as I am. I let out a deep breath as I lead Maize over to the stands. We finish watching the riders, and I can tell she's really into it. After it's over, Cooper's brought to the center of the arena where he's declared the Eldorado Rodeo winner. He does just as I said and shows all his teeth when he's handed his first buckle. I'm sure he'll win many more after riding like that. The crowd cheers for him, and he eats up the attention. Hell, when I was his age, I did too.

As the people disperse, Cooper finds me and lets me know he won't be staying on-site tonight, so I can have the camper if I want. I happily take the keys, glad not to be driving home after all the excitement. After Cooper's gone, I wrap my arm around Maize and pull her tight.

"So, whatcha think?"

She melts in my arms. "I'm impressed, like totally blown away by all of it. I'm just not sure how you did that for so long."

I grin. "Me neither."

We walk around the rodeo and grab some food because we're both hungry. When I look at the clock, I see it's just past nine.

"You nervous 'bout tomorrow?" I ask her just as we finish our blooming onion and fried shrimp.

"Yeah. But after seeing guys nearly get trampled by thousand-pound animals, I realize I don't have it so bad." She snickers. "And if I don't place, I'll just try harder next year."

"But if you do?" I ask.

"Then I might gloat a little," she admits.

"You should 'cause you deserve it. You work too hard not to be recognized on a high level like this."

A blush hits her cheek, and in the distance, I think I hear a band play. "You like to dance?"

She points at herself. "Who me?"

I laugh.

"Not getting amnesia again, are you?" I pop an eyebrow at her. She picks up a shrimp tail and throws it at me but misses.

"I've been known to two-step a few times," she admits.

After we clean our mess, I lead her over to where a cover band is playing. A temporary stage was erected, and some people have blankets on the ground watching while others dance in the grass.

I place my arms around her body as the group plays "Keeper of the Stars" by Tracy Byrd, a country classic. Her body fits with mine perfectly as we sway to the music. Maize looks up at the sky, and I follow her lead, humming the melody. The lyrics make way more sense with her in my arms like this. I silently thank the keeper of the stars for this moment.

"Oh look, you can see Regulus perfectly," she says, pointing up at the sky. I smile because all this time, I've been so amazed by her to notice the sky is full of stars. When another song begins, she looks up at me, and I place my hand under her chin and capture her lips in mine. Our tongues twist together, and that same fire I felt the first night we were together nearly burns me alive.

She becomes breathless, and I want to lose control with her again, but I refuse to be the one to pursue it.

"Gavin," she whispers when we finally pull apart.

"Hmm?" I say, leading her away so we can have more privacy.

"Take me home with you tonight," she tells me without hesitation.

"You're sure?" I ask, needing to know she wants me as much as I've always wanted her.

"Absolutely."

The confidence in her voice is all I need to hear. I thread our fingers together, and we rush back to the RV, barely able to keep our hands off one another. It seems as if the sexual tension between us has finally snapped, and I'm not complaining one bit.

CHAPTER ELEVEN

MAIZE

RIGHT NOW, I need Gavin like I need air. He's the only reason I didn't completely lose my mind after delivering the food to the judges. Knowing I'd have the opportunity to spend time with Gavin tonight gave me something else to look forward to. As much as I've tried to turn off my attraction to him, I've found it impossible. My resolve has completely crumbled.

When he unlocks the RV, and I step inside, my eyes go wide. This is a huge change from the small campers we used to camp in as kids. It's like a damn mansion on wheels with a kitchen island, residential fridge, and recessed lighting. I rub my hand against the marble countertop, and my mouth falls open. "This is crazy."

"I know. They have way more options now than when I was traveling." He grins, the continues, "You thirsty?"

I pop a suspicious eyebrow and he chuckles, which is contagious.

"Loaded question," I say with a laugh.

Gavin removes the space between us and captures my mouth with his. Immediately, my heart races as his strong hands seem to memorize my body. A moan escapes me, and I want him to dominate me and make me his again. Carefully, he removes my hair from the ponytail I've been sporting all day, and it falls around my face.

"You're so goddamn beautiful," he says, studying me. "And you smell like barbecue."

A howl of a laugh escapes me. "Does this thing have a shower?" I ask, knowing it probably does.

Gavin takes my hand and leads me to the front. We climb a few stairs, and he opens the door to a full walk-in shower with glass doors and his and her sinks. There's even a real toilet. I turn and look at him with wide eyes because I'm actually shocked. "You're kidding me right now. This is nicer than my bathroom at home."

"I know, it's fancy. Shocks the shit out of me each time I walk into one of these things."

Slowly, he moves toward me and undresses me. His calloused fingers brush along my skin, and goose bumps form where he touches. I'm floating as he takes my chin and lifts my mouth to meet his again. I get lost as our tongues twist together, and I don't know how much longer I can wait to have him. I've been fantasizing about this as much as I've been trying to forget it.

Though we've had our ups and downs since he started working on the ranch, I've never stopped thinking about how he made me feel. Hell, I'd be willing to bet that's impossible. Now that he's standing before me, undressing me, I don't want to think about anything but his mouth and hands on me. I want to live in the moment with him.

After he unsnaps my bra and it falls to the floor, Gavin takes a step back and admires my body, lingering on my breasts.

"You're beautiful, Maze," he says, and it only builds my confidence.

"Thank you." I move forward and slip my fingers in the loops of his jeans and pull him to me before undoing his belt buckle and top button. I move the zipper down and forcefully push his jeans to his ankles, leaving him in only his boxer shorts.

Gavin bends over and takes off his boots and pants, then takes off his shirt. When I gaze down his body, I notice just how hard he is, and it makes me smirk. Gavin hooks his fingers in my panties and slides them down my body. It's the first time I've been naked with him in way too long.

His fingers thread through my hair, and I nearly melt into him as we greedily kiss. There's so much pent-up sexual tension between us that it nearly slices through the air as he leads me into the shower. The water is the perfect temperature as he washes my hair and body. One thing about the man is he pays attention to detail and doesn't miss an inch. When his fingers brush against my clit, I'm nearly putty in his hands. It doesn't go unnoticed as he palms my breast. After I'm washed, I return the favor.

It feels amazing to be able to touch him wherever and however I want. Considering it's been so long since we've been together, I drop to my knees and put the tip of his length in my mouth. Gavin places his palms on the wall to steady himself as I tease his cock with my tongue. His grunts only encourage me to devour as much of him as I can. Knowing how good I make him feel gives me all the confidence I need to continue.

His head rolls back on his shoulders, and his body tenses, but I don't let him come, not yet. When I stand, I brush my fingers over his thighs and up his stomach muscles, then give him a devilish grin. Gavin leans forward and plucks my bottom lip into his mouth.

"You wanna play dirty, sweetheart?" he asks.

With a popped eyebrow, I smile. "Maybe."

"Alright," he says, turning off the water and handing me a towel from the cabinet.

After we're dry, Gavin leads me to the bedroom. Seconds later, he removes my towel and moves me to the king-size bed. I sit and climb up, watching him intently. Swiftly, he grabs my ankles and slides me down to the edge. His warm mouth sucks on my clit until I'm squirming, then he flicks it with his tongue. Gavin goes painfully slow, allowing the orgasm to build to monumental levels before he slides a finger inside. Reaching up, he grabs one of my nipples and pinches. The sensation soars through me. My pants seem to please him, and before I come, he pulls away.

"Welp, that was fun."

I prop myself up on my elbows and look at him with wide eyes. "You wouldn't."

"You started it in the shower," he reminds me.

"Alright," I say, slowly moving my hand down my stomach and resting my fingers on my hard nub. "I'll finish myself. Trust me when I say I've had *lots* of practice."

Slowly, I massage my clit and close my eyes. Moans escape me as I love how good it feels even though I still wish it were his mouth.

"That's hot as fuck," he admits. Grabbing my wrists, he pulls them away. "But that's my job."

His tongue goes inside me, and he hums as he tastes me. "Delicious."

I don't know how much more I can take of him waging war on my pussy, but I try to hold the orgasm back as long as I can. Seems like an impossible feat and becomes one when my muscles tense and the build begins.

"Yes, baby, come for me," Gavin encourages. He finger fucks me as he flicks his tongue against me, picking up the pace. Seconds later, I'm crumpling beneath him, screaming his name. The orgasms nearly blind me, and I feel as if I'd been shot to the upper atmosphere. When I'm brought back to reality, all I can do is grin.

I move my head to the side and coax him toward me. He obliges and slides his tongue up my body until both of his arms are on either side of me as he hovers above.

"I've missed you so damn much, Maize," he admits.

I bite my bottom lip. "I'd be lying if I said I didn't feel the same."

"We're good together. You should just give up your game."

Before I respond, I wrap my arms around his neck and bring his mouth to mine, wanting to kiss him and taste myself on his tongue. The tip of his dick sits outside my entrance, and I want nothing more than to have him inside me.

"I should get a condom," he says before he continues.

"I'm on the pill," I admit. "I want to feel you. *All* of you."

"You're sure?" he asks, being the perfect gentleman.

I nod, begging him with my eyes. I've never wanted a man to take me as much as I want him to at this very moment. Slowly, he moves forward until we're one again. I gasp, forgetting just how big he is, and open my thighs wider to give more clearance.

"You okay?" he asks, making sure he's not hurting me, which I appreciate.

I nod. "Yes, feels amazing," I encourage, wanting him to lose control with me tonight.

Gavin takes it slow at first, his eyes meeting mine. Something boils between us, an energy I can't quite describe. It's magical and dangerous because I'm feeling things for him that I haven't experienced in a long ass time. I push the thoughts away, and my eyes flutter closed. Scratching my nails down his back, I hum his name.

"Fuck me, Gavin," I beg.

A second later, he's flipping me onto my stomach and moving me to the edge of the bed. I stick my ass into the air as he grabs my hips and slides inside. In this position, he might split me in two. He slaps my ass with his hand, and the pain causes so much fucking pleasure.

"You like it when I do that?"

"Yes," I call out. "Slap my ass harder."

He does exactly what I say. The orgasm comes quick, without much of a warning, and I feel as if I internally combust. Sex this good should be illegal.

"You're so goddamn tight," he groans, moving in and out of me so quickly our skin smacks together. He grunts.

"Fuck, Maize," he moans, and then he loses it. Grabbing my hips, Gavin comes, and I feel his warmth inside me. It takes us a minute to catch our breath, and I swear I'm dreaming. After we're clean, I collapse on the bed like my body is gelatin.

We stare at the ceiling, and my mind is mush. Gavin rolls over on his side and wraps his arm around my stomach, pulling me close to his body. I lay my head on his chest, listening to his heartbeat as he holds me. As his fingers brush against my arm, I close my eyes.

Being with him was the perfect ending to my day, and somehow I instantly fall asleep.

The next morning, the sun blasts through the windows and wakes me. My eyes flutter open, and it takes me a minute to realize where the hell I am. When I look over, Gavin wakes up.

He almost looks shocked and pulls me into his arms.

"Good morning," he says. "Glad to see you're still here."

I playfully smack him, and he laughs. "I guess I kinda deserve that. What time is it?" I ask, knowing my phone is probably still in my jeans on the bathroom floor.

"Almost eight."

My eyes go wide. "Eight? Shit."

"You gotta at least let me cook you breakfast. I kinda owe you for all the blueberry pancakes of yours I've eaten over the past few months," he says, and I laugh.

It's so tempting, but I know I have to go. "Can I take a rain check? Crap. I need to run home and grab a change of clothes so I don't get questioned by my entire family for wearing the same thing as yesterday."

Gavin sits up, giving me the perfect view of his bare chest and abs. My eyebrow raises, and right now, he's the only thing I want for breakfast.

"You like what you see?"

"Mm-hmm. I'm really enjoying the view right now."

He pulls me close and devours my lips. "So, if breakfast is out of the question, how about a quickie?"

I create some space so I can look at him, and I narrow my eyes. "Are you a mind reader or something?"

"No ma'am, it's your body that gives you away every time."

Seconds later, I'm crawling on to his lap, straddling him. He's already hard, and I want him so badly my entire body aches. We kiss as he slides inside, filling me full of his length and girth.

"Damn," I whisper as he digs his thumbs in my hips, steadying me as I greedily ride him. It feels so goddamn good being with him like this, taking full control as he gives me my body everything it needs and desires. The pace slows, and he thumbs my clit, and the build happens fast and quick.

"Maize, you feel so fucking good," he whispers as my mouth runs across his neck and up to his ear.

"I'm close," I breathlessly tell him, and then the orgasm rips through me. My head falls on his shoulder as he holds me tight, but I don't stop rocking my hips. Seconds later, he's riding out his release too, letting out a guttural moan.

After we clean up and I put on my clothes from yesterday that smell like brisket, I tell him goodbye. He kisses me so softly, and I just want to spend all day rolling in the sheets with him. No one has ever made me feel the way he does, and it's scary as hell.

"See you later?" he asks.

I nod and smirk. "I'd really like that. Want to meet me at the judging area at ten thirty-ish? They're supposed to announce who won then."

"I'll be there," he promises and pulls me in for one last kiss.

As I go to walk away, I look at him over my shoulder and smile.

"I already miss you," he admits, and I playfully roll my eyes at him as I go to the front door. He's everything I've ever wanted and needed, and I wonder what we'd be like if I actually gave him a chance. When I step outside, the sun is hot against my skin. I rush to my truck and try to think of what I'm going to tell my parents when I get home. It doesn't matter how old I am; they question me when I'm out all night.

I pull up to the house, and I'm relieved to see Kenzie's the only one home. Of course, she's still asleep, though. At least, I hope she is because she'll give me just as much shit about this.

I hurry and go to my room, grab a fresh set of clothes, and then jump in the shower. My only goal right now is to get back to the rodeo before my parents arrive. When I turn off the water and hear their voices, I realize that's not gonna happen today. I take my time fixing my hair and getting dressed. Then I grab my keys and try to sneak past my parents in the kitchen.

"Where've you been all night?" Dad asks, stopping me.

"John, leave her alone," Mom cuts in, thankfully.

He studies me. "You'll always be my baby no matter how old you are."

"And this is exactly why I want my own place," I say with a big grin. "Also, my business is only for me to know."

He sucks in a deep breath. "You are not moving out until you're forty-five."

I snort and pat him on the shoulder. "Nice try, Daddy."

Mom shakes her head and turns her attention to me. I'm scared she can see through me, or maybe she notices the glow I've been sporting all morning from having the best sex of my life. "Going back to the rodeo?"

"I am. Gonna check on everything, walk around a bit, then make my way to the judging area," I explain.

"We'll see you there," she tells me as she refills her cup of coffee.

"Okay, well, bye!" I sing-song and rush outside.

It's so quiet I can hear the birds chirping and the light breeze blowing through the trees. When I get in the truck, I become all sorts of nervous. Gavin was the perfect distraction to keep me out of my head about this competition, but now that I'm alone, it's all I can think about.

I drive to the rodeo as fast as I can. Once I'm parked, I text Gavin and let him know I'm back.

Gavin: Good. I missed you. I'm still at the camper. Wanna meet me here?

Maize: I'll be right there.

A blush hits my cheek, and I realize I'm biting my lip. My heart flutters as I walk to the RV, and when I knock on the door, he comes out.

"Want to grab some coffee?" he asks, looking sexy as sin in tight jeans, boots, and a black button-up shirt.

"Thought you'd never ask."

We mosey to the food trucks, his fingers brushing against mine as we walk. I want him to grab my hand, but I also know we could get caught too. The smell of bacon and eggs makes my stomach growl, and Gavin offers to get us some breakfast burritos because I'm starving. As we sit at a picnic table and eat, I try to imagine what it would be like to be with him. How our life could be if we were together. Would my parents accept our relationship? Would I be enough to keep him here?

"Only one hour to go," he reminds me around a mouthful.

"I know. I'm getting super anxious."

He places his hand on my thigh, and that's when I realize my leg was bobbing up and down, and I stop moving.

"Sorry, bad habit," I admit with a smile.

He finishes his burritos and crumples up the foil wrappers. "Your breakfast has spoiled me. Nothing tastes good anymore unless it comes from the B&B."

"It's the secret sauce," I say, then nudge him.

"Do you bottle it up and sell it?" he jokes.

"Nah. The secret sauce is cooking for the love of cooking, not for the money," I explain.

He tilts his head at me and nods. "I understand and respect that so damn much."

After I finish, we make our way to the judging area. People are already in the seats they have set up at the pavilion, and I try to steady my breathing. The reality is I'm a nervous ass wreck. Time feels as if it's passing by so slow, and Gavin rubs my back to calm me down, but I tense. I quickly look to see if any of my family are around because if they saw this type of affection, the questions would come like crazy.

He moves his hand to his lap. I grab and squeeze it. "I just. I don't..."

"No, I get it. You don't have to explain, Maize. It's hard not to touch you after what we've shared. You know?" he whispers. "I'll be your best-kept secret. I have been for this long."

I smile, and my skin burns as I relive last night and this morning.

Soon, the family arrives and sits beside Gavin and me. The ceremony starts, and the judges go through each entry. As they talk about my brisket and the way it tasted, butterflies fill my stomach. After the judges have explained the rules, they announce the third prize winner. I'm relieved but also scared not to be called. Second place is next.

"And the first place winner is..." They hesitate. "Well folks, this was a hard one, very hard. There were so many incredible entries."

Uncle Jackson's sitting behind me and leans forward. Talking just loud enough for me to hear, he says, "Shut the fuck up and get on with it."

"Maize Bishop," the judge announces. Climbing to my feet, I look down the row at my mom and dad, who stand and wrap me in a hug. The crowd screams my name, and hoots and hollers fill my ears.

"Go, sweetie. Go get your prize," Dad tells me. I'm in complete shock and speechless, not able to comprehend what the judges are saying. Blood pumps through my body as I walk to the stage. They hand me an oversized check and a trophy, and I'm so overwhelmed with emotion, I instantly burst into tears. I never thought this would happen to me.

"Would you like to say anything?" the older man asks and hands me the microphone.

I take it and swallow. "I'm not good at public speeches so forgive me, but I'd like to thank my grandma for encouraging me to enter and my parents. Also thanks to all my cousins who helped out and made this possible. *And* Diesel." I blow them all kisses. "And thanks to the cowboys who insisted I had a chance and believed in me." I look at Gavin, and our gazes meet.

Jackson lifts his hand to his mouth, and yells, "And what about your favorite uncle?"

Kiera elbows him hard in the ribs.

"And you too, Uncle Jackson," I say, handing back the microphone. As another judge speaks and entertains the audience, I'm brought to the back to sign some paperwork. They tell me a real check will be in the mail, and I guess I didn't realize the oversized one was just a novelty item. After I thank them nearly a million times, I return to my family, who are all waiting for me with smiles.

I'm surrounded by Bishops, and all I can do is cry because I'm so damn happy. A few older guys who have been competing in competitions like this all over the state come over and congratulate me.

After the onlookers disperse, I realize how much my cheeks hurt from smiling.

Gavin walks up and wraps his arms around me, nearly swallowing me whole. "Congrats. I knew you'd win."

"Thank you!" I exclaim as we linger for a few seconds, but he looks around and backs away, creating space between us.

"Congrats, baby," Grandma tells me, then looks back and forth between Gavin and me with a lifted brow but doesn't say a word. "Knew you had it in you."

After I've spoken to every single family member, we return to our cooking area and finish packing up the supplies. Once everything is loaded, Gavin walks me to my truck. Before I unlock the door, he looks around, then dips his head and gives me a soft kiss, and I get lost in it.

I pull away breathless, and I meet his eyes, mesmerized by him like he put a spell on me.

"Hopefully, we can do this again sometime," he suggests.

"Maybe," I say, liking I can keep him on his toes.

He chuckles and shakes his head. "It's all about the chase with you, woman."

"And it's a marathon, not a sprint." I climb inside the truck and give him a wave, which he returns. I back out and drive home, feeling the happiest I have in years. I think about the contest, my family, watching the bull riders, and being with Gavin. I've had a perfect weekend.

Right now, I don't know what we are or where this is going, but the chemistry we share is undeniable. The way he makes me feel is incredible. But is he in this for the long term?

Deep down, I want to give him a chance, but I also have to protect myself and my heart.

CHAPTER TWELVE

MAIZE

IT'S BEEN a week since the rodeo, and I'm still riding the high of winning the barbecue contest and being with Gavin again. We haven't talked about it and have just shared side glances and texts with each other. He knows I'm wary, given my past, but I have a feeling I'm about to break my rules for him. If our feelings are mutual, then we need to decide where to go from here.

Our work schedules are hectic, and we haven't been alone since the rodeo. While I have some free time, I decide to drive to the training center, hoping to get a few minutes alone with him. This isn't a conversation to have over texts, and it'll be better to grasp his reaction if we're face-to-face.

I smile when I see him brushing one of the horses in the stables but quickly come to a halt when I notice Knox and Kane walking toward him. Those boys are the *last* people I want to run into here. They have loud mouths, and everyone would know I was visiting Gavin before dinner.

Instead of turning around like I should, I quietly hide behind a stack of hay. They can't see me, but I can hear them clearly.

"Hey, guys. How's it goin'?" Gavin asks as they lean against the gate.

"We heard a rumor," Knox says, crossing his arms.

Gavin chuckles. "Okay. And what's that?"

My heart hammers because I don't know who saw us together at the rodeo. If they speak my name, I'm going to have to make sure I keep my mouth shut. The dramatic pause makes me roll my eyes.

"Are you leavin' the ranch?" Kane finally blurts out.

I blink hard, inching closer to make sure I heard correctly.

"Yeah, Dad said you got another job offer," Knox adds.

What in the actual fuck?

Is it possible he's leaving the ranch for me? Or for good? I have so many questions right now.

"I did," Gavin confirms calmly.

"So you're takin' it?" Kane asks.

"Not sure." Gavin moves to the other side of the horse to finish brushing it. "Cooper wants me to train with him full-time year-round, which would mean traveling around to all the competitions and rodeos in Texas."

That news makes me sick to my stomach. He'd be gone most of the time, and a long-distance relationship would be complicated. Dating or even trying would be pointless.

"So you haven't decided yet?" Knox kicks his boots against the ground, clearly upset about this. I guess they've grown close with Gavin. We all have.

"Not yet, but I'm considering it because I love the lifestyle. It's been in my blood for years, but then again, I also love being on the ranch, so I haven't made up my mind yet. Right now, I'm juggling working here and training him, and it's hard to balance both. He wants me full-time, or he'll search for another coach."

"Tell him to find someone else then," Kane blurts out.

Gavin chuckles. "It's not that easy, but once I make a decision, I'll let y'all know."

Crossing the line with him was a mistake. I should've stood my ground, but the more I pushed him away, the more he pursued me.

Stupid, stupid, stupid.

I should've learned my lesson in getting tangled up with cowboys, but I obviously didn't. My heart can't take this.

Before any of the guys can catch me, I sneak out of the barn and go back to the B&B. Trying to keep busy, I decide to text my sister.

Maize: We're drinking tonight.

Kenzie: Uh-oh. What happened?

She's the only one who knows Gavin and I hooked up after the rodeo and the only one I can talk to about him. Kenzie graduated from college a few days ago and is home now, thankfully. I missed having her around.

Maize: Gavin. I'm an idiot for getting my hopes up.

Kenzie: Why?

Maize: I just overheard him tell Knox and Kane that he got a job offer to work with Cooper full-time and travel with him. What was the point of chasing me if he planned on leaving? I'M SO STUPID!

Kenzie: No, you're not, so stop that right now. Did you ask him about it?

Maize: No, I don't want him to know I was listening, and I especially don't want him to think he has to stay for me. If he wants to go, then he should. I refuse to hold him back. Plus, he should've told me himself.

Kenzie: Oh Maze. Tonight, I'm all yours. We'll talk and watch movies.

Maize: I'll bring the booze.

I should've known better. Why would a retired bull rider be content in small-town Texas after years of traveling? Gavin craves excitement and probably enjoys the attention of multiple women too.

As I finish cleaning up while Donna and Becky prepare dinner, I get a group text.

Riley: Just a reminder, Zoey and I are throwing Zach a birthday party this weekend. You're all required, I mean expected to come. Yes, even you, Grayson.

I snort at Riley calling out Grayson. They already know I'll be there since I'm helping with the food. Gavin will hopefully be too busy with Cooper to stop by since he's having a hard time juggling it all.

As I'm cutting potatoes to roast, I dodge Gavin's calls and ignore his texts. I'm annoyed he hasn't told me this news and that my cousins heard it before I did. If he's leaving anyway, then I might as well cut things off between us before they have a chance to blossom.

Though my heart already feels like it's cracking, so it's probably too late for that.

At seven, I say goodbye to everyone and head to my truck. As soon as it comes into sight, I see Gavin leaning against it. He's waiting for me.

"Can I help you, sir?" I keep my tone flat. He's wearing dark jeans and a gray shirt. He looks good in anything, especially when it accentuates his muscles.

"As a matter of fact, you can, ma'am. I've been trying to get ahold of you all afternoon." His arms are crossed as if he's preparing to stay there until he gets an answer.

"I've been busy, ya know, working and all." I shrug, not giving him the attention. "I have plans tonight, so I need to get home."

"Why are you avoiding me again?" he blurts out, blocking me from my door.

"Look, Gavin," I say with a straight face. "Hooking up at the rodeo was a bad idea. A huge mistake. It shouldn't have happened, but it did, so let's allow the past to be in the past."

He squints, tilting his head as if he's waiting for the punch line. "Well, I can't say I'm surprised."

Now it's my turn to narrow my eyes at him. "What's that supposed to mean?"

"Running away is your MO, Maize. The second things get too real, you bail. You keep people at arm's length to avoid getting hurt again, and if you keep it up, you'll never find love."

I cross my arms over my chest, shaking my head in disagreement. "I'm not running or bailing. I just don't think you and I will work." I stand my ground, not willing to let him see this is breaking me.

He pushes off my truck and closes the gap between us, moving my chin up until I look at him. "I'm too old to play these games, Maize. You either grow up and take a real chance on us, or you don't. I won't chase you this time."

"Good," I blurt, my emotions boiling inside me. I'm seconds from telling him what I heard and have to stop myself from asking him not to go with Cooper. I won't be that type of woman who stops him from doing something that makes him happy. I saw how his eyes lit up at the rodeo, and I'll never take that away from him. "Being together meant nothing, Gavin. So let's pretend it didn't happen."

"That's what you really want?" His gaze burns into mine, and I swallow hard.

"Yes. Stop bothering me. It's time you moved on." I take a step back so I don't do something stupid, like kiss him.

Gavin retreats, brushing his hand over his scruffy jawline. "Alright, Maize Bishop. Have it your way." He sucks in a deep breath, then walks away.

I fight the urge to look at him over my shoulder and quickly slide behind the wheel, holding back tears. Even though this is what I told him I wanted, it nearly destroys me. But I have no right to be sad about it.

Once I get home, I take a long shower and let my thoughts wander. The only thing that'll numb the pain is alcohol, and I plan to imbibe once I'm dressed.

"Hey," I say, popping my head into Kenzie's room.

"I've got *The Longest Ride* on standby." She snickers, knowing damn well the premise revolves around a bull rider and a sappy love story.

"Hard pass." Walking in, I hold up the bottle of whiskey I found in Dad's liquor cabinet. "I've got the good stuff."

Kenzie pats the space next to her and gives me a sympathetic expression as I sit on her bed.

"Don't give me that look," I scold, opening the bottle. "And we're not watching anything from Nicholas Sparks."

She laughs and flips through Netflix before landing on *Scary Movie 4*. It's so ridiculous and stupid, and it's just what I need.

After twenty minutes of watching Anna Faris be a doofus while passing the whiskey back and forth, I finally speak. "Gavin was waiting for me by my truck after work."

"What'd he say?"

"He wanted to know why I was ignoring him. Instead, I told him what happened between us was a mistake and to move on."

"Maize!" she squeals. "What the hell is wrong with you?"

"I'm being smart, Kenzie!" I defend.

"No, you're pushing him away before he can do that to you."

"Duh." I take another long sip.

"But you're not even giving him a chance. He could stay. You don't even know what he's going to do yet."

"No, but he's considering it, which means it's only a matter of time before he does leave. And at that point, I could be stupidly in love with him or some shit, and it'd be a hundred times worse. It's better that I break it off now before anything more can happen," I tell her matter-of-factly. "I have to be the rational one. Though I don't want to hurt him, it's better than getting in too deep where the pain is unbearable."

"How'd he react to that?"

"I'd say less than pleasant."

She snorts, shaking her head as I tell her his exact words.

"You're too jaded and really will become a nun if you keep pushing guys away. Especially one who seems to like you and obviously wants to be with you."

"We're clearly at two different places in our lives, so it's for the best," I say with certainty.

"Or…" Kenzie grabs the bottle out of my hand. "You could just communicate, tell him you overheard his conversation, and ask if he plans to go or not. That way, you aren't making an irrational decision to end things and can choose together."

I flash her a glare, curling my lip. "Who the hell are you, and what have you done with my sister?"

She blows out a breath, then rolls her eyes. "I'm just being reasonable because someone has to."

Now that has me snorting. "Oh really? Do I need to bring up Grayson?"

Kenzie scowls, taking a gulp of the booze. "Shut the hell up."

Her sudden change of tone has me bursting into laughter. "That's what I thought."

"Guess we'll both become nuns," she confirms.

"Fine with me. I don't believe in love anymore anyway." I grab the bottle from her and take another drink.

"Yes, you do," she says, trying to reason with me. "You're just scared."

The whiskey goes to my head and makes me dizzy. Leaning against the headboard, I close my eyes. "Maybe you're right."

"Hope Mom and Dad didn't want grandchildren." Kenzie laughs as she rests her head on my shoulder.

"They know I'm working to get my catering business off the ground. What will your excuse be?" I tease.

"Focusing on my teaching career," she says with a giggle.

"You're already hired at Mom's school."

"Exactly, I need to let lesson plans and teaching on my own be the center of my attention. I don't want to disappoint her or the students."

I shrug. "Alright, that sounds like an excuse she'd buy."

We both laugh, are tipsy, and finish watching this ridiculous movie. It's just the kind of night I needed—to let loose, complain about my pathetic non-love life, and have my sister—my best friend—by my side.

CHAPTER THIRTEEN

GAVIN

THREE WEEKS AGO, Maize was in my arms, and we had another amazing night together—a night I'll never forget.

Two weeks ago, she told me it was a mistake and to move on.

Now I'm left deciding if I'll take Cooper's offer or stay at the ranch. Though I'm tempted to live the rodeo life again, even if I'm not the one competing, I'm also not ready to give up on Maize Bishop. She's running because she's scared I'll hurt her, but that's the last thing I want to do. I've given her space as she requested, but when I catch her staring at me, I know something's still lingering between us.

In the next twenty minutes, the family vet is coming to check on a horse with an infection. Sugar and Georgia got into a little tiff, and now Sugar has a nasty bite on her back. I've separated them and won't allow them in the same pasture.

"Dr. Wallen, hey," I say, reaching out my hand, and he shakes it. "I'm Gavin Fox.

"Gavin, how's it goin'? I'm Connor."

"Nice to meet you. It's goin' alright. Just dealin' with these horses fightin' each other. Ya know the drill."

He chuckles, grabbing his bag and following me into the stables. "I sure do."

"Jackson tells me you've been working with the family for a while," I say as I lead him to the barn.

"Yeah, several years. Big family."

"I didn't realize that until Thanksgiving last year. It was a never-ending line of Bishops."

Connor grins as I take Sugar's lead rope and bring her out. He examines her, softly petting her to calm her as he inspects the area.

"So Elle works with you?" I say after he injects an antibiotic.

"Elizabeth? Yeah, she's been working with me for a couple of years now."

"I've only seen her a few times, but she seems nice. I hear she's brilliant, too."

"She is a very smart young lady."

His expression tightens as he talks about Elle, and I wonder if there's a reason for it. I've overheard Elle call him a dick, but Maize and Kenzie think he's a hot piece of ass.

If I had to guess, he's around my age, and since the majority of the friends I have here are much younger than me, I invite him to my party tonight. He seems friendly enough and as though he'd get along with everyone.

After he finishes with Sugar and packs his things, I put her back into the stall and turn toward Connor.

"So I'm having a little get-together tonight with a few of the Bishop guys. You should stop by for a beer if you can," I offer as we walk to his truck.

"Uh, sure. I should be able to swing it."

"I'm staying at one of the ranch hand cabins on the east side," I tell him.

"Yeah, I know where those are. I'll see you later."

I wave once he jumps in his truck and takes off. Next, I head to the shop where I know the guys sometimes hang out during their breaks. When I open the door, I immediately hear Diesel and Riley being rowdy and messing around, which causes me to laugh. Though they've been up since the ass crack of dawn, they're always having a good time.

"Hey, Gavin," they greet when they see me. "How'd it go with the vet?"

I shove my hands in my front pockets and nod. "Fine. He gave Sugar an antibiotic and said to inject her with it for five days. Hopefully, that does the trick."

"Since it's Friday, we're gonna hit up the pub tonight," Diesel says. "You should meet us there."

"Actually, I was gonna have a party at my place and invite all the workers."

"Party!" Riley shouts. "Hell yeah!"

"No, no…" I shake my head. "It's just a *small* gathering for my birthday, so if you'd rather drink at the bar—"

"Are you kiddin' me? We'll be there!" Diesel slaps my back.

"With a cake," Riley adds. "How old are you now, old man? Fifty?"

I snort at the way he gives me shit. "Thirty-six, asshole. I'll bring the beer since I'm not sure you're even legally allowed to buy it."

They laugh, and I tell them to come around nine. I plan to have finger foods and play some horseshoes. I'm happy to just hang out with the guys since we're always working and don't get to relax too much.

"Let Grayson, Ethan, and the others know. Cooper will be there, too."

"We're on it," Diesel confirms.

"But really, just a small gathering," I tell them. "We all gotta get up for work tomorrow."

Moments later, Alex comes in and scolds them for slacking off, so I head out and get back to work. I finish earlier than usual so I can get ready for tonight. When I picked up the alcohol and snacks, I grabbed extra just in case they came super hungry.

I throw on a button-up shirt and clean jeans with my boots. Tonight will be a nice distraction from thinking about Maize. Since no one knows about us, no one will bring her up.

At nine, Diesel and Riley come barreling in with a pan and whiskey.

"Hey! Birthday boy!" Diesel shouts, holding up the bottle.

"We made you a cake!" Riley adds, setting it on the counter.

"You *made* it?" I pop a brow, rounding the table to see this shit. "Is it edible?"

"Hell yeah, it is." Diesel removes the tin foil, and I nearly bust my gut as I laugh at their "cake."

"What the fuck is that?" I squint at the weird-shaped concoction.

"It's a dick and balls," Diesel tells me. "Well…kinda. It's a little slanted because dumbass over here"—he throws a thumb in Riley's direction—"messed it up."

"And I'm guessing these brown squiggles are pubes?" I point.

"You betcha." Riley grins. "It's Funfetti."

"Wow, I'm speechless." I cackle. "Thanks, guys."

I set the pan next to the sandwiches and chips. After I offer them each a beer, more people show up. Cooper comes, and I introduce him to the others. Ethan and Grayson arrive wearing grins, then soon we're all standing around with bottles and paper plates full of food.

Thirty minutes later, we go outside and play horseshoes in teams. Of course, I'm kicking all their asses, which isn't hard considering how much they suck.

When I purposely lose so others can play, I head into the house for more beer and to catch up with Grayson, who's standing in the kitchen.

"Hey, man," I say. "Need another?"

"Sure."

"How are things going? Anything new with Kenzie since she's been home?"

"Pfft." He grunts as I hand him a bottle. "She's a complicated egg I'll never crack. These damn Bishop women are confusing as hell. Maize and Elle are nice to me, but Kenzie? She'd murder me if given the option."

"Dude, you must've done somethin' to her." I lean against the counter and take a sip of my beer.

"Wish I knew. I'd apologize if she'd just tell me already, but instead, she insists on busting my balls every chance she gets." He groans.

"You like her," I say. "Or it wouldn't bother you so much."

Grayson shrugs casually. "I do. From the moment I met her, I thought she was beautiful and wanted to get to know her, but it's never been reciprocated. So instead of pursuing anything, I've just pushed her buttons since she won't tell me what the fuck her problem is."

I chuckle, having seen their back-and-forth banter firsthand. It's comical.

"What about Maize? Figure out why she hates your guts?" he asks.

"Which time?" I sigh, frustrated as hell. "Honestly, we do have a history."

He snaps his fingers and grins. "I fuckin' knew it!"

"We had a one-night stand a couple of weeks before I got hired, and on my first day of work, she acted like she didn't know me. She introduced herself like normal, and for months, she pretended she didn't remember me. Drove me crazy until she finally admitted it on New Year's Eve. But she doesn't date men who work on the ranch because she's been burned. Then at the rodeo, something happened, and we hooked up again."

Grayson's jaw nearly smacks the floor as his eyes bug out. "Dude. I should've known. I could always tell there was something between you two."

"I've been chasing her since the day I got here, and all she does is run." I sigh, chugging my beer. "I thought we'd gotten past all that at the rodeo, but then two weeks ago, she said it was a mistake and that I needed to get over it." Doesn't help my ego that I've never had to pursue a woman before, but Maize's different. The connection we share isn't like anything I've experienced before.

"Ouch." Grayson cringes. "That's not good."

"Especially since I still want her."

"These damn Bishop women are difficult, I'm tellin' ya. Just when you think you're making progress, they go and rip the rug out from under ya."

I laugh at the truth of his words. I haven't felt sparks with a woman in years, nothing like what I feel when I'm around Maize, and I hate that she won't give us a chance. Some people never find love once in their lifetime, and it's even more rare to find it twice. I'm not ready to walk away from someone who I'm falling so hard for—not after all this time. Especially not when I know how it feels to be inside her. I'll always remember the way she screams my name as she comes. She felt it too, and I'll do whatever I can to prove I'm worth the risk.

"Maize's a sweet girl, and from what I know about her, she's reserved and keeps to herself a lot. Don't give up on her yet," Grayson genuinely tells me.

"Trust me, I don't plan on it."

We leave the kitchen, and when I get to the door, I see a group of ladies walking across the yard toward Diesel and Riley.

"Ah shit." Grayson says what I'm thinking. "Looks like they told their women about the party."

Rowan, Kenzie, Elle, Maize, and Zoey come into view.

"Who are the guys with them?" I narrow my eyes at Kenzie and Maize as frustration and jealousy ripple through me.

"No idea, but I think they're townies. I've seen them at the pub before."

Just great.

We walk outside and say hello. Kenzie smiles at me but avoids Grayson, while Maize pretends I don't exist.

"Sorry, man." Diesel pats my shoulder. "Rowan overheard me and decided to invite the girls. Hope that's okay."

I nod. "Sure, no problem. Plenty of beer and food inside."

Looking around, I realize my *small* gathering is now at least thirty or more people.

"Get used to it because nothing on the Bishop ranch is a small affair. Ever." Grayson chuckles.

A few people walk inside and return with plates and drinks, but one guy has two bottles, then hands one to Maize. She smiles and squeezes his arm. What. The. Fuck.

Did she seriously bring a fucking date to my party?

After getting no closure and waiting six months for her to acknowledge we hooked up the first time, this is how dirty she wants to play?

I want to confront her, but that'd make a scene, and I don't want everyone seeing or hearing our conversation. I'm too old for these childish games, but dammit if it's not working.

For the next hour, I do my best to keep my eyes off Maize and her little boy toy, but it's nearly impossible when she purposely stands in my view. I've learned her friend's name is Leo, and if his arm wraps around her one more time, I might snap off his fingers.

"I'm gonna use the bathroom, be right back," I overhear her tell him. As she walks away, his gaze lingers on her ass, and my jaw nearly cracks in half.

A few moments later, I head inside, using the opportunity to be alone with her. The bathroom door is wide open, and when I walk down the hallway, I see Maize snooping in my bedroom.

"Can I help you?"

She jumps, quickly spinning around. "Jesus!" Her hand presses against her chest as she catches her breath. "You scared the shit outta me, Gavin."

"Well, imagine my surprise when I catch you *not* in the bathroom but in my bedroom. Lookin' for something?" I lean against the doorway with a smug grin on my face. She's not getting out of this easy or walking away this time.

"I got lost."

"Is that so?" I don't feed into her bullshit for a second as I push off the doorframe and step toward her. "You wanna tell me what you're doing here tonight?"

Maize crosses her arms, pursing her lips. "I was invited. That a problem?"

"Considering you've ignored me for two weeks and brought a date to my party, I'd say yes, it *is* a problem. You and I need to talk."

I nearly close the gap between us as her arms fall to her side, and the way her breath hitches doesn't go unnoticed. She licks her lips as her eyes flick up to mine.

"We have nothing to talk about, Gavin."

"Sure we do. For starters, why don't you tell me who your little friend is?"

"None of your damn business."

"You gonna sleep with him, then bail the next morning, too? Should…" I throw a thumb over my shoulder. "Should I warn him? Give him the Maize 101 on what to expect?" I lean down until my lips nearly brush her ear, then whisper, "Tell him you like it fast and deep and to slap your ass real hard. Save him the trouble of having to hear you talk."

"You asshole," she spews when I back away. "What's your problem? We hooked up, twice, and that's it. Move the fuck on!"

I smile in amusement because seeing Maize fired up is fucking hot as hell. She's trying to keep her walls up by being bold, but I see right through her façade. When I catch her staring at me when I'm eating at the B&B, it's with intent, not disgust. I see the way she bites on her lower lip, and how her chest rises and falls any time I'm near. She tries so damn hard not to be affected by me even when her body aches for my touch.

"You're adorable, Maize. A little spitfire even, but a *horrible* liar."

"What?" She gasps. "I'm not lying. I've already moved on, and you should too."

"You mean, that little Leo dude?" I bark out a laugh. "He couldn't find your clit even if you drew him a map with color keys."

She rolls her eyes, folding her arms.

"Alright then, go out there and kiss him. Stick your tongue down his throat and prove to me you're over us."

"You're ridiculous." She steps around me and moves toward the door.

I spin around, walking into the hallway to watch her ass. "But make sure you're not thinking about me the whole time when you do!"

"Fuck off, Gavin!" She flips me the bird over her shoulder, and I stifle a laugh.

Her mouth says one thing, but the way her body reacts is another—*the actual truth*. She doesn't want me to play this game and start dating for the hell of it. Or maybe she does?

Perhaps it's time to test that theory.

CHAPTER FOURTEEN

GAVIN

It's been two weeks since Maize pulled her little stunt and showed up at my birthday party with Leo in tow. I'm still annoyed as hell about it and determined to make her feel the fire that scorches me each time she's around. I'm not stupid and know she planned to make me jealous. Maize makes the rules to this game, and it's time for me to break them.

I've chased her enough, and if she really wants me to get over her, I've come up with a plan to see if she'll believe her own bullshit. When we were at the rodeo, I remember how she looked at Sarah Cooke like she may steal me away. Though I'm not the type of guy to lead a woman on, I asked Sarah if she'd like to join me at the big Fourth of July celebration at the Bishop ranch. Riley encouraged me to bring a date, and she was the only woman who I've really spoken to who wasn't a Bishop or married to one.

I drive over to pick up Sarah from her house, and she's dressed in a mini skirt, boots, and a strapless shirt showing off her summer tan. Though she's beautiful, I'm not really into blondes. When she climbs inside the truck, she immediately grins.

"Hey! How have things been going?" she asks. As soon as she buckles, we head toward the ranch.

"Good. I don't have any complaints." I smile at her as we continue to make small talk. We chat about the rodeo and Cooper placing and how he won first place again.

"I heard him tell my daddy he was planning to go pro and wanted you to travel with him full-time," she tells me when we park and get out of the truck.

"Yeah, that's all true." I leave the conversation there. I've lived in this town long enough to know that rumors travel like speed trains 'round here, so I'd rather not get into the specifics.

I grab a blanket from the back seat so we can sit on the grass comfortably. A tip Diesel offered when he told me he'd be proposing to Rowan today. As soon as we walk up to the crowd of people, I watch everyone's eyes zip to Sarah, but no one says a word. I've never brought a woman with me anywhere, so I'm sure it's a shock. Considering Maize is like a vault with her secrets, I doubt any of them would notice something's off except for her or Kenzie.

I spread the blanket and lay it flat, then we sit next to Rowan, Chelsea, and her boyfriend, Trace. I met her once before and say hello to the group. She recently moved back so Diesel could see his son more and she could see where things go with Trace. Sarah leans into me and laughs as Riley runs all over the place chasing after Zach. He's a cute kid, but I can already tell he's gonna be a handful when he's older.

John and Jackson are grilling burgers while a few of the others set up the fireworks. I watch as Alex takes Diesel and Riley off to the side. A moment later, "Life of the Party" by Shawn Mendes blasts through the speakers. Diesel walks across the pasture to Rowan and takes her hand. Dawson moves on to his mama's lap and twirls his fingers in her hair.

Watching Diesel and Rowan dance is mesmerizing. It's obvious how much they love each other. She smiles as Diesel dips and spins her around. Above, an airplane flies low, and everyone looks up to see the message drifting behind it.

It reads: Will You Marry Me, Rowan Bishop?

All eyes are on them as Diesel clumsily fidgets and tries to pull the ring from his pocket. As soon as he flips open the box, tears spill down Rowan's face. Diesel drops to one knee and tells her he knew she was his the first time they kissed. My eyes fall on Maize, who's standing with her hand on her chest over her heart, and she looks so goddamn beautiful with her hair pulled back. Even from a distance, I can see the softness of her neck and have the urge to run my mouth across her skin.

She may be anti-love, but I'm convinced it's all a ploy.

Rowan hesitates with her answer, and eventually, her grandma Bishop speaks up. "Rowan Bishop, you better give that man an answer and not keep him and the rest of us waitin'."

With a grandma like that, no wonder she's a spitfire.

"Yes, yes, yes! I will marry you," Rowan yells, loud enough I'm sure everyone in San Antonio could hear her answer. They have a little make-out session, then Diesel slips the ring on her finger. It's adorable, and I'm glad they're so happy and will officially start their life together.

After they walk away for some privacy, Jackson and John serve everyone what they've been grilling. I get up and grab food for Sarah and me, then deliver it back.

"I'm so happy for them," she says, taking a bite of her burger. "I love engagements and weddings. Mama says I'm a hopeless romantic, always have been, if I'm being honest," she admits.

"I can see that," I say. "It's not a bad thing to have a heart. Shows you're compassionate."

After we finish, the fireworks are nearly set up, and they'll start lighting them any minute now. I see Maize, who looks like she's ready to internally combust when Rowan walks up to her. It's obvious she's pissed. When Rowan pulls her away to talk to her, I nearly chuckle. While her anger shouldn't bring me joy, it does. It's proof she's jealous as hell. Once they head to the drink table, I turn to Sarah. "You thirsty?"

She nods, leaning back on the blanket.

"I'll be right back," I tell her and stand.

As soon as I'm close to Maize, I gently pull her away from Rowan so I can get a few words in.

"I've put the pieces together, Maize," I say in a lowered tone. She looks at me like she wants to throw daggers at my face.

"What are you talkin' about exactly?" she asks, playing dumb like usual.

I glare at her, allowing the silence to pass between us as she stares me down. Unfortunately for her, I'm immune to her act because, at this point, I could write a book on her reactions. The thought has me laughing, which only infuriates her more. "I've tamed wild horses, Maize Bishop, and I'll tame your attitude too. I like a good challenge."

She scoffs and rolls her eyes at me, but I can tell I've gotten under her skin. "Is that a threat or something?" she asks with shakiness in her voice.

"Not a threat, sweetheart. That's a damn promise," I confirm, meaning every word. I give her a smirk, then walk away. Before I make it back to Sarah, I grab two waters from an ice chest. I can only imagine how angry Maize is right now, and it fills me with joy knowing I can see through her.

I hand Sarah the water, and she thanks me. When I sit next to her, she scoots closer and leans her head on my shoulder. When I turn around, I catch a glimpse of Maize watching us and chuckle. I've got all the goddamn proof I need. She tells me to move on, then is ready to murder me when I invite another woman to join me. One thing is for certain—Maize needs to make up her mind because, at this point, I'm damned if I do and damned if I don't.

The firework show starts, and it's incredible. I've seen displays this big at rodeos, and I'm amazed they're able to pull it off so flawlessly. The booms from the mortar shells echo in the distance, and the colors are bright and spectacular. Some crackle and pop while others glitter and fade.

The summer breeze brushes against my skin, and I realize how much I love being on the ranch. It's been almost a year since I took the job, and I haven't once regretted it. I've found my second family, and I can't imagine how hard it's going to be to leave this behind.

When it's over, the big group of us burst out into applause while some hoot and holler. Considering nearly fifty people are here, it takes a while to tell everyone goodbye. I pick up the blanket, and we walk back to my truck so I can take Sarah home.

"Want to go to the bar and have a drink?" she asks when we climb in, and I start the engine.

"I'd love to, but I have to be up early. Should probably get some sleep."

She sticks out her bottom lip and pouts as I turn toward her house.

When I pull into the driveway, I park and smile at her. "Thanks again for joining me. That was a lot of fun."

"It was. Do you want to come in?" she whispers. She leans in and tries to kiss me, but I pull away before our lips can connect.

"Whoa, whoa," I calmly say. "Sarah. Because I'm a gentleman and I don't like to lead ladies on, I think I should set the record straight. While I think you're a very beautiful woman, we're just friends, and that's all we can be."

She rolls her eyes, obviously annoyed by the rejection. "Wow. Okay. Is it because of Maize?"

My heart rate quickens, and I meet her eyes. "All that matters right now is that you understand where you and I stand. I'm sorry if I gave you the wrong impression."

She sucks in a deep breath and lets it out. "It's fine. I feel really stupid now, but thanks for a good time."

"I'm sorry." I want her to know I genuinely mean it, but I don't think her embarrassment will allow it. She gets out of the truck, turns, and gives me a wave before going inside. On the way home, I feel like an utter asshole. If I were in my twenties, just passing through, I probably would've followed her inside. I'm a different man now, and my door no longer revolves. The only woman I want pushes me away continually, and it's frustrating as fuck.

By the time I walk into my house, I'm more than annoyed. I go to the fridge and pull out a beer, then sit on the couch. After I kick off my boots, my phone vibrates in my pocket, and I pull it out and see it's Cooper.

I open the message he sent.

Cooper: Hey man. Just checking to see if you made up your mind about traveling the road with me and coaching me to pro level.

I read his text message a few times. I think about Maize and the way she looked at me with disdain today. Her words repeat in my mind, and how she's said several times she wants me to just go away. Regardless of what I think, Maize believes we were a mistake, and it only fuels the fire burning inside me. Closing my eyes, I set my phone down and lean my head back.

I weigh the good and the bad. I loved rodeo life, but I hated how dangerous it was, and I won't be risking myself. If Cooper wins, I get a percentage of his money. He's a good rider, and he has learned quickly, taking all my instruction to heart.

My mind is made, and I know what I have to do. After finding the right words, I send a text to Cooper, lock my phone, and then go to bed. I don't wait for his response because I already know what he's going to say. Tomorrow is a new day, a new beginning, and I know I made the right decision.

There's no going back now.

CHAPTER FIFTEEN

MAIZE

Rowan shows up carrying a bottle of tequila, and it makes me smile wide. She knows exactly what a girl with a broken heart needs, and it usually starts and ends with Patrón. In her other hand is a bag of limes, salt, and shot glasses.

"The traveling bartender. I love it!" I exclaim, helping her with the items. I move some things from the top of my dresser and set everything down. A minute later, Kenzie bursts through the door with cookies, popcorn, and a giant ass bowl of M&M's. Elle's trailing behind her, and she looks exhausted.

"This should do the trick," Kenzie tells me.

Elle nods. "Booze, snacks, and reality TV. You literally can't be upset after all that."

"I hope you're right," I say, sucking in a deep breath as Rowan pours the shots.

Elle kicks off her shoes and sits on the bed, and Kenzie follows her.

"So, catch me up." Elle waves her hand. "I need to know all the details of what happened, considering we're having a drinking party over a man."

I let out a huff and roll my head on my neck. I've been cautious to keep everything to myself—except for Kenzie, but she'd never spill my secrets.

I'm grateful I had someone to talk to. Otherwise, I might've driven myself crazy over the past year while dealing with Gavin's shenanigans.

"You're stalling," Elle sing-songs and Rowan snickers, then turns around and hands us the tequila. She goes back to the makeshift bar as we shoot it down, then takes our glasses.

"Just needed a little liquid courage first," I admit, then start from the beginning. I tell them about the one-night stand and how it was the best sex of my life, how we kissed, the stolen glances, and unspoken words we've exchanged over the past few months. Then I go into detail about the rodeo and how elated I was to spend time with him.

"So what's the problem?" Rowan asks.

I suck in a deep breath. "I overheard the twins asking him about traveling with Cooper full-time, and he hadn't made up his mind at that point. So I pushed him away and stupidly brought a date to his birthday party. I honestly didn't know it was his birthday, though, so I wasn't trying to be a bitch. Anyway, he confronted me about it, and I told him I'd moved on, and he should too. So what did he do?"

I glance at them. "He brings Sarah motherfucking Cooke to the Fourth of July party. She was so hateful to me growing up and did some messed-up things just because she could."

Rowan shakes her head. "Maze. You told him to move on, and he did."

I throw my hands up in the air. "I know. I'm a damn idiot, and now I don't know what to do to fix this. I've messed up big time, and I've realized this entire time that he deserves better from me, but I'm scared."

"I was actually pissed when I saw Sarah there," Kenzie admits. "And she was being so flirty and touchy. I wonder if they had sex afterward."

Elle throws a pillow at Kenzie. "That is *not* helpful. Gavin is a gentleman, so I bet even if she begged him, he would've denied her. I'd bet money on it."

"Yeah, I don't think he did either," Rowan says, bringing us more shots, then continues. "Gavin's more mature than that. He didn't seem like he was *that* into her. After you two had your little confrontation, I watched him. Each time she tried to make a move, he tensed. He was playing games with you, Maize. It was so obvious."

We gulp down the tequila, and I try to think back to Saturday. I was in a blind rage and didn't notice the way he reacted to her. I just saw the two of them together, and that was it. Shaking my head, I roll my eyes. "If he did that…"

"Wait, so is he going to travel with Cooper?" Elle asks. "Did you ask him?"

"I'm pretty sure he is because Uncle Jackson mentioned he was looking for another trainer. Why would they need someone else if Gavin wasn't planning to leave? I thought about it, and that's the only solution. It's not like I can just come out and ask him because we're not really on speaking terms at the moment," I explain.

"That does make sense, but it could be coincidental." Elle places a hand on mine. "I'm sorry. Men are dickheads."

"Speaking of dickheads, how's that boss of yours?" Kenzie asks.

"I am not talking about him tonight. This is about Maize, not me," she announces.

"He's just so hot. I literally thought about getting an assistant job just so I could stare at his tight ass in those jeans all day long." Kenzie grins, then shrugs. "It's not a lie."

I snort, and I'm so happy to have them as my support system. "Maybe you should apologize," Rowan suggests. "Tell him how you feel. You won't know what you're missing out on if you don't give him a chance. You have no idea if he's going to break your heart until he does. Sometimes, finding love is worth the risk. I know you're asking yourself, what if it doesn't work out? At least you would've had a good time. The flip side of that is, what if it does? What if he's your match, and you're so determined to push him away that you lose that opportunity?" Rowan stares at me, waiting for my answer.

I have nothing, though. She's right.

"When did you become so logical?" I ask.

She gives me a small smile, and I see her glance down at the gigantic diamond on her finger. "Love does that to a person, I guess. If I hadn't given Diesel a chance or allowed him to explain himself, I wouldn't be where I am right now. I was convinced marriage wasn't in my cards too, and the whole time the man of my dreams was right in front of me."

"I'm so damn happy for you," Elle exclaims, and Kenzie pipes in too.

"It was the sweetest proposal I've ever seen," Kenzie tells Rowan.

I look at her as she grabs our glasses and the tequila, and that's when I realize she hasn't drunk a sip. "Are you gonna have some Patrón, or are you trying to get us all drunk for a reason?"

The alcohol streams through my blood, and my face is starting to feel numb. "Well…" She hesitates.

My eyes go wide, and my mouth falls open. "Are you pregnant?"

A hint of pink meets her cheeks.

"You are!" Elle says, and Kenzie gasps.

Immediately, we stand and move to her, then exchange a group hug.

She places her finger over her lips. "Shhh…I don't want your parents finding out before mine do."

"You haven't told them yet?" Kenzie asks.

"No, and I was hoping I'd get you all trashed before you noticed I wasn't drinking."

"This is so amazing!" I admit, really meaning it. "More Bishop babies!"

She places her hand on her belly and laughs. "Told you they'd love you."

"Diesel knows?" Elle asks.

She nods. "After he proposed, I took him off to the side and told him. He's ecstatic to give Dawson a little brother or sister and so am I. Diesel's already an amazing dad, and I'm so happy he'll get to experience all the nuances of having a pregnant wife. He's already excited for the doctors appointments and making me tacos whenever I demand them." She laughs, and I notice how she's glowing. "You all better keep that secret because if Grandma finds out she didn't know before you three, she will kick my ass."

"You're right." Elle nods. "She'd lose her shit."

"But, back to you, Maize. Time to admit you were wrong and give the man a chance. Also, what did he say to you when he pulled you to the side?" Rowan asks.

I roll my eyes again. "He said he tames wild horses, and he'll tame my attitude too."

Kenzie slaps her hands together. "That's fucking hot. If you pass up the opportunity, I might let him tame me."

I playfully smack her. "You are too much sometimes."

"You need some grand gesture to show Gavin that you're sorry for being an asshole," Elle suggests as we move back to the bed. "You were literally being an asshole because of your insecurities, and that's not fair to him."

"If I've learned anything over the years, it's that communication is key. Apologize and put all your feelings on the table, then see what he says. You're gonna have to talk to him, and it won't be easy. Hell, it might even be a little humiliating, but you're gonna have to humble yourself a bit and do it anyway," Rowan says.

"Do you think it's too late?" I look at her.

She shrugs. "I dunno, but you don't want to look back five years from now with regret like that."

"You're right. It's just all so…"

"Awkward?" Elle says. "I understand that."

Kenzie looks at her. "Because of Mr. Hot Vet, huh?"

"Shut it." Elle points her finger at her.

"I have a lot of thinking to do," I admit. "A lot."

Kenzie hands me the M&M's, and the four of us sit on my queen-size bed and get lost in trashy reality TV. Rowan gets up to go to the bathroom every so often, then comes back and makes us shots. I lean against the headboard, not paying attention to anything on the screen. All I can think about is Gavin and how I'll even begin that conversation. I feel lost and confused, and it's all my own doing.

After the girls leave, I lie down, unable to go to sleep. I toss and turn all night, thinking about Gavin and wishing I had the courage to text him, but I don't. The things I need to say should be said in person, but after the way I treated him, I wouldn't be surprised if he ignores me. At least that's what I deserve.

It's been almost a week since I hung out with the gang, and many of the things Rowan said have played on repeat in my mind. I know communication is key, but I'm also stubborn as hell. Half of me wonders what good it would do to talk to him about it, especially if he's planning to go on the road anyway. Then I remember how he said he doesn't regret retiring the night of the rodeo. My stomach is in knots thinking about it.

All week, I've looked for him at the B&B, but I haven't seen him once. I feel as if I ruined my chances by not giving him a fair one, and the thought crushes me.

"Did you hear me?" Dad asks from the doorway of the kitchen.

I was lost in my head again, something I've been doing a lot of this week. "No, sorry. What did you say?"

"We need more tea out here, please," he says with a smile.

I nod and suck in a deep breath. Instead of turning and walking away, Dad comes over to me. The lunch rush is nearly over, and I was prepping for dinner while my employees washed dishes.

Dad stands beside me as I grab the teabags. "What's going on with you this week?"

I shrug, not really wanting to talk about this with him, though he is a really good listener.

Dad grabs the sugar. "Is it about a guy or something?"

I could lie, but at this point, I don't even have the strength for it. "Yeah, actually it is."

"Not that I'm an expert or anything, because I'm not, but I can tell you that when I met your mom, I pushed her away as much as I could because I wasn't ready for a relationship. Sometimes though, you find the person you're supposed to be with when you least expect it. Your mom was only supposed to be here for a little while, and I didn't want to get involved with someone who didn't have roots here. My heart did what it wanted, and I fell so madly in love with her that I couldn't deny her anymore. The point is, you gotta be willing to give people a chance. I know Timothy broke your heart. I know it destroyed you, and I've also noticed how you've rejected every single man who's been interested since then. But honey, in the long run, you're only hurting yourself."

My eyes soften when I look at him, and I'm so emotional I almost burst into tears. He notices and opens his arms, and I fall into them. I'll never be too old for my daddy's hugs. "Thank you," I tell him.

"I love you so much, sweetie. And if your grandma doesn't get more great-grandkids, she might freak the hell out. I'd like some grandkids of my own one day too. No pressure, though." He gives me a wink and presses start on the tea maker.

"I'll bring it out once it's done brewing," I say, feeling the weight sitting heavily on my heart.

Once Dad is out of sight, I know exactly what I have to do, so I text Gavin.

CHAPTER SIXTEEN

GAVIN

I'm knee-deep in mud and frustrated as hell. Jackson and I struggle to capture one of the new wild horses in the pasture that's transformed into a playa lake. We've gotten a shit ton of rain lately, and it's caused a huge mess for us. Doesn't help this horse is an asshole and doesn't follow instructions.

"C'mon, Lacey. Let's go," I beg softly, ready to go home and shower.

"I think her foot is stuck," Jackson says, sticking his arm down and reaching for her hoof. "Gimme just a second."

As I tightly hold her halter, Jackson tries to get her free.

"Ah, I think I got it."

As soon as his words come out, Lacey becomes more agitated. Quickly, I tighten my grip before she hurts one of us.

"Alright, girl. You're okay." I smooth my palm down her nose.

Jackson stands and shakes his hand, whipping muddy slop all over me.

"Ugh, thanks." I wipe mud from the only clean part of my shirt. At this point, my clothes need to be thrown out.

"Sorry." He chuckles. "Hazards of the job."

"So I've learned."

Together, we pull Lacey out and take her to the barn. Like the other six we rescued this morning, she'll need to be bathed. According to Jackson, that'll be Knox and Kane's job, which means they probably got themselves into trouble again.

"I'm going to head home early," I tell Jackson. "I'm gonna have to shower three times to get this smell out of my hair." Taking off my hat, I brush my fingers through it.

"I hear girls like that." He smirks.

"Very doubtful." I snort. "See ya tomorrow."

I hop into my truck, and when I check my phone, I blink hard to make sure I'm not imagining a missed text from Maize. We haven't talked since the Fourth of July party two weeks ago. Though I've seen her plenty at the B&B, she's ignored me as though I don't exist. She was so pissed when I showed up with Sarah Cooke, but I'm not sorry about it. She shouldn't have brought a guy to my fucking birthday party. The moment she saw me with another woman, jealousy radiated off her.

Before I drive off, I unlock my phone and open her message.

Maize: We need to talk in person. Can you meet me at the B&B tonight? Around 7:30?

What in the world would she want to talk about now, after weeks of this cat and mouse game she's played?

I'm too shocked to reply, so I decide to text Grayson since he's the only one who knows about Maize and me.

Gavin: Maize just texted me to meet up with her tonight. What do you think she wants?

Grayson: *eggplant emoji*

Grayson: *peach emoji*

Grayson: *tongue emoji*

Gavin: Wow, you're a lot of help. Thanks, asshole.

I shouldn't be surprised, considering Grayson's basically a country frat boy. Though it did make me laugh a little.

Grayson: My pleasure. Take condoms.

Gavin: *middle finger emoji*

Deciding to just man up, I respond to her.

Gavin: Do I need to bring groin protection, or are you not going to bust my balls for once?

Maize: Guess I deserved that. But no. I genuinely want to talk to you.

Gavin: Alright, I'll be there.

Once I'm home, I take an extra-long, steaming hot shower. My mind races with the possibilities of what Maize wants to talk about. Considering her sudden change of tune, I'm half wondering if she needs me to donate a kidney or something.

I put on a black T-shirt and blue jeans with boots. Making sure I don't reek, I add cologne and put some gel in my hair. Once I'm finished, I grab a beer and eat something. With some time to spare, I decide to watch TV to keep my mind off her, but it's no use. My thoughts wander as the memories of us together play on repeat. Talking and laughing at the bar and rodeo, then falling into bed together. Waking up with her next to me was a nice contrast to the first time, and I wished it weren't so short-lived.

At twenty after seven, I jump in my truck and drive to the B&B. I'm nervous to hear what she has to say, but I don't let her know that. Once I park, I walk in with all the confidence I can muster and look around.

"Hey." Maize greets me in the dining room. I hold back a smile as I take in her beauty. She's in a sundress that makes her blue eyes pop, and I resist the urge to lean in and kiss her.

"Hello," I say, pushing my hands in my front pockets. "You look beautiful."

She brings her gaze to mine with a smile. "Thank you. So do you."

I furrow my brows because the sudden flip in her attitude is confusing. "So, wanna tell me why I'm here?"

"I want to talk about us but not in here. Outside." She glances over her shoulder to the back door that leads to the wraparound porch.

"Alright." I motion for her to lead the way.

The moment she opens the door, I spot a small round table filled with food.

"Take a seat."

I sit across from her and look down at the spread. "What's all this?"

She blushes nervously and shrugs. "Wanted to make you dinner."

"Okay, I'm gonna be honest with you. I feel like I'm in the twilight zone right now, Maize. After everything, I'm not sure what the hell is goin' on." I swallow hard. "One minute you're hot and the next you're cold. Your mood swings are givin' me whiplash."

She nods. "You're right. I have been, and it's what I want to talk about."

"Okay, well I'm all ears then," I tell her.

Maize grabs a roll and pulls it apart. "I'm sure you know by now that I'm not great in the sharing my feelings department or talking things out when my emotions get the best of me. While my past is no excuse for how I've treated you, it really messed me up. I had basically given up on dating, and the morning after our night together, I was embarrassed I jumped into bed with a man I had just met. We didn't know that much about each other, and I was judging the shit out of myself."

She stuffs her mouth with food, and I silently wait for her to continue. I can tell she's nervous, so I don't want to speak until she's done.

"It was really shitty of me to pretend I didn't know you. I should've owned up to it long before I did. You didn't deserve that kind of treatment, so for that, I'm truly sorry. Even though I'm in my mid-twenties, I'm not experienced with dating or having one-night stands. I get shy and anxious, so I resorted to playing dumb instead of acknowledging you. The fact that you even wanted to talk to me after that shows what kind of man you are. I should've realized you had good intentions."

She pauses to take a sip of her drink. I look down at my untouched plate and dig in while she continues.

"I'm far from perfect, and while you don't owe me a damn thing, I'd really like it if we could start over. I'd love for us to get a second—well, *third*—chance. No more ignoring or avoiding you, no more acting like a brat, and I'll definitely work on communicating better." She chuckles, and it makes me smile to hear that sound again.

"Well..." I swallow. "Honestly, I'm not sure if that's possible. You've been running this whole time, and I'm kinda tired of chasing you. I thought we started over at the rodeo, and then you blindsided me and pulled a one-eighty on me. So..." Shrugging, I hold back a smirk as I watch her squirm. As much as I want to give in and taste her lips, I won't make this easy for her.

"Okay, well first, Leo is just a friend, and I didn't know it was your birthday until after. Don't forget you brought Sarah Cooke to the family Fourth of July party!"

The anger firing through her voice causes me to chuckle. She really didn't like me bringing her.

"You told me to move on, so I was just following orders." I smirk, stabbing a piece of meat and taking a bite.

Maize groans with an eye roll, and it's adorable how worked up she's getting. "The only reason I said that was because I overheard a conversation and got spooked. I should've talked to you about it, but I didn't."

I tilt my head, curiously. "What are you talkin' about?"

"Knox and Kane asked about your job offer with Cooper, and you confirmed it. I knew if you took it, we'd be over, so I thought if I ended it before anything started, then maybe I'd save myself from heartbreak."

Fuck. If I had known that, things would be different between us right now.

"Wow. I'm glad I finally have an explanation at least."

"I'm sorry. I know I fucked up big time. My sister and cousins basically had to smack some common sense into me before I lost you for good. Or perhaps I already have...to Sarah."

The sad expression on her face is just too much, so I put her out of her misery. "Sarah and I are just friends. She understands I have no romantic feelings for her."

"Okay." She flashes a small, relieved smile. "We weren't friends in school, and she made my life hell. Seeing her with you made me hate her even more."

I frown. "I'm sorry to hear that." Had I known that, I would've never invited her. Now I'm twice as glad I turned her advances down.

She shrugs. "It is what it is."

"This is really delicious, by the way," I admit as I inhale another bite. "Beef tips are one of my favorites."

"That's a relief. I wasn't sure."

"I'm not picky, but you're an amazing cook, Maize. If I hadn't picked you up at the pub that night, I definitely would've tried after eating your pancakes."

Maize snorts and laughs again. This is the side of her that I adore. I'm just not sure if it's here to stay.

"You picked a great spot," I tell her, looking out at the sunset.

"I love it out here." She watches the clouds float across the sky. "Figured if you were gonna tell me to take a hike, at least I'd have a nice view to console me."

Smiling, I shake my head. "You knew feeding me would keep my ass here until my plate was at least cleared."

"Ha-ha." She playfully rolls her eyes.

Once we're both finished eating, I've made up my mind. Standing, I lean in and grab her hand, then place a soft kiss on her knuckles. "Thanks for dinner. It was delicious."

She looks up at me in confusion. "You're welcome. Thank you for coming."

Then I push in my chair.

"Are you leavin'?" she asks in a panic.

"Yep. I accept your apology, but I'm not sure where we stand right now."

She quickly rushes to her feet when I walk down the porch steps toward my truck.

"Wait, you're leaving before we finish our conversation?" The hurt and shock in her voice along with her scrambling to keep up with me has me holding back a smile. It's the first time she's chased *me*.

When I make it to my truck, I spin around to face her. "I've accepted your apology, but if you want to start over, then it's time for you to work for what you want."

Maize folds her arms over her chest and narrows her eyes. "Are you serious?"

Smirking, I open my door and hop in, then roll the window down. "Sure am, Maize Bishop. I've been chasing you for months. It's your turn."

"What?" She throws her arms to her sides.

"Gonna have to prove you're serious, sweetheart. You're a smart girl. You'll figure it out." I flash her a shit-eating grin and reverse out of the parking spot.

Her jaw drops, but before I drive off, I add, "Appreciate dinner. Already lookin' forward to breakfast." I throw her a wink, then speed off.

Watching her pout in my rearview mirror has me releasing a bellow of laughter. I can't imagine the thoughts running through her mind right now.

I've never stopped wanting her, but if she truly wants us to be together, she'll have to show me she's one-hundred-percent committed this time.

And I can't wait to watch her try.

CHAPTER SEVENTEEN

MAIZE

Dust flies in the air as my jaw drops in shock. I can't believe he fucking left!

Gavin drives off, and the anger pumping through my veins has me stomping my feet back to the table where I poured my heart out to him. If he forgave me, then why do I need to *prove* I want to be with him? Shouldn't my apology and spilling my truths be enough?

Ugh!

Did I need to spell it out for him? I thought I was clear when I said I wanted to start over. Didn't he realize that meant I wanted us to go out on a date or hang out and get to know each other again?

I basically pleaded for another chance, tried to work through my humiliation, and now he wants me to grovel. Gavin knows exactly what he's doing.

While I deserve it, I don't know how the hell I'm supposed to show him I want a chance and that I'm not going to run again.

After I clean up and put the dishes in the dishwasher, I call Rowan.

"Hey!" she greets eagerly as if she'd been waiting to hear from me. This was her idea after all.

"Listen to what this asshole did!" I blurt out, then tell her the whole story.

Once I finish, Rowan bursts out laughing.

"Are you seriously laughing?"

"I have to commend Gavin actually. He's a genius. You admitted you were wrong and apologized, but now he wants you to fight for him."

"That was me fighting for him," I deadpan. "What else am I supposed to do? Show up in lingerie and seduce him?"

"Girl, I'm not sure, but I'm living vicariously through you, so whatever you do, I wanna hear about it."

I groan, rolling my eyes. "Ugh. You're no help!"

"You fucked up, and now it's your turn to win his heart. You hurt him, and he needs to know you're serious about him now."

"But I am! I said I wanted us to have another chance and to start over. Should I have explained in detail what that meant?"

"You're gonna have to put some effort into it."

"Fine, fine. But hell if I know how or what to do…"

"Well, better get brainstorming." She chuckles.

Once we hang up, I head home and find Kenzie in her room. I explain what happened, and though part of this night was her idea, she says she's still "Team Gavin" and can't wait to see how I win him back. After getting zero advice from her, I lie in bed, thinking about everything. Before any ideas come to mind, I fall asleep.

The next day, I go through my early breakfast routine at the B&B and run into Gavin earlier than expected. He gives me a shit-eating grin, and I somehow restrain the urge to strangle him for leaving so abruptly last night.

"Howdy." He tips his hat after taking a seat.

"Howdy?" I arch a brow.

"That's what I said, ma'am. How're you on this beautiful day?"

Now I'm really confused. "Are you runnin' a fever or something?"

He chuckles, stuffing two pieces of bacon in his mouth.

"What? I'm always in a good mood when I see your gorgeous face in the mornin'."

Grayson barks out a laugh, and I finally realize he heard everything as he sits down across from Gavin. By the way he looks at us, I know he's aware of our situation.

"He knows, doesn't he?" I place a hand on my hip and scowl.

"You sayin' your cousins don't?" he counters.

I rock on my feet. "They might know a little." With a shrug, I continue, "But girls talk. Didn't know you and Grayson were that close."

"Hey," Grayson chimes in.

"He's the only guy around here who isn't consumed with a chick, so we have more time to talk and hang out. Plus, he's not related to you."

"Dude, thanks." Grayson grunts. "The girls around here are batshit crazy."

"Hey," I scold. "Maybe we're just not willing to put up with your antics. Ever think of that?"

"Antics? Y'all must be talkin' about Grayson." Kenzie comes to Maize's side, crossing her arms over her chest.

"And you've just made my point." Grayson flicks a piece of sausage in his mouth.

"So Gavin…" Kenzie directs her attention to him. "Heard Maize made you a nice dinner last night."

I groan with an eye roll.

"She sure did," he responds with a smug grin. "Best meal I've ever had."

"Well, I just want to say…" Kenzie looks over her shoulder at me with a mischievous smirk. "I'm rooting for you. But if she fails, I'm single. Just a heads-up…"

Oh my God. I'm gonna kill her.

"Is that so? Well, thank you. It's refreshing to have one Bishop girl on my side."

"Don't you have a job to get to?" I elbow her ribs and push her out of the way. "Mom won't like it if you're late."

"I'm not afraid of her," she taunts. Kenzie talks a big talk, but she'd never be late, considering she's teaching now.

"Ha, don't let her hear you say that."

Kenzie quickly looks around in a panic, and I laugh. Point made.

"Well, *I* have to get back to work. If you need someone on your side, Grayson you have my number." I flash him a wink to get under Kenzie's skin, and luckily, it works.

"Why does he have your number?" she asks. At the same time, Gavin says, "He doesn't."

Chuckling, I head into the kitchen to clean. Lunch is baked chicken casserole and doesn't take long to prep, especially with Sandra and Jane bouncing around. Once it's baked and served, I meet Elle at the diner for a late lunch. My employees are more than capable of handling the kitchen while I'm gone. Right now, I need another woman to talk to about Gavin since my sister insists on antagonizing me about it.

"Hey!" She stands from the booth and immediately hugs me.

"I'm so excited you were able to come," I say, taking a seat.

"Me too. Honestly, it's been so hectic."

We grab our menus and flip through them even though we know what they offer.

"Yeah, same. Lunch rush is over, and my employees were fine." If I'm lucky, they'll start washing dishes too.

"Oh good, so we have time to chat." She smiles up at me.

"Yeah, I owe you an update on Gavin."

"Girl, yes. I wanna hear *all* about it."

I go through all the details– the nice dinner I made and our conversation that quickly shifted to him getting up and leaving. It takes me nearly twenty minutes to explain it all.

"Wow…Gavin's not messin' around this time." She snickers. "Sounds like he's trying to protect his heart just like you. What would you want a guy to do if the tables were turned?"

I hadn't thought about it that way. Shrugging, I draw a blank. "I don't know, I guess…a nice gesture of some sort. Something that shows he's thinking of me, but not just materialistic things. Something from the heart and thoughtful."

She waves out her hand. "There ya go."

"I don't even know where to start," I groan. "I tried to win him over with my cooking, and that didn't work, so I'm kinda screwed."

"What's he interested in? Obviously bull riding and horses since he trains them. But you gotta go deeper than that. What kind of music does he like? Or movies? Figure out some personal things, go out of your way to find out his favorites, then make it special."

"Hmm…that's not a horrible idea." I tap my bottom lip. "I have a lot to think about. But anyway, enough about me, what's going on with you? How's Dr. VetDreamy?"

"If it's possible, he's even moodier and more asshole-ish than before. He glared at me the whole time at Gavin's birthday party, then barely said a word to me the next day. It's like, no matter how well I do every task he gives me, it's not good enough or even acknowledged. I'm ready to open my own business, but even if I did, he has all the contacts. Everyone around here trusts him, and I'd go bankrupt within my first year."

"Have you ever just asked him? Like hey, you want to hate bang this out so we can work together or hey, need help gettin' that stick outta your ass so we can be civil?"

"When he was super edgy, I snapped at him a few times, but it barely fazed him. He'll hardly look at me when he gives instructions, then freaks out when I don't pay attention. Like talk about a double standard. I have to listen to his every word, but he pretends I don't even exist."

"My best guess is that he's actually attracted to you and is trying really fucking hard not to be. He's pulling a Maize."

She frowns. "A what?"

"A Maize. Me! He's pushing you away so you can't get close because he's scared he'll get hurt, or that he'll hurt you. Probably worried it'd ruin your professional relationship too. I mean, he's basically me in a man's body."

"I think you're reading into this *way* too much. He gets phone calls throughout the day, but one woman calls almost every hour, and he'll walk out of the room or distance himself to answer it. So I think he has a girlfriend, which makes your theory moot."

"You're sure it's a woman?" I ask.

"Yep, based on the few seconds of conversation I overheard."

"You don't know it's a girlfriend, though. For all we know, it's his drug dealer."

Elle snorts. "Yeah, that makes me feel better, thanks."

I shrug. "Gotta think of all options here."

The waitress comes over and takes our order. Surprisingly, I'm not super hungry, so I order a salad and a sweet tea.

"Maybe you should join a dating app," I suggest. "Then let it slip into your convo and watch his reaction."

"After your disasters, you want me to suffer through that?"

"Well, you don't really have to participate to see what he thinks about it. Maybe he'll try to find you and swipe right." I waggle my brows.

Elle rolls her eyes. "Very doubtful. Good looks aside, his personality is dull, humor is dry, and don't get me started on our one-sentence conversations."

"You need some kind of drastic change and see if he notices. Wear something different and tight, cut or dye your hair, put on a padded bra. If he looks even a tiny bit fazed, then that means he's looking."

"Okay, I can do the first two, but I'm not wearing a padded bra. Aside from being uncomfortable, I wear scrubs, and they're tight enough as it is."

"I would love to see you with bleach blond hair!" I exclaim. "It'd look hot with your tan, too. Get some layers or side bangs." I move my head from side to side as I imagine it in my mind. "Yep, it'd look sexy as hell."

"You know how long it'd take to get my dark hair to blond?"

"Well, good thing Zoey has all the mad skills!" I smirk. "I'm sure she'll help you out."

Elle groans but nods. "Alright, but I'm *not* doing this for him. I could use a change."

Smiling, I grab my phone to set a reminder to call Zoey after lunch. "Maybe I'll get some highlights myself. See Gavin resist my charm then."

She snorts as she takes a sip of her water. "Trust me, he's probably just as anxious to get you back in his bed. He just wants to play hard to get first."

"If Gavin grew up here, I could do recon and ask his best friend questions and get intimate details about him. Grayson would be my best bet, but I don't want to get him involved. Maybe Cooper would know? I don't have his number, though, and he might be traveling right now." The thought of Gavin leaving nearly suffocates me, but I push it away. I realize he never told me what decision he made. Regardless, I think I'd try long distance for him.

"Ooh, this is starting to sound like some kind of detective mission." Elle rubs her palms together. " I think Connor's been called out to their ranch before. I'll look in his files and see if I can find his number, or maybe you can just stop by randomly."

"Oh my God, that'd be amazing. You're a genius!"

Elle snorts. "I didn't go to vet school for nothing. But you probably know more than you think. You can't tell me in the past year you haven't eavesdropped on him while he was eating at the B&B."

She makes a valid point. I've heard a lot of his conversations. But I don't want to screw this chance up because it might be the last one he gives me.

Once our food is delivered, we take our time eating and chat.

After we finish, we pay, then stand. Neither of us wants to go back to work, but we know we have to. I miss hanging out with Elle and make her promise to do this again sometime soon.

"Well, good luck wrangling your cowboy." She pulls me in for a hug. "I'll text you if I find Cooper's number."

"Thank you."

We say our goodbyes, and before I drive back to the ranch, I text Gavin. Just in case she can't find Cooper's info, I need a plan B.

Maize: I want to give us a real chance this time. Are my words not enough?

Gavin: You're adorable. Actions always speak louder than words, sweetheart.

I groan while simultaneously getting butterflies at the way he called me *sweetheart*. Damn him.

But if that's how he's going to be, then fine.

I just hope whatever I come up with is enough to win him back because right now, I'll do whatever it takes.

CHAPTER EIGHTEEN

GAVIN

AFTER TWO DAYS OF SILENCE, I'm wondering if Maize's given up altogether. Though I've accepted her apology, and she's said she wants a real chance, I won't be falling back into bed with her that quickly. I've been burned too much by her already. She's spent the past year giving me whiplash with her mood swings, so she needs to prove she's serious.

I'd love nothing more than to hold Maize Bishop in my arms until the sun rises, but I'm patient.

It's Monday morning, and I'm heading to the B&B to meet up with the guys for breakfast. It'll be the first time I've been around Maize since Friday, and I'm anxious as hell to talk to her.

"Mornin'." John greets me when I enter. I tip my hat and flash him a small smile while scanning the room.

Grayson's already sitting at a table and looks up at me with a grin. "Hey, man."

"Hey."

I go to the coffee station, fill a mug, and add a little sugar. When I walk toward Grayson, I finally see her.

"Good mornin'," I drawl when she approaches. My eyes widen as I get a glimpse of her hair. It's pulled back as usual, but I notice blond strands. "You changed your hair."

"Morning. I did. I made you a special breakfast." She clamps her hands together.

I eye her suspiciously, pulling out a chair and sitting. "Is that code for poison or something?"

"Of course not." She flashes a wink, then leans down until her mouth brushes against the shell of my ear. "I promised to win you back, and since I know how much you love my food, I figured I'd better start there."

Shit, I'm impressed. There's no denying I'd eat anything she cooks. They say the way to a man's heart is through his stomach, so I guess she's testing that theory.

"What kind of favoritism shit is this?" Grayson complains the moment Maize returns carrying two plates.

"There might be enough for you too if you don't piss me off," she retorts, setting them in front of me.

My eyes widen in shock when I study the spread. I can hardly contain my excitement to try it all.

"Strawberry-stuffed French toast with maple syrup…" She points at the second plate. "Cheesy grits 'n sausage and blueberry streusel coffee cake."

"Maize, wow…" I look at the breakfast my grandmother used to make. Every Saturday morning, I'd go for a visit, and without fail, she'd cook this feast. Unfortunately, she passed away five years ago. I wished Mimi would've been able to meet Maize. She would've loved her.

Maize takes a step back, but I grab her hand and pull her close. "How? How'd you know?"

"I did my research." She smiles proudly. "Told you I was serious."

"Serious about what?" Grayson blurts out, trying to tear off a piece of my streusel.

I smack his hand away. "None of your damn business."

"Oh like I can't put two and two together." He scoffs.

Looking up at Maize, I smile wide. "Thank you. It smells amazing and really means a lot to me."

"You're welcome. I hope I did it justice."

Standing, I cup her face and press my lips to her. She melts into me, but I pull away all too quickly. Normally, she would've freaked out because she's at work, but she didn't this time. Though I'm sure her dad wouldn't appreciate the PDA.

"I'm sure you did. Thank you."

With flushed cheeks, Maize goes to the kitchen, and I sit.

"What the…?" Grayson's jaw hits the floor. "You wanna explain what is goin' on?"

"She's tryin' to win me back," I reply with a shrug. "I need to know she's not gonna run away from me again."

"You got a Bishop to admit she wants you, and you're not jumping at the opportunity to have her right now? You have some strong willpower." He chuckles.

"I've been chasing her for a year, and after being told it was a mistake, I'm a little hesitant."

"So you're playing hard to get?" He chuckles.

I nod. "Something like that."

The next day, she's bubbly and full of smiles, which makes me think she has something up her sleeve.

"Mornin', beautiful," I greet and quickly plant a kiss on her lips when no one's looking.

"Morning. You have plans after work?" she asks softly.

"Hmm…" I brush my fingers over the stubble on my jawline. "Stripper joint, beers, and hookers."

Maize groans, crossing her arms with an unamused expression. "That sounds like a productive Tuesday night."

"I mean, unless you have something else in mind? I'd cancel for you." I flash her a wink, and her cheeks tint red.

"Well, since you didn't call me last night to say you were taking me back, I do. Way better than a guys' night out. And if you wanna join me, be ready by eight."

I chuckle at her annoyance. "Alright. Where should I meet you?"

She licks her lips, then smirks. "I'll pick you up."

By the time the workday is over, I'm a giddy, anxious fool. I have no idea what Maize has planned, but I can't wait to find out.

I drive home and shower. Without knowing how I should dress, I play it safe by wearing jeans, boots, and a dress shirt. At eight, a knock sounds on the door, and when I open it, Maize nearly takes my breath away. Her hair is in two braids with loose strands around her face, showing off her new blond highlights. She's wearing cutoffs with a Texas tank top that leaves nothing to my imagination.

"I feel a bit overdressed," I tease, scanning down her body again. I'm not used to seeing her like this, but I'm not complaining.

"As long as you're comfortable, that's all that matters." She smiles in return. "I hope you're ready."

"I don't think I have a choice." I chuckle, closing the gap between us and kissing her cheek. "You're so pretty. I love your hair."

Maize flips one of her braids and blushes. "You do? Thank you. Elle and I got our hair done over the weekend."

I hold a piece between my fingers and imagine how it'd look spread across my bedsheets.

"You better take me somewhere quick before I come up with another idea."

She snorts, shaking her head. "Is this all it's gonna take for you to give me another chance?"

"I don't know. I guess we'll both see." I wink, then close and lock the door behind me.

Following Maize, I squint when I see a jacked-up truck. "What's this?"

"I'm borrowing it for the night."

"You know how to drive that thing?"

"Well, mostly." She laughs. "C'mon, Cowboy. Don't you trust me?"

I help her into the driver's side, and when I round the truck and hop into the other, she hands me a blindfold.

"Are you serious?"

"Yes!" She laughs. "It's a surprise, so put it on."

"Hmm...alright."

After a bumpy ten minutes and hearing her laugh at my uncertainty, she finally parks.

"We're here."

"Can I take this thing off now?"

"Yep."

I open my eyes and squint as I look around the partially wooded area. There's a large firepit surrounded by grass and hay bales.

"Where are we?"

"It's what I like to call the secret spot."

Scanning the area, I notice we're on a hill, and the ranch is in the far distance. "Okay, so what're we doing here?"

Maize opens the door and hops out. "Follow me and find out, Cowboy."

I do as she says, and when I turn around, I see a large white screen on a pole. Then she opens the tailgate and gestures for me to get in the back.

"Wow..." Blankets and pillows are spread out on the truck bed along with a cooler and picnic basket.

"I thought it'd be more fun to watch a movie under the stars."

I walk toward her, tilting up her chin. "No one's ever done anything like this for me before. I love it." I kiss the tip of her nose.

"Good. I even picked out a really awesome movie for us to watch."

"Is that so?" I climb into the back and help her up.

She messes with the projector while I grab some drinks and food.

We get comfortable on the blankets, and I pull Maize into my body during the previews.

"No way." I glance at her. "How'd you know?"

"Know what?" She plays innocent.

I smirk. "*No Country for Old Men* is my favorite movie. Now, how'd you know that?"

"I maybe did a little internet stalking."

"There's no way you found that online. Who'd you talk to?"

She sighs, realizing I'm not gonna drop it. "You're really gonna make me reveal my sources?"

"Yes, ma'am."

"It was Cooper. He gave me some great...intel about you."

I groan with a chuckle. "Shoulda known, that bastard."

"What's wrong with that?" she asks.

"He likes to joke around, so I'm wondering what else he said. I'm a little concerned, to be honest."

Maize laughs and snuggles closer. "Don't worry." She pats my chest and meets my eyes. "I already knew you secretly cried to *Big Daddy*."

I fucking hate Cooper.

We end the night wrapped up in each other, and I can't seem to take my hands or lips off her. I want to be as close to Maize as possible. While I want to lose myself with her, I keep control of the situation and only allow her to kiss me.

"Thanks for a nice evening," I tell her once she drives me back to my house. It's late, and we have to be up early, but that doesn't make it any easier to leave.

"You're welcome." She smiles in return. "I'll see you at breakfast."

By six, I'm dragging my ass outta bed and wishing I had an extra hour or three of sleep. Though I'll be paying for it today, last night was worth it. I'm enjoying Maize's effort and appreciate the lengths she's already gone to. When I look around the B&B, I don't immediately see her, so I load a plate with food. After chatting with Grayson, Riley, and Diesel, Maize appears wearing a wide, bright smile and greets everyone.

"Do I get a *special* breakfast this mornin'?" Grayson flashes a cocky smirk, and I kick him underneath the table. By the looks the other guys give him, Grayson spilled the news about Maize and me.

"You wish." She snorts.

"How about me? Your favorite cousin?" Riley muses.

"Or your favorite future cousin-in-law?" Diesel adds with a grin.

"You know…" Maize puts her hands on her hips. "It really surprises me you two managed to find women. Sorry, Grayson. Kenzie will get the stick outta her ass one day."

They laugh at the way Grayson glares at her. "Don't put that juju in the air."

Maize snorts, shaking her head. "Well, anyway. I do have a surprise for you." She licks her lips, bringing her gaze to mine. "Be right back."

"So you datin' my cousin, now?" Riley asks pointedly.

"Maybe."

"Shut the hell up," Grayson blurts out. "They've been screwin' for months."

I kick him harder this time. "Dude."

"For *months*?" Diesel asks, chuckling. "I think these Bishop women get their rocks off from sneakin' around. Don't get me wrong now, it's hot as fuck, but I'm bracing myself for the day Grayson and Kenzie come clean."

"Not happenin', bro." Grayson groans.

"We'll all find out when she's giving birth to his baby," I tease.

"You guys fuckin' suck. I hate you all." He grunts, then shoves food into his mouth.

Maize returns and sets a platter in front of me. It's a round cake covered in cream cheese frosting with purple writing on top.

Meet me where we first met. Tomorrow. 8pm.

The guys lean over to read it. "Where's that?" Diesel and Riley simultaneously ask.

Maize leans down and whispers in my ear, "I want to recreate that night. But this time, no cheating."

I smile wide as I think back to when we played pool together almost a year ago.

"What kind of cake is it, Maze?" Diesel dips his finger into the frosting, and Maize smacks his hand away.

"Carrot cake, Gavin's favorite."

My mouth waters, and I glance up at her with a grin.

Maize flashes me a little wink. "Told you I did my research."

Then she walks away.

It's Thursday, and I'm meeting Maize at the pub in an hour. Since she wants us to recreate the night we met, I wear the same shirt. The real test will be if she notices.

By the time I arrive, she's sitting at the bar talking to Kenzie and drinking. I walk up to her, and Kenzie's eyes light up when she sees me. Maize quickly turns and releases a gasp before I cup her cheeks, and our mouths collide.

Our tongues tangle together, and before we get lost in the moment, we break apart.

"What was that for?" she asks, doe-eyed.

"Just a thank you for the delicious cake." I smirk. "Grayson's all butt hurt I didn't share, but I refused. Best carrot cake I've ever had."

She blinks up at me with a shy smile.

"I don't recall that happening last time," Kenzie blurts out, watching us closely. "Am I getting the R-rated version?"

A blush hits Maize's cheeks, and I laugh at Kenzie's boldness.

"Might be X-rated. Not sure yet." I shrug, stepping closer and wrapping an arm around Maize. "One thing's for certain, I'm not wasting any time tonight. Plus, I'm like an elephant and remember every detail. The conversation about you becoming a nun, crooked dick pics, and—" I lean in so only Maize can hear me. "Spanking your ass."

She gulps and bites down on her lower lip.

"But right now, we have drinks to order and a game of pool to play."

"Dude." Grayson slams his palm on the table. "I can't believe you still haven't put her out of her damn misery. She's given you the first-class treatment all damn week, and you *still* haven't agreed to give her a second chance?" His eyes widen with disbelief.

I shrug, scanning the dining room for Maize and frown when I still haven't found her. We've been here for almost twenty minutes.

"Trust me, I appreciate her effort. I'm shocked, honestly. And I want to be with her. I'm just concerned she'll change her mind next week. But I'm enjoying every second."

"You better stop makin' her chase you before she gives up and the tables turn. This back-and-forth shit is giving me a headache. It could all backfire because Maize isn't that patient."

His words nearly gut me, and I realize he's right.

"Shit, I didn't think about it that way." I rub my sweaty palms down my jeans, looking around for her again but only see Jane.

"Hey," I say, grabbing her attention.

Jane walks over with a bright smile and rests her hand on my shoulder. "Hey, Gavin. How's your breakfast?"

"It's delicious, ma'am. Do you know where Maize is this mornin'? I haven't seen her yet."

She gives me a suspicious look. "She took a vacation day, so Sandra and I are handling everything today."

"Oh. Is she sick or somethin'?"

"Not that I know of." She shrugs.

After she walks away, Grayson points at me with his fork. "Told ya. You got greedy." He snorts.

I brush a hand through my hair before putting my hat on. Then I set my plate in the dirty dish bin and leave.

If Grayson's right, I'm gonna kick my own ass. Or better yet, let one of the horses do it.

CHAPTER NINETEEN

MAIZE

I'M STANDING in Gavin's cabin wearing red lingerie with black cowboy boots, and though I'm not snooping, I feel like I'm invading his privacy.

But maybe he should've thought about that when he started this whole *prove I'm ready to be with him* crap. For the past four days, I've gone out of my way to create some memorable moments.

Has he put me out of my damn misery and taken me to his bed? No.

Gavin kisses me like his life depends on it, then leaves me hot and bothered.

That ends *tonight*.

He'll give me a damn answer about us being together or I'm walking out of here.

I have candles lit, his favorite music playing softly, and my outfit doesn't leave anything to the imagination. Either I'll successfully seduce Gavin or he'll turn me down for good.

If the latter happens, I'm never going to be able to face him again.

When I hear the front door open, I lick my lips and wait for him to find me.

"Uhh, hello?" His voice echoes.

"In the kitchen," I respond sweetly as our dinner warms in the oven.

I even made dessert, assuming we'll have the energy for it later. I lean against the counter and hear his footsteps down the hallway.

"Holy fuck."

I blink at him with a small smile.

"Uh..." Gavin brushes his hand over his scruffy jaw, and I blush as his eyes study me. "H-how did you get inside?"

"My uncles have a master key for all the housing." I shrug. "I decided to borrow it."

He swallows hard and looks around. "You wanna explain what's goin' on here because I'm..."

I boldly step toward him. "I'll tell you exactly what's happening. I've been doing my best to show you just how ready I am to be with you and how I'm not gonna run, yet each night, I wait for your call and nothing. So I decided to try one more time—a less subtle approach," I say, placing a hand on my hip. "But it comes with an ultimatum."

Gavin crosses his arms, wearing an amused grin. "An ultimatum?"

I tilt my head. "You decide right now if you're giving me a second chance or I leave for good this time. I don't know how else to convince you. Hell, I've literally waxed my entire body and found a vinyl of Diamond Rio to play in your ancient record player—which was not easy to figure out, mind you."

"Of course you knew I was a fan."

"I overheard you talkin' about how you saw them in concert when you were a teen. Then something about how they were your grandpa's favorite and that was when you started listening to their music."

"Eavesdroppin'?"

"Please." I roll my eyes. "You and the guys are loud as hell. Everyone hears your conversations at the B&B. Including the ones about me."

The corner of his mouth twists up. "So tell me, Maize..." He sets his hat on the counter before threading his fingers through his messy hair. "You ready to be my girl?"

My heart races, and my breaths turn shallow as his husky voice sends shivers down my spine. He walks toward me, never breaking our eye contact.

"If you haven't gotten the hint by now..."

"Oh, I have." Plucking the strap of my dress, he leaves goose bumps as he brushes the pad of his finger down my arm. "I just wanna hear you say it."

Releasing a groan, I roll my eyes, then smile. "Fine, I'll stroke your ego this one *last* time, but then that's it."

"Mm-hmm." He smirks.

Instead of giving in to his cockiness, I inch closer and make demands of my own. "Make me yours, Gavin. I want you."

He cups the back of my head, pulling me toward him until our mouths collide. I gasp as he holds me into his body and captures my bottom lip between his teeth.

"*Mine*, Maize," he growls, sliding his hands down my back until his palms reach my ass. "Fuckin' mine. Got it?"

I nod and release a rush of air. "*Yes*. All yours."

Gavin lifts me, and I wrap my legs around his waist. His erection presses against his jeans, and I know he's as desperate and eager as I am.

Instead of taking me to his bedroom as I'd hoped, he sets me on top of the kitchen counter and stands between my legs.

"Waxed everywhere, huh?" He moves his mouth down my neck.

"Yes," I pant, tilting my head back.

Gavin slides his hand over my thigh and over the thin fabric. His fingers roam under my panties, and I release a moan of anticipation.

"Fuck," he groans in my ear. "So damn soft."

His thumb finds my clit, and soon, my breathing turns ragged and needy. He plunges two fingers inside me as he sucks on the softness of my neck.

"You're so tight and wet, baby. Shit, I wanna fuck you so hard."

"God, yes." My head rolls back.

He thrusts his fingers faster and harder until I can no longer take it and dig my nails into his biceps as I scream out my release.

Our mouths slam together, hot and greedy, as I claw at his clothes.

"Off...now," I order.

As he strips, I do the same, not wanting anything between us. He cups my face and crashes our lips together again. His tongue tangles with mine.

"Goddamn, baby."

"You've been teasing me all damn week," I tell him. "With your little kisses, then leaving me all hot and bothered. So *rude*."

He chuckles. "Imma make up for it, baby. Turn around and put your palms flat on the counter."

I do as he says, and anxious butterflies swarm low in my stomach as I look over at him studying every inch of my body.

"Now spread your legs and let me see your sweet pussy."

I obey, watching him stroke his hard cock.

Gavin closes the gap between us, brushing the tip of his erection along my slit. "Say it again, Maize. Say you're mine," he whispers in my ear.

Licking my lips, I look at him over my shoulder. "I'm yours. Have been since that first night a year ago."

"That's fuckin' right," he hisses, pushing in slowly. "'Bout time you realize it."

I smile at his possessiveness. "Now fuck me, Cowboy."

Gavin squeezes my hips as he thrusts deep inside, jolting me forward until I'm nearly flat on the counter. God, it feels so good.

"Shit," he whispers. "You're so tight."

Gavin pulls out slowly before ramming back in. Our bodies form a rhythm as we slam together over and over. Wrapping an arm around my waist, Gavin aggressively rubs my clit until I lose myself. My release is intense and harsh, and when I float back to earth, he squeezes my breast.

"Don't think I've forgotten about your ass…" He pulls back, then slaps a cheek, hard and sharp.

My body jerks, and I moan in response.

"We fit together perfectly," he says in my ear, his voice hoarse and raw. "We always have."

"Yes," I whisper-moan.

My back arches as the sensations build inside me, but then Gavin slides out and falls to his knees. Just as I'm about to ask what the hell he's doing, he grips my thighs and spreads my legs apart.

My stomach is flat on the counter as he slides his tongue up my center. He flicks and sucks, tasting every inch of me as I claw at the granite. I can barely fill my lungs with air as he draws out another orgasm, his mouth devouring my pussy like it's the last thing he'll ever taste.

When Gavin stands, he grabs my arm and spins me around until I'm facing him. Our lips fuse, and he lifts me.

"Oh my God," I squeal as he leads us out of the kitchen.

"Hang on." He grins.

When we enter his bedroom, we fall on top of the bed, and he quickly positions me to straddle him.

"Ride me."

I move until his cock presses against me, and I slowly slide down his hard length. He grips my hips, and we rock together, fast and hard.

Gavin massages my breasts, smacks my ass, and pulls my hair until I scream his name. I love how demanding and rough he is, but he's also sweet and soft. After my fourth orgasm, he flips me on my back and kisses me until he groans my name. He spills inside me, and slowly, we resurface to reality together.

"Wow..." I breathe out.

"Yeah, wow," he echoes, lying next to me.

Gavin brushes his knuckles over my cheek and gazes into my eyes. "I'm really fallin' for you, Maize Bishop. I hope you feel the same."

"As much as I didn't want to admit it, I do. No doubt about it," I confess with a smile.

"More stubborn than a mule, aren't ya?" He chuckles, pulling me into his arms.

"Well, I've learned what it takes to get your attention. Lingerie and an ultimatum."

His bright blue eyes light up. "Can ya blame a man? You're downright gorgeous with a smart mouth to boot. I was hard the second I saw you tonight."

"Romantic." I snicker.

Gavin tilts my chin and brushes his mouth softly over mine. "I really want this to work out, so no more games. I want to be together, and we can wait to tell people when you're ready."

His declaration has my heart beating wildly. It's been years since I've wanted a man as much as I've wanted him. Though it scares me, I want this to work.

"I agree," I tell him. "And we'll figure out the long-distance thing and take it one day at a time."

He quirks a brow, giving me a puzzled expression. "Long-distance?"

I suck in my lips, releasing a sigh. "When you start traveling with Cooper."

"Maize..."

"It's okay." I pull back slightly so I meet his eyes. "You have to follow your heart, and you love bull riding, so it only makes sense—"

"I turned it down," he blurts out. "A month ago."

My brows rise. "You did? But...when I brought it up at dinner last Friday, you acted like it was something you were pursuing."

"After you admitted to overhearing my conversation, I never said I was or wasn't, and you didn't ask."

I blow out a breath of annoyance. "And you couldn't put me out of my misery and just tell me you weren't leaving?" I scold.

Gavin laughs with a shrug. "It was nice to see you sweat for once."

"Soooo funny," I mock. "Why'd you say no?"

"Realized the ranch was my second home, and while I enjoyed being on the road, I want to settle down, and I want to do that here. With you. I love seeing you every morning, and it's something I looked forward to, even if you ignore me. Your family feels like my own. It just feels right to be here."

My heart swells as my eyes fill with tears. "I'm really happy you're staying."

He tips my chin. "Me too. Now I get to slap that fine ass anytime I want."

With a loud smack to my bare cheek, I yelp and laugh. "I kinda like sneaking around with you. Well, my cousins and Grayson know, but I want to wait until we get to know each other better to tell my parents. Are you okay with that?" After my last relationship backfired, I don't want to introduce my parents to any man until we've been dating a while.

"I'm good with waiting until you're ready." He flashes a wink. "Just promise me it won't be another year?"

I can't stop the ridiculous smile from forming as I look at him. "I can definitely promise that."

After we eat dinner and devour the dessert, Gavin cages me against the counter while I rinse the dishes. He feathers soft kisses on my neck. "I could get used to seeing you in my kitchen half-naked. It's giving me ideas."

"Yeah? What kind?" I muse.

"Really dirty ones. Bending you over the table for one, putting whipped cream on your delicious tits, then licking it off, you riding me. Those are just a few."

His hard cock presses against my back. "Mmm…I think that could be arranged."

He wraps his arms around my waist and pulls me close. Gavin's tall and big, which I love, and it makes me feel so small and cared for when he does that.

"Promise you'll always hold me like this?" I whisper, leaning my head against his chest.

"Always, Maize. I'm not going anywhere."

And when he presses his lips to my temple, I fall even deeper in love with him.

CHAPTER TWENTY

GAVIN

Sneaking around with Maize for the past month has been incredible. I wish we wouldn't have wasted so much time chasing each other, but it's better late than never. While all her cousins know about us, and so do the guys, none of the Bishop adults do. And tonight is the big reveal to her parents.

While I'm nervous as hell, I'm also ready to yell from the mountaintops how much she means to me. We've spent all our free time together, but it never seems like enough. I genuinely want to know everything about Maize Bishop—her likes, dislikes, dreams, and aspirations.

Though it took a while, I think she finally understands I'm not some twentysomething looking for a one-night stand. I'm a man searching for my forever woman, and I've found that in her. I'm ready to settle down, and she is too. While she doesn't want to rush into things, I'd marry her tomorrow, but I keep it to myself. I selfishly want to wake up next to her every day and see her pretty smile before I leave for work.

After I get out of the shower, I put on my Sunday best, comb my hair, and rehearse articulating the way Maize makes me feel. While John and Mila are amazing, being introduced as her boyfriend could be a disaster. I'm not sure what their reaction will be, and that makes me nervous.

I'm falling hard and fast for Maize in ways I never imagined was possible. I've not loved anyone or anything as much as I loved bull riding and training, but I'd hang my saddle for her.

What we have is the real deal.

As I slip on my boots, there's a knock on my door. I open it and see Maize standing in a sundress with velvety red lips. A cute smirk forms as she looks me up and down.

"Damn," I say, pulling her into my arms and devouring her mouth. "Do I have lipstick on me?" I ask when we finally break apart.

"No, silly. It'll last fifteen hours." She steps inside.

"Really? I'd like to put that to the test then." I waggle my brows at her.

"I'd be up for the challenge," she admits. "Are you ready for this?"

I check the time and grow more anxious. I let out a cool breath, and Maize notices. Tilting her head, she moves closer and wraps her arms around my waist. "It's gonna be fine. I promise. My parents already love you."

I create just enough space so I can look into her baby blues. "They love me as an employee on the ranch, not as their twenty-five-year-old daughter's boyfriend. There's a big difference."

Her face softens. "I know that, but I also know how unconventional my dad's relationship was along with all my uncles. It's kinda a Bishop thing, if I'm being honest."

I grin. "How so?"

"Mila was my nanny before she was my mother." Maize shrugs. "So Dad has no room to talk."

"Wow." I remember Maize telling me about this before, but it slipped my mind.

"And Uncle Alex knocked up his now wife on vacation in Florida, then she showed up here, pregnant. Uncle Evan met his wife at a wedding, had a one-night stand, then found out she was the new doctor at the hospital."

My eyebrows go sky high. "What about Jackson?"

This question makes her laugh. "He's the only normal one. I know it's *very* hard to believe. He and Kiera were best friends growing up. There was drama, but it wasn't a random hookup. He chased after her for fifteen years." She chuckles.

"How do you know all this?"

"One time, Grandma Bishop was wine drunk after a quilt meeting and told me all their dirty secrets." Maize throws me a wink.

I grin at her. "Still doesn't mean your dad and uncles won't kick my ass or fire me."

She pulls me closer. "As long as you don't break my heart, I think you'll be safe."

"I'd *never* do anything to hurt you," I promise her and seal it with a kiss.

"I believe you," she whispers. "But we should really get going. Don't want to be late. It's one of Dad's major pet peeves."

I nod. "Okay, okay. I guess I am stalling."

She interlocks her hand with mine and leads us outside. I jump in the truck with her, and my mind spins on the drive over. Any other time, it would seem far away because the ranch is so large, but we arrive in a blink. We get out, and she stops and turns to me before we walk in.

"A kiss for good luck." She paints her mouth across mine, and her tongue darts inside. For a moment, I forget where I am, but when she pushes away, I remember.

"Let's do this," I say, finding my confidence as she grabs the knob, and we enter. Whatever her mother's cooking smells amazing, and I realize just how hungry I am. When her parents turn around and make eye contact with me, I immediately lose my appetite.

"Wait, Gavin's your boyfriend?" John asks, staring me down, and I'm not sure if it's with approval or rejection.

Maize nods with a smile. Then she takes my hand and leads me to the table, and we sit.

"Oh thank god," Mila says. "I was worried to death trying to guess who you were bringing tonight. Happy to see you again, Gavin."

It's a relief to know her mom is on board, but I still can't read John. He's typically quiet, especially compared to Jackson, but this seems more intense than usual.

"I made lasagna," Mila announces. "I hope you're both hungry."

"Sounds amazing," I say.

"Yeah, Mom. Can't wait. I'm starving." Maize looks around. "Did Kenzie already leave for work?"

"She did," John mumbles, not making eye contact with either of us.

A knot forms in my throat, and I can't seem to swallow it down. "What would you like to drink?" Mila asks.

"I got it." Maize gets up and pours us all glasses of iced sweet tea. I drink it down, wondering what John's really thinking. Maize helps set the table, then brings the salad, and eventually, the lasagna is set in the middle. John and Mila sit across from us as we pass serving spoons around and fill our plates family style.

"So, you're now dating my daughter?" John finally says once we all have our food.

"Yes, sir," I confirm.

"How long has this been going on?" he asks.

"Dad. That's really none of your business, is it?" Maize snaps. I can tell she's getting frustrated, and I try to put myself in his shoes. I understand his response.

Mila places her hand on John's lap. I'm sure to help calm his unease.

"You're much older, Gavin. Do you plan on stayin' in town?" John continues with questions.

"If we're counting, Gavin's about ten years older," Maize answers for me. "That's no secret. Older means more mature, and he's not a fuckboy like all the other men around here who only want me for one thing."

"Maize, language," Mila says.

"I've thought about my age more times than I can count. Maize's mature and thinks on a higher level. She knows what she wants in life, and I support that one hundred percent. And yes, I plan to stay here indefinitely. I love the ranch, and I love your family. I've already lived a full life and have traveled around the world and have no desire to go back to that. I'm ready to settle down, start a family, and do what I love, which is training."

Mila looks at me with adoration and smiles. "That's nice, Gavin. There's something magical about this place. It's one reason I moved here, well and because my grandmother lived here, but I fell in love with the ranch and John, and you too, Maize. It was home in my heart," Mila tells me. "Seems like it's yours too."

"Yes, ma'am. It is. Growing up in Houston has made me appreciate all this land, the quietness at night, and the stars. I've never seen so many. I know our relationship seems like it's coming from left field, but I can promise this has been brewing between us for a long time," I admit.

Maize snickers. "Over a year. And I'm happy, Daddy."

The room is silent for a minute before I speak up, but I know I can't leave without admitting my true feelings. I want her dad to know this isn't a fling, and I'm not sure how to convince him, so I let my heart speak for me instead. "I love Maize with everything that I am. I can't imagine my life without her." I smile and look over at Maize, who has tears forming in her eyes. It's not easy for me to be so vulnerable and honest, but it was the only way.

"I love you too," she tells me, then leans over and presses her lips right against mine. I kiss her back, but damn, the fire this woman has is blazing hot right now.

"I know you both have concerns about me breaking Maize's heart, but that's not going to happen. Finding love like this is rare, and I'm not going to let the opportunity pass me by," I profess, meaning it with all my being.

John's mouth tilts up into a smile, and he lets out a sigh. "Okay. Okay, you two. You don't have to prove anything to me. I just don't want you getting hurt, sweetie. And if you break her heart..." John glares at me and doesn't finish his threat.

I nod. "I'd kick my own ass if that happened," I admit. "But it won't, I can guarantee that. I'm a man of my word."

"I'm so happy for you two," Mila says in a high-pitched tone. "Now, let's eat before this masterpiece of a meal gets cold."

I grab Maize's hand as Mila chats about the school and how many kids they have enrolled this year. There are so many stolen glances and unspoken words that I can't wait to be alone with her.

"How's your planning going with the business?" Mila inquires.

John points his fork at me. "You support her starting this catering business?"

"Yes!" Maize raises her voice an octave with a laugh. "Gavin's been helping a lot. I ordered a ton of equipment, and he's kept me on schedule with my launch. Also, he's strong and has helped me lift all the heavy items that have already arrived. Free labor." Maize gives me a wink.

"I know you're gonna be successful," I say, beaming at her. I can't wait to see what she accomplishes. Grandma Bishop has already gotten her booked solid for months with ladies from church.

"And I'm about to be twenty-six, and even though I still live at home, I'm grown. I can do whatever I want, date whoever I want, and make whatever decisions I want."

John cracks a smile. "I wouldn't expect anything else from you, but I'll always be your father and will always have your best interest in mind." He pauses for a second, then looks at us. "I know the two of ya are waitin' for my blessing, so you have it. Once your grandma finds out, that's if she doesn't already know about this, she will be publicly asking for more great-grandbabies. Just please, wait until you're married."

"And don't wait until I'm old and gray to get married and have kids," Mila says. "I'd like to enjoy having grandkids."

Maize nearly chokes on her food and places her hand on her throat before chugging tea. "I've announced I have a boyfriend, and you're already planning a wedding and kids. You both need to chill out. We're taking it slow. There's no need to rush because I want this to last forever."

"It will," I say with a big grin.

Mila shrugs. "I was serious, though."

"Okay, so ring shopping next week?" I turn to Maize.

Her eyes are as wide as saucers, and her cheeks turn rosy pink. "Don't you even!"

I wrap my arm around her, and she leans in. "One day."

"Not right now," she says with a smile, but the look in her eyes gives her away. It's as if she's imagining a future with me, and it makes my heart swell with happiness. My face actually hurts from smiling.

After dinner, Mila makes coffee and pulls out a coconut cream pie.

"Just because Maize's a chef, doesn't mean I don't buy store made pies," she admits as she slides pieces onto plates and hands us forks. I take a bite and grin.

"It tastes great. I wouldn't have known the difference," I say.

"Maize still has a lot to teach you then," Mila says, grinning at her daughter.

Maize snorts. "I'm a little snobby when it comes to desserts that aren't made from scratch."

"A *little*?" John scoffs and holds his arms as wide as they'll go.

It makes me laugh. John watches the way Maize and I interact, and eventually, something snaps in him. It's almost as if he can see how much I love her. After we finish eating, I get up and help Maize with the dishes. Once the kitchen is clean, we go to the living room and tell her parents good night.

John stands up and gives me a firm handshake. "Take care of my daughter."

"Yes, sir. I won't let you down," I say, meeting his eyes, and we hold a silent conversation. I have his permission to date Maize, and it's enough.

"I'll be home later," Maize says, tugging at my shirt and pulling me away.

"Thanks for dinner. It was great," I say to Mila. "Good night, y'all."

"We'll do it again sometime soon," she tells me as Maize leads me to the door.

Once we're outside, I can breathe again. Maize leads me to the truck, and I pin her against the cool metal and kiss her. "So your dad didn't kill me."

"*Yet*," she says with a snicker before returning her mouth to mine.

CHAPTER TWENTY-ONE

MAIZE

It's been two weeks since my parents learned that Gavin and I were officially dating. Dad took it as expected, but he quickly accepted it. When Gavin promised he wouldn't break my heart, I nearly melted on the floor like a popsicle in the middle of summer. Not having to hide my feelings has been such a relief. We've even gone on a few dates in town and hung out at the bar together. The two of us are inseparable.

News spread around town like wildfire, and I was actually happy about it. I want everyone to know he's *mine*.

Today, we're driving to Houston so I can meet his parents. It's a five-hour road trip, which gives me way too much time to think. I kinda understand why Gavin was so damn nervous to be introduced as my boyfriend to my folks, but at least he wasn't a stranger to them. This is on a different level. Gavin's promised he's said nothing but amazing things about me.

It's scary how fast I'm falling for him, and I don't ever want this to end. Gavin's my past, present, and my future, and it's a big deal to meet his parents. He hasn't dated seriously in over a decade, so to say I'm feeling anxious is an understatement.

"What're you thinking about over there?" He grabs my hand and kisses my knuckles as he turns on the cruise control.

"What if your mom and dad don't like me? What if I'm nothing but a big disappointment or something?"

Gavin lets out a howl of a laugh. "Are you kidding me? They already love you and are ecstatic to meet you. My mom can't wait and even called me this morning to make sure we were still coming and I wasn't going to chicken out. They're down to earth and will be just as supportive as your parents are." He glances over at me. "Well, now that your dad is on board with the idea of us," he adds.

"That makes me feel a tad better. And hey, Dad just needed to warm up to the idea. He knows he can control me as much as he can control Kenzie," I tell him, and we both laugh, knowing Kenzie does whatever the hell she wants and doesn't care who knows.

"Okay, so I need to ask a million questions, and I have about four hours to do it," I say, wanting to ask everything I can before we arrive.

His smile is contagious. "Ask me anything you want."

I let out a breath. "Tell me about your parents' relationship."

"That's not a question," he says, chuckling. "But they were high school sweethearts. Mom barrel raced growing up, and Dad rode bulls too. He never went pro like I did because of an injury. They got married before they both turned twenty-one and had me soon after."

"Aw, that sounds sweet. Do you have any brothers and sisters?" Even though I know so much about him, I realize I still have a lot to learn.

He shakes his head. "Not that I know of. It's a good thing, though, because your family is so goddamn huge."

"This is very true," I admit. "There are *a lot* of Bishops."

Gavin grins. "And we're gonna add some more to that list."

I shake my head. "One day."

We blow through San Antonio without getting stuck in traffic, and the rest of the way to Houston goes by way too quickly. When we take the loop away from the city, I'm amazed at how quickly it transforms into open pastures. It's not Eldorado, but I see barns and horses and even some cows grazing in the distance.

Those five hours passed in a snap. Gavin makes another turn, and we drive down a long rock road until the two-story home with white shutters comes into view. We park, and I suck in air.

Gavin's palm rests on my thigh, and he squeezes. "They already love you. Trust me."

I smile. "Okay, let's do this then."

Gavin comes around and opens my door, and he holds out his arm for me to take. Having him this close is comforting in every sense, but as we climb the steps leading to the front door, I grow more nervous. He rings the bell, and his mama swings open the door. Before saying a word, she pulls me into a big hug and squeezes me. "It's so nice to meet you, Maize. Sorry, we're huggers 'round here. I'm Rose, but you can call me Mom."

I laugh and hold her for a second. "I'm a hugger too. Nice to meet you, finally."

"Come on in now. Y'all must be tired from that drive. Your daddy will be back any minute. He's out feedin' the horses," she explains, going to the stove and stirring something. Instantly, my mouth begins to water.

"Whatcha cookin'?" I ask, taking a few steps forward.

"Seafood gumbo," she tells me.

"Oh, I love shrimp!" I admit.

"Don't be shy. Come see. Gavin told me you were a highly regarded, award-winning chef," she adds.

This makes me laugh. "He's just being kind."

Gavin's mouth falls open. "No, I'm not. She won first place at the rodeo's barbecue contest."

His mom turns and looks at me. "Honey, that's not easy to do. Some people travel around the state and enter those competitions just for the prize money. Now, I want barbecue."

A blush hits my cheeks. "Thank you. I didn't think I'd win because of that, but the brisket spoke for itself. Gavin gave me the confidence I needed to continue because I was hesitant about entering."

With a quick turn of her head, she glances over at him leaning against the counter. "That's my boy. He's good at encouraging people to follow their dreams. Now, come and have a taste of this homemade roux."

Grabbing a spoon from the drawer, she dips it inside the giant stockpot and hands it over. I blow on it for a second, then sip it up. My mouth explodes with the different spices. With wide eyes, I can't seem to speak fast enough. "That's the best I've ever had."

"Really? It's a family recipe, top secret. Once you and Gavin get married, I'll have to share it with you."

Gavin moves forward. "Don't say the m-word, Mom. Kinda freaks her out."

"Hardy har har. It does not. Okay, well maybe a little," I admit. "But when you know you've found the one, why does it matter?"

"Is Maize Bishop turning a new leaf?" he asks, just as the back door opens and shuts.

Moments later, Gavin's dad waltzes in wearing a grin. Gavin's the spitting image of his father, and if he ages just as well, I'm in for a treat. He's tall and handsome with slivers of gray in his hair. "Oh, you must be Maize, the woman my son has fallen head over heels with," he announces, walking forward and hugging me.

"I already warned her about us being huggers," Rose tells him with a chuckle.

"I'm Wyatt. Welcome to the family," he says with a huge grin.

"Thank you!"

When his parents aren't looking, Gavin gives me a thumbs-up.

His dad grabs a cup of ice water and chugs it. "Horses are fed, and I'm starving. Smells so good." When it's empty, he refills it before sitting at the table.

Gavin pulls bowls from the cabinet and sets them next to the stove.

Feeling out of place, I turn and ask, "Is there something I can help with?"

He gives me a wink. "Nope. You're the guest of honor. Let someone else cook for you for once."

"Maize, do you want rice?" his mom asks.

"Sure. I'm not picky," I say.

"Only with your men," Gavin adds.

She carries two bowls, and Gavin grabs the others.

After his dad says grace, I gobble up the gumbo so fast it seems like I inhaled it.

"Help yourself! Have seconds and thirds. Don't be shy around here," Wyatt says.

"This is true," he tells me.

"So tell us a little about you, Maize. How'd you and Gavin meet?" his mom asks.

I swallow down the big bite I'd just taken, and thankfully, Gavin steps in. "We met before my interview at the ranch. Her family owns it."

"Oh, that's right. You know me, I forget so much these days," she admits.

"I work in the family bed and breakfast and plan all the meals each week. I'm responsible for making sure everyone is fed and full. Not any of that processed stuff either. We serve homemade everything and lots of comfort food. I have a few employees to help me because the workers will eat ya out of house and home."

"Bed and breakfast? Sounds like a place I'd like to visit." She grins.

"You should. Could get you the family discount." I laugh and give her a wink.

Rose claps her hands together. "Don't tempt me with a good time," she warns with a big smile. "You might spoil me so much I'll move in permanently."

"The more, the merrier," I offer, finishing my second bowl of gumbo. "I grew up on the ranch and am in love with the scenery and how peaceful it is. Small-town living is the best."

"It really is," Gavin agrees. "I don't think I ever want to leave."

"Well, if you won't move back home, then we might sell the house and come up there, especially if you have kids." She looks directly at Gavin, but I don't think she's joking.

My face heats. "My parents gave us the kids and marriage talk too," I explain. "It seems everyone's ready for that."

Gavin gives a chuckle and a head nod.

Once we're finished eating dinner, Gavin and I volunteer to clean up while his parents go to the living room to catch the evening news. We stand next to each other as he scrubs and I rinse the dishes.

"Told you they'd adore you." He softly bumps his hip against mine.

"Your parents are so nice. Seriously." I speak loud enough for only him to hear.

He bends down and kisses my forehead. "That makes me so happy. You have no idea."

After we finish, he takes me on a tour of the house. On the mantel sits framed pictures of him riding bucking broncos and bulls. When he shows me his childhood bedroom, I nearly gasp at all the trophies, medals, and winning belt buckles decorating the room.

"Welcome to my shrine," he says, holding out his hand.

I step inside. "Gavin. This is...*amazing*."

"I guess," he mumbles, entering behind me.

I feel like I'm walking into a time capsule full of his past memories. Moving around the room, I take it all in. "I didn't realize you won this much because you've acted like you weren't a big deal. Gavin, I'm so impressed." I wrap my arms around his waist and pull him close. "I didn't realize I was dating a cowboy celebrity of sorts."

He shakes his head. "I'm not."

"But you are. Look at this. Wow. No wonder people try to reach out to you all the time for training and stuff." I stand on my tiptoes and slide my mouth against his. We get lost in the kiss, in the moment, and the only thing that pulls us away is the sound of footsteps down the hallway. Not wanting to make it awkward, I create some space between us. A knock rings on the door, and it cracks open. She peeks her head inside.

"I made pudding parfaits if you'd like some dessert," she tells us.

"Thanks, Mom. We'll be right down," he says sweetly. She slowly closes the door, and after a second, Gavin pops a brow at me and brings me back to him.

"Right now, you're the only thing I want for dessert," he hums in my ear.

"If we weren't at your parents' house, I'd consider it," I admit. "But we better go downstairs before they get suspicious."

"This is true." He grabs my hand and leads me to the kitchen, where we fill ourselves full of pudding and cake. It's so good that I'm contemplating adding it to the B&B menu when I get home. Gavin and I watch TV with his parents until we nearly fall asleep. Both of us keep yawning, and eventually, we say good night, then he leads me upstairs. We fall asleep in his bedroom surrounded by all his accomplishments. To say I'm proud is an understatement.

The next morning, we wake up to a breakfast that's as big as the ones I serve at the B&B. We chat about the weather and Eldorado, and everything under the sun. When we're done eating, Gavin leads me outside to the barn.

"Want to go for a ride?" he asks.

A smile fills my face, and I nod. "Absolutely. I would love that."

"Then let's catch some horses." He grabs two lead ropes from the tack room, and I follow him out to the pasture where at least five quarter horses are grazing.

"Choose whichever one you want. They're all as tame as can be," he explains.

I walk with the rope behind my back and my hand out, the same way Kenzie and I did as kids with the trail riding horses. It works like a charm, and I snap the lead rope on the halter, then turn to Gavin.

"Meet you at the barn," I tell him with a hop to my step.

By the time he walks inside, I've already saddled up, adjusted my stirrups, and am waiting for him.

"Look at you! Hot as fuck!" he exclaims.

I chuckle. "I thought for a second I was gettin' rusty 'cause I haven't ridden in a while, but putting on a saddle is something you never forget. It's like riding a bike. By the way, this is a nice one."

"It was a prize saddle," he explains, then points at the branding and the date burned into it.

"You never seem to stop surprising me." I meet his eyes, wishing he could see what I see.

After Gavin's ready, he gets in position, and we head down a trail that looks well-traveled. As we ride into the path that goes through the forest, I can't help but grin the entire time. Beams of sunshine leak through the tree limbs as I follow him. Thankfully, a cold front came in over the weekend, so the weather is perfect. Eventually, we come to a clearing, and I see a giant pond with a canoe tied to a small floating dock. This is not what I expected.

We hop off our horses and tie them to a few posts. Gavin takes my hand, and we walk toward the water. He sits, takes off his boots, and rolls up his pants before sticking his toes in the water. I follow his lead and lean my head against his shoulder as we look out at the reflection of the tall pines on the water.

"Mom really loves you," he says, smiling. "And I do too. I love you so damn much, Maize."

"I love you too, Gavin. You're everything to me," I admit.

He turns and places his rough palm on my cheek, then dips down and memorizes my lips with his. Our tongues twist together, and by the time we pull apart, I'm nearly gasping for air.

"Thanks for joining me this weekend. I know it was a big step," he says, running his toes across the water.

"We should visit more often. I can tell how much your parents miss and love you." I steal another kiss.

"You mean it? You'll make the drive with me again?"

"Yeah, I'd love that. Your parents have already adopted me and made me a member of the family."

He kisses my forehead. "Thank you."

After twenty minutes of enjoying the view, we put our shoes and socks back on. He stands and offers his hand. I take it, and the moment I meet his eyes, there's not a doubt in my mind that he's the man I'm supposed to spend my forever with.

"One day, Maize, I'm gonna make you my wife."

I bite my bottom lip and smile. "That a promise, Cowboy?"

"You better believe it, baby. And I'll spend the rest of my life making you happy."

"Lookin' forward to it," I admit. He takes my hand, and we go back to the horses.

CHAPTER TWENTY-TWO

GAVIN

I<small>T'S BEEN</small> four months since Maize and I have been official. Today's Maize's birthday, and it's the first time I'll get to celebrate it with her, which means I'm going all out.

Though she told me not to make it a big deal since she's "only turning twenty-six," I absolutely am. There might be ten years between us, but age is only a number. Without a doubt, I know my future involves her, and tonight, she's going to know that.

I was able to get off work early so I can get everything ready at my place. She's always cooking for me and everyone else, so I'm returning the favor and plan to make her something amazing. While I'm no gourmet chef, I can follow a recipe.

Since she loves food so much and has a thousand favorite dishes, I had to get creative. Seafood isn't served regularly at the B&B, so I start there. She mentioned she loved shrimp when we visited my parents, so I found something I think she'll love. Knowing her love for spicy foods, I've decided to make Cajun seafood pasta with homemade garlic toast. It'll take me a good hour to cook the scallops and shrimp, so I hurry and take a shower, then get dressed beforehand. I want her to eat as soon as she gets here.

Gavin: Dinner's almost ready! It smells so good…can't wait to see you.

Though she slept over last night, and I saw her this morning at breakfast, I always miss her and want to be with her all day. It's a sickness really—one I don't want a cure for. With our busy work schedules, there's never enough time.

Maize: On the way! Had to do laundry and pack a bag since you never let me sleep at home anymore ;)

I smile at her smart mouth, and hell, she's right. I'm downright addicted to her body being next to mine and getting to kiss her before we start our days.

Gavin: See you soon, baby.

Ten minutes later, I hear the rumble of her truck and rush to the door. I open it and go down the steps to meet her before she gets out.

"Allow me," I say, opening her door.

She takes my hand. "Ooh, well thank you. What a gentleman."

"Only the best for my lady." I tilt my hat and press a kiss to her soft lips.

She giggles, then I grab her duffel. Taking her hand, I lead her into the house and set down her bag.

"Wow, you weren't wrong. It smells amazing in here." She lifts her nose and inhales. "Seafood for sure."

Reaching the oven, I take out the skillet, and her eyes widen.

"You made this?"

"Don't sound so surprised." I scoff. "I can cook. You just never let me." After setting the pasta on the stovetop, I remove the garlic bread.

"If it tastes as good as it smells, I'll gladly put you in charge of the kitchen from now on." She grins, eyeing everything.

"Not sure I'd go that far. This took a lot of planning. I honestly don't know how you make three meals a day for so many people."

"Lots of practice and prepping ahead of time," she responds effortlessly. "Also helps that I have help."

"Now, I didn't make dessert because I'm only so capable in the kitchen, but I did get Grandma Bishop to bake a cake for you."

"You didn't!" She gasps when I uncover it. "My favorite! German chocolate cake with chocolate mousse."

I chuckle at how adorably excited she is. "Of course."

She wraps her arms around my neck and pulls me down for a kiss. "That was really thoughtful. I haven't had that in years. Thank you."

"Anything for my love." Lowering my hands to her ass, I squeeze with a smirk. "You look beautiful, birthday girl. I love it when you wear easy-access dresses for me."

Maize snorts. "Let's see how good this meal is first before you get any ideas."

The table is set, and I pull out a chair for her to sit so I can serve her. Once our plates and wineglasses are full, we dive in, and I swear she's seconds away from an orgasm when she takes her first bite.

"Holy God, this is incredible," she moans around a forkful. Before she even swallows, she takes another bite, inhaling it. "I'm gonna need this recipe. My parents would lose their minds over this."

I don't admit that I've already spoken to her parents and told them what I was cooking. They're anxiously waiting to hear all about how tonight goes.

"Glad it turned out good," I agree. "Don't forget the garlic bread. I made that baby from scratch."

She grins, putting a piece in her mouth. "Mmm...so good."

"Did you have a good shift?" I ask when we're almost finished eating. Though we text nonstop, I always like hearing her talk about her day.

"Yeah, I did. My dad surprised me with flowers and balloons, as usual. My mom wrote me the sweetest card that made both of us cry. Kenzie bought me something that I'm currently wearing under this dress..." She waggles her brows. "And a few of the guests sang me 'Happy Birthday.'"

"Wow, sounds awesome."

"And now I'm ending it on a high note and get to be with the man I love." She gives me a sweet grin, and I can't stop the burst of happiness that radiates through me.

After we finish eating, I take the opportunity to do what I've been anxious about for the past month.

"What would you think about spending *every* birthday night with me?"

"What do you mean?" She tilts her head in confusion.

"And all *my* birthdays too," I add.

"Well, of course." She licks her lips.

"Forever?" I ask.

She furrows her brows in confusion. Deciding it's now or never, I stand and pull the velvet box from my pocket, then kneel in front of her.

"Wh-what are you doing?" She turns her body to face me.

"I have a special gift for you—well, two actually—but the most important one is this." I open the box so she can see the diamond I picked out for her.

"Oh my God…" she whispers barely over a breath as her eyes zero in on it.

"I'm not looking for a girlfriend, Maize. I don't need to date you any longer to know you're the one for me. I want to fall asleep with you every night and wake up to you every morning. I'm ready to settle down and start a life with the woman I'm madly in love with. I want forever with you, baby. Now the question is if you're ready for that too."

Maize licks her lips, her eyes catching mine for a split second before she looks back down at the ring.

"I love you so much, Maize. Will you marry me?"

Her hands fly to her mouth as tears spill from her eyes. She nods furiously. "Yes! Yes, I will marry you."

Her arms quickly swing around me, and she buries her face in my neck. I capture her to my chest and squeeze her tightly as my emotions start to boil over.

"I love you," she tells me, cupping my face, then kissing me. "I can't believe you just proposed!" She's half-laughing, half-crying, which causes me to chuckle.

"I have something else for you, sweetheart." I dig into my other pocket and pull it out. "This key is hypothetical since you already have a key to my place, but it's a promise."

She takes it from me and squints. "A promise for what?"

"A promise to build us a house with your dream kitchen so you have all the counter space and top-of-the-line appliances you want. But really, it's a token that I'll provide for you and our family, as well as support any goal you have in life. I know you want to stay close to your family and work, and your dad's already helped me scope the land for us to build on."

Tears fall down her cheeks as she looks at me with awe. "I honestly can't believe this is happening. It seems too good to be true."

I brush the pad of my thumb under her eye. "I know what I want, Maize. And that's you. Since the moment we met, you're all I've thought about. I've told myself that if I had the chance to be yours, I'd do anything in my power to make you happy."

"I love you with all my heart, Gavin. *You* make me happy." She leans into my palm, and I kiss her once more.

"Good." I grin. "Wanna put on the ring?"

Her eyes light up as if she forgot about it. "Yes! Oh my God, it's so beautiful."

I slide it onto her left ring finger, and our emotions get the best of us.

"I hate to ask, but…" She lingers on her words for a beat until our eyes connect. "You didn't happen to ask my father, did you? I know it's kinda lame in this age, but my family is—"

"Traditional, I know," I interject. "And yes, of course I did. I'm sure your mother's pacing the living room waiting for your call."

Maize bursts out laughing and grabs her phone. "You're probably right. Let's quickly FaceTime them so we can dive into that cake!"

Seeing Maize this happy is all I've ever wanted, and I'm not sure I could ever come down from this high. I knew it was risky to propose only months into us dating, but I've loved her much longer than that. I don't want to waste any more time. When I spoke with her parents, they were shockingly supportive. Mila cried and John gave me a bear hug, which was hilarious considering I tower over him. But I'm damn glad I'll be a part of the Bishop family now, even more so that Maize will be my wife.

"Alright, you crazy kids, you have a great rest of your night," Mila says with a knowing grin.

John takes the phone and looks directly at me. "Remember what we talked about, son?"

"Of course, sir."

He nods. "Good. Go have fun celebrating now. I have Sandra and Jane lined up in the kitchen tomorrow."

"Thank you. I love you guys," Maize tells them before hanging up. "Wow, we get to sleep in tomorrow? When's the last time that's ever happened?" she teases.

"Oh, don't be getting any ideas, future Mrs. Fox…" I pull her into my arms. "There'll be minimal sleeping happening tonight."

"Hmm…Mrs. Fox," she tries it out. "Or you could take my last name and be Gavin Bishop." She quirks a brow. "Or we could hyphenate?"

"Not to sound biblical, but my wife is taking my name. If you wanna hyphenate, that's fine, but Maize Fox sounds sexy." I squeeze her harder.

"Okay, Mr. Arrogant." She rolls her eyes but laughs. "Bishop-Fox would be a mouthful."

"It would. Plus…" I lower my lips to her ear. "I can think of other things to fill that mouth of yours."

As soon as the words leave my mouth, Maize's lips crash against mine. "Naked now, cake later."

"Fuck yes," I growl, scooping her into my arms and carrying her to my room.

"In my bed, tangled in my sheets, naked underneath me…" I whisper against her mouth.

"Forever," she says in return.

We rush to strip off our clothes and jump under the covers. My cock is so hard, but I need to taste her first. I slide between her thighs as they wrap around my shoulders, giving me full access to her sweet pussy. She fists her fingers in my hair, which I love, and I suck her throbbing clit between my lips.

"Yes, right there," she hums, tilting up her hips.

The best part about being in love with someone is how much better the sex is. When those feelings started to surface with Maize, I knew what we shared was special. I didn't want to acknowledge the void I felt before I retired, but it started to fill again when Maize entered my life. She's the woman I'm meant to be with.

I make love to my fiancée all night long. From the bed to the shower to the kitchen, and when we finally make it back to bed again, we pass out in each other's arms. Everything's perfect, and if someone had told me a year ago that I would be engaged to Maize, I wouldn't have believed it.

Goes to show what can happen when you don't give up and keep fighting for the one you love. It's even sweeter when the feelings are mutual, and her stubborn ass finally admits she wants to wrangle you in.

But I wouldn't have it any other way.

EPILOGUE
GAVIN

ONE YEAR LATER

"Did you turn on the heat?" Maize calls from the kitchen as I take care of our laundry in the living room.

"No," I answer with a chuckle.

I'm folding clothes while watching the football game, but Maize's hot flashes have me cracking up, especially in the middle of November.

"God. Why's it so hot in here?" She comes into view, and I nearly burst out laughing when I see she's taken off her pants and shirt.

Meanwhile, I'm in joggers and a sweatshirt since she's turned on the air conditioner.

"I think it's you, sweetheart," I tease, standing to meet her. My palm automatically lands on her belly, and I'm overcome with pride. "You're not only eating for three, but your hormones are raging." I smile, thinking about the two babies inside her that I can't wait to meet.

She pouts with a groan, and I pluck her bottom lip from between her teeth. "I'll turn down the thermostat, baby. Go sit, and I'll grab the fan, too."

"You're amazing." She sighs. "I feel like a freaking oven."

"It'll pass," I reassure her. It typically does anyway. "I'll grab you a sweet tea, too." Pressing my lips to her forehead, I grab the fan from our bedroom, then go to the kitchen for her drink. Lately, she's been getting hot flashes all the time and even in the middle of the night. To combat it, Maize has started sleeping with the fan blasted on her face, nearly naked, while I'm wrapped in a blanket.

Once I'm back in the living room, I make sure she's comfortable before I sit next to her. One hand rests on her bump as she sucks down her tea. Without even trying, Maize is the most stunning woman I've ever laid eyes on. Making her my wife was the best day of my life, tied with the day we found out she was pregnant with twins.

We hadn't expected it to happen so fast, but I was ready since I'm not getting any younger. Though if you ask Maize, she'd argue that her biological clock is ticking since she's closer to turning thirty. Undoubtedly, she was ready to get knocked up as soon as humanly possible. Apparently, the Bishop legacy of having multiples lives on.

My parents were undoubtedly thrilled when we told them the news. They visit at least once a month but I have a feeling they'll be coming a lot more or even moving here after the twins are born.

I go back to our clothes. We're finally having our housewarming party now that everything's unpacked. We moved in right before the wedding five months ago, but it wasn't completely finished. I helped the crew between shifts, and since I didn't want Maize to have to juggle unpacking and working, I took care of it all.

Once we learned we were having girls, we started decorating the nursery. Now that it's painted, it's time for all the furniture to be built and baby gear stored. I'd be lying if I said I wasn't nervous about taking care of two infants at once, but Mila's already offered to help as well as Grandma Bishop. They're over the moon excited, and her mom can't wait to be a grandma.

John keeps going back and forth about what he wants the girls to call him, and he's excited about our growing family. Kenzie was her typical overdramatic self and screamed with joy.

"You excited for this weekend, babe?" I ask, trying to match socks.

"Yes, I am," she says with a gleeful smile. "I can't wait to show off my hot house-building husband."

I scoff. "I *helped*, but I'm definitely not taking all the credit. The crew did the hard shit. I basically pointed and made sure nothing got messed up."

"That's pretty sexy in my book." She waggles her brows while lowering her eyes down my chest.

I chuckle, shaking my head. Another symptom of pregnancy is raging hormones that make her want sex all the time. Not that I'm complaining, but we have a party happening in three days. We've invited the whole damn town, it seems, but I don't mind. It's a potluck, so Maize isn't stuck preparing food for a crowd since her catering business is booming. Kenzie helps on the side, but Maize does all the cooking. Her doctor has warned her to take it easy with the stress of extra work since it's likely she'll go into preterm labor.

Moments later, my phone vibrates with a text, and I see it's Connor.

Connor: Would you mind if I brought someone with me to your party this weekend?

I read the message to Maize, and her smile drops. "He's bringing a *date*?"

I'm not sure what's happened between him and Elle, but their work relationship hasn't been the best as far as I've heard.

"I guess." I shrug.

Gavin: No problem. The more, the merrier.

"I hope you told him absolutely not!" she pouts.

I snort. "Why not? Elle isn't dating him."

"Well, she could be if he wasn't such a jerk. And now she's gonna have to see him with another woman. It's a dick move."

I'm not sure how to reply and don't wish to get in the middle of whatever's going on, so I stay quiet.

"Whatever. I'm gonna tell her to bring someone then. Ha! See how Dr. Dickhead likes that."

I narrow my eyes in confusion. "Thought you called him VetDreamy?"

She scowls. "Not anymore."

That doesn't sound good, but I also don't ask. Connor and I see each other at least once a week at the ranch, and if there's drama, I stay out of it.

"There," she says as she sets down her phone. "Now it won't be awkward, and she won't be alone when he's hanging on some other woman."

After the clothes are done, I sit back and pull Maize into my chest. "Any kicks today?"

"I feel a little fluttering on my right side," she tells me, and I move my hand around.

"You're gonna be the hottest pregnant mama-to-be when you're ready to pop. I can't wait." I smirk.

"Ugh, shut up. I'm fat and only gonna get fatter."

"You're growing two babies," I remind her. "I can't wait for a houseful of girls." Smiling, I press a kiss to her cheek. Due to Maize being high-risk with twins, they took a bunch of bloodwork, and we found out the genders early on. "Which means we're gonna have to try for a boy next."

She relaxes against me and laughs. "I thought of what I want their names to be," she says, then looks up at me. "Madison Bailey and Mila Rose. Bailey after my biological mother. Mila after the woman who raised me."

"And Rose after my mother?" I ask, honored.

"Yes, and it's Grandma Bishop's first name too." She beams. "I thought it was a perfect tribute to the amazing women in our life."

My heart beats with pride and excitement. "I love them. It's a great idea, sweetheart. Mila's gonna love that you named one of the babies after her."

"I wanna surprise her, though. Announce it after the babies are born."

"She's gonna cry." I chuckle, and Maize does too.

"Oh, she definitely will."

MAIZE

I can't wait to see everyone today. Though I frequently see my family, I'm usually too busy working to visit for more than five minutes. Plus, I'll get to spend more time with my cousins and sister without being interrupted by guests. Not that I mind, but a break is definitely nice.

Now that I'm pregnant with twins, I need to slow down, which is hard when I'm trying to keep up with my catering business too. I book parties for up to fifty people a couple of times a month, and it's rewarding for me. I hope I can continue after the twins are born, but I'll hire someone if not.

One of the best things about growing up with a ton of cousins is that our kids will get to grow up together just like we did. My grandparents are in their late seventies and want to be more hands-off with the business side of things. They've already discussed passing the operations entirely over to my dad and uncles, which is a significant milestone. Bishops have run the ranch for generations, and the legacy will continue.

Although the idea of getting pregnant again after twins seems crazy, I do want to try for a boy. My nephew Zach is two, and he'll have a little brother soon since Riley and Zoey are expecting baby Zealand in just two months. There are Bishop boy cousins for him to grow up with, plus I know Gavin would love to teach our kids about bull riding and training horses. Mutton bustin' is already on the list for the girls when they're old enough. I'd be willing to give Gavin a houseful, but for now, I'm focusing on these two precious babies inside me and soaking up every minute I get to carry them.

"My girls," Gavin says, wrapping his big hands around my belly and grinning into my neck. "You're beautiful." He looks at my reflection in the mirror, and I smile in return.

"This bump is cute now, but in a couple of months, I'll be surprised if I can see my feet."

"You'll be waddling all over the B&B like a cute penguin," he mocks.

"Thanks," I deadpan, adjusting my dress so it covers my boobs that have doubled in size.

"Your mom's here. Kenzie too."

"Oh yay! Tell them I'll be right down." I turn around and kiss his lips. "Assuming it doesn't take me an hour to climb down the stairs."

"I could carry you. You're on your feet too much as it is, no wonder they're swelling."

"My feet are swelling?" I squeal in panic, then look down at them. "Do I have chubby ankles already?"

"Uh…" Gavin removes his hat and brushes a hand through his hair, a tell that he's about to bullshit his way outta this question. "I think I hear more people at the door. Meet ya down there, sweetheart." He quickly kisses my cheek before leaving.

He's lucky I love him too damn much to scold him. I didn't think it was possible to love him more than I did the day we got married, but when I found out we were pregnant, I fell for him even deeper.

By the time I enter the living room, it's filled with Bishops and friends of the family. I greet people and swipe Rory out of Rowan's arms. He's seven months now, and his little personality reminds me so much of Diesel.

"Hey buddy." I blow raspberries on his cheek, and he giggles. Rory is a perfect blend of his parents with adorable little dimples. Rowan and Diesel got married two months ago, and I hope they'll try for baby number two soon. Grandma Bishop hasn't stopped reminding them.

"Is Elle here?" Rowan asks.

I look around. "I don't see her yet, but…" My eyes widen when they land on Dr. Wallen, her boss. "Oh my God," I mutter quietly, and Rowan's gaze follows mine.

"I thought you said he was bringing a date?" Rowan whispers, taking Rory from my arms when he starts to fuss.

"I-I assumed he was…" I have to pick up my jaw from the floor at the little girl's hand he's holding. "He asked to bring someone."

"Elle's gonna be *so* mad at you." Rowan chuckles.

Kenzie comes over to us, and we fill her in. "Wow." She eyes Connor up and down. "He's somehow hotter now."

"Kenzie, ew. He's way too old for you anyway." I scoff.

"Really? You gonna talk to me about age?"

I roll my eyes. "Shut up. I better text Elle and warn her."

"Too late," Kenzie mutters, staring at the front door.

"Shit."

Elle walks in with a man I've never seen before, and he's dressed in black slacks and a sleek black button-up shirt. He's tall, with broad shoulders, and fit. He looks like a guy her mom would set her up with. Perhaps he's a doctor from the hospital Aunt Emily works at, but nevertheless, things are about to get awkward.

"Maize..." Gavin comes to my side and brushes my elbow.

"I saw," I say before he can speak. "Is that his...daughter?"

"Yeah, Olivia. She's six. He shares custody with his ex-wife," he informs me.

Well, *fuck*.

Elle spots us and walks over with a bright, friendly smile. "Hey, guys." We exchange a hug.

"Hey, who's your date?" I ask.

"This is Stephen. He's a doctor and works with my mom."

Nailed it.

"Hi, Stephen, nice to meet you." I shake his hand. "I'm Maize, Elle's cousin."

"A pleasure to meet y'all."

He shakes Kenzie's, then Rowan's, and Gavin's hand next.

"You have a lovely home. Elizabeth's informed me it was recently built."

Elizabeth? I nearly cringe at the way he uses her full name, considering none of us do.

"Yes, well, it's been a few months, but it took some time to finish. Plus, the Bishops love any reason for a party." I chuckle because it's true.

I turn to Elle, and my eyes widen. "Can I talk to you for a quick sec?"

"Uh—sure." Just as we're about to walk off, Connor comes over with a pointed glare as he holds his daughter's hand.

Elle's eyes bug out of her head as she stares at Dr. Wallen and the little girl next to him.

"Hey, Connor," I greet sweetly. "I heard you brought a little guest with you." Smiling, I lean down and take her hand. "I'm Maize. Thanks for coming to our party."

"Hello, ma'am. I'm Olivia."

"Oh my gosh, what a sweetheart," Rowan coos.

"How did no one know you had a child?" Kenzie blurts out.

"Well, you never asked." He shrugs. "Her mother lives in New Mexico, and we share custody. She visits over the summer and holidays. I picked her up early for our Thanksgiving celebration."

That explains why he asked at the last minute.

"She looks a lot like you," Elle says, breaking the awkward tension. "Hi, Olivia. I'm Elle. I work with your daddy."

Olivia shakes her hand with a cute smile. "Nice to meet you."

"Connor," Stephen says curtly.

Dr. Wallen stands up straighter with furrowed brows. "Dr. Burk."

"You two know each other?" I ask, waving a finger back and forth between them. I shouldn't be that surprised, considering we live in a small town, and everyone knows everyone.

"We were friends in high school," Stephen explains.

"Yeah, well…that was ages ago." Connor takes Olivia's hand. "Anyway, I'm gonna get a couple of snacks for her. It was nice seeing y'all."

Before anyone can say another word, Connor walks away and heads toward the kitchen.

Rowan, Kenzie, and I exchange a look. "I'm gonna go say hi to Grandma and make sure she gets something to eat."

An hour later, people are scattered throughout the house having a good time. Some are outside on the deck and admiring the views of the ranch.

"Hey," Gavin whispers in my ear behind me as I stare out at the orange and blue sky. "You wanna sneak into the guest room?"

Chuckling, I glance at him over my shoulder. "Are you crazy? We have a house full of guests."

"So? You used to like sneakin' around with me." He winks.

That causes me to laugh hard. "That's true."

I grab his arm and lead him down the hallway into the room. Once the door is locked, he latches his mouth to mine, and our tongues feverishly fight for control.

"Think you can stay quiet, baby?" he asks in a growl.

"If you cover my mouth." I grin.

Gavin lifts my dress and moves my panties to the side, then plunges a finger into my wet pussy. I'm already aching for him, desperately needing his cock to fill me.

He wraps his hand around my head and slides his tongue between my lips as he finger fucks me hard and fast, building the orgasm until I fall over the edge. I moan out his name, and he quickly covers my mouth with his.

Without wasting another second, he undoes his jeans and boxers, and when his cock comes into view, I immediately wrap my hand around him.

"Mmm…baby." His head falls back on his shoulders. "As much as I love that, we need to make this quick."

He lifts me until my legs wrap around his waist, and his cock presses between my thighs. The tip rubs against my clit before gliding down and entering me.

With a throaty groan, I take in all of him, and we rock together in rhythm.

"You make me so damn happy," he mutters in my ear. "Happier than I ever thought I deserved."

I'm on the verge of tears as he fucks me against the wall. "You make me happier than I ever thought was possible," I tell him.

"I'll spend the rest of my life making sure you and our girls are always happy. No matter what, sweetheart."

"I know you will."

I have no doubt Gavin will do anything to give us everything we could ever want and need.

He captures my lips once more, and soon, we're falling over the edge, moaning out our release as quietly as possible.

"Fuck, baby mama. That was hot." He smacks my ass after I adjust my dress.

I snort and shake my head.

"You think anyone noticed we were gone?" I ask, smoothing down my hair as he zips up his jeans.

"Nah. I think everyone's distracted as hell from seeing Connor with his daughter, Olivia. Especially Elle and Stephen."

I cringe, feeling awful that I'm the one who told Elle to bring someone. "Elle's gonna murder me. I still can't believe no one knew he had a kid."

"Connor's a private guy." Gavin shrugs, pulling me into his arms once he's dressed.

"As if things weren't tense enough between Elle and Connor, it's about to get a lot more awkward," I say.

"Considering that Stephen guy seems like the type Evan and Emily would approve of, I imagine he could be here to stay."

"You think so?"

"And if I'm being honest, Stephen seems more of her type than Connor."

"I wonder why he's always so short-tempered and rude to her. If he truly didn't care for her personality or the way she does things, why would he have hired her in the first place? Unless…"

"You think he likes her?" he asks.

"He could purposely be pushing her away like I did you when I didn't want to admit my feelings. I've had this theory before, but I think it's safe to say he just might be doing the same."

"Maybe." Gavin shrugs, pressing a sweet kiss to the tip of my nose. "We should go back out there."

I nod in agreement.

"Well, either way, when they go back to work on Monday, it's gonna be hella interesting." I cackle. "And I can't wait to hear all about it."

Continue the Circle B Ranch series with Connor & Elizabeth's story next in *Bossing the Cowboy*

If you haven't started at the beginning, make sure to read Riley and Zoey's story in *Hitching the Cowboy* and Diesel and Rowan's story in *Catching the Cowboy*.

AVAILABLE NOW

**Next in the Circle B Ranch Series is
Connor & Elle's story in *Bossing the Cowboy***

After surviving a messy divorce and custody battle, Dr. Connor Wallen quickly became married to his job. Helping animals is the perfect distraction from his crazy ex, but he finds it difficult to concentrate when an attractive woman joins his veterinary clinic. Getting involved with someone who works for him would only lead to disaster, so staying professional is key.

He tries to ignore her, but their chemistry is undeniable.

Elizabeth Bishop can't stand her boss or how he treats her, but there aren't many job options in small-town Texas. No matter what she does, it's never good enough for Connor, but she continues trying to impress him anyways him anyway.

She'll never admit she's attracted to him and denies it every chance she gets.

Avoiding him is impossible, but Elle keeps her distance whenever possible. After his walls start to crumble, she knows her feelings aren't one-sided. She's tired of playing his games and is ready to prove who's really in control.

Although he pushes her away, she's determined to pull him closer—showing him exactly what they've both been missing.

ABOUT THE AUTHOR

Brooke Cumberland and Lyra Parish are a duo of romance authors under the *USA Today* pseudonym, Kennedy Fox. Their characters will make you blush and your heart melt. Cowboys in tight jeans are their kryptonite. They always guarantee a happily ever after!

CONNECT WITH US

Find us on our website:
kennedyfoxbooks.com

Subscribe to our newsletter:
kennedyfoxbooks.com/newsletter

facebook.com/kennedyfoxbooks
twitter.com/kennedyfoxbooks
instagram.com/kennedyfoxduo
amazon.com/author/kennedyfoxbooks
goodreads.com/kennedyfox
bookbub.com/authors/kennedy-fox

BOOKS BY KENNEDY FOX

DUET SERIES (BEST READ IN ORDER)

CHECKMATE DUET SERIES

ROOMMATE DUET SERIES

LAWTON RIDGE DUET SERIES

INTERCONNECTED STAND-ALONES

BISHOP BROTHERS SERIES

CIRCLE B RANCH SERIES

BISHOP FAMILY ORIGIN

LOVE IN ISOLATION SERIES

ONLY ONE SERIES

MAKE ME SERIES

Find the entire Kennedy Fox reading order at
Kennedyfoxbooks.com/reading-order